BLACKOUT

K. MONROE

BLACKOUT

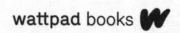
wattpad books

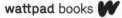

Content Warning: underage drinking, bullying, mental health, amnesia, car accident, violence, unwanted sexual advances

Published in Canada by Wattpad Books, a division of Wattpad Corp.
36 Wellington Street E., Toronto, ON M5E 1C7

www.wattpad.com

First Wattpad Books edition: January 2022
ISBN 978-1-98936-573-1 (Trade Paper original)
ISBN 978-1-98936-574-8 (eBook edition)

Library and Archives Canada Cataloguing in Publication information is available upon request.

Printed and bound in Canada
1 3 5 7 9 10 8 6 4 2

Cover design by Ysabel Enverga

Images © Jess Craven via stocksy, © Filip Zrnzevic via Unsplash, © Olga and © naiauss via Adobe Stock

JUL 1 5 2022

To those who have supported me from the beginning of my journey and those who found me along the way.

01 | BEGIN / END

The last thing I remember is noise.

Images are hazy, and they only come in flashes. Most of them are dark, dripping with night and impossible to make sense of—a glimpse of a tree branch here, a wiry crack in the glass there. Bloodstained fingers. Fragmented pieces of my reflection gazing back at me.

But the noises are vivid, and when I squeeze my eyes shut, I can still hear them. It begins with tires squealing, struggling to gain traction on damp pavement, followed by the devastating crunch of metal connecting with metal. A car door clicks open, and the melodic chime of keys being left in the ignition resonates through the air layered with frantic voices melding together. One of them sounds similar to mine, only warped and laced with pain.

A desperate urge to flee the scene propels me forward, but my limbs fail, and I fall to the ground.

When I wake, I no longer know my own name.

The abrupt shaking of a pill bottle makes the present come back into focus.

Dr. Meyer sits across from me, holding up the bright orange container, and the room is quiet, all eyes trained in my direction. Outside, thick, menacing clouds on the verge of bursting hang low, peering over the canopy of evergreen trees in the distance. There's a garden adjacent to Dr. Meyer's office—a courtyard that must bloom with color later in the year but looks stark and barren against the backdrop of early spring.

After a month of staying here, I've learned that the neurology wing is the nicest place in Pender Falls General Hospital, significantly more inviting than the room I first woke up in—where I was called a name I didn't remember and was surrounded by faces I'd never seen before—or the one in which I spent weeks learning how to use my body again. This meeting is the last checkpoint I have to complete before getting out of here for good.

"Sorry. I lost focus for a second."

"That's all right." Dr. Meyer's smile is gentle, practiced. "This is a lot of information to take in at once, that's why we have your family here with you. The more ears, the better."

Sofia—my mother, though it's far too early to call her that—studiously scrawls notes on the lined paper of the notebook in her lap, while my sister, Audrey, sits on the other side of me, fingers resting on my leg gently in a show of support.

"As I was saying, you'll continue taking these in order to help with your awareness and memory. Over the counter pain meds like acetaminophen and ibuprofen can be taken for headaches and any muscle stiffness you may be feeling."

"How long does she need to take them?" Sofia gestures to the pill bottle. The words are firm, demanding, and I don't know if it's motherly instinct or a desire to be in control of the situation.

"We'll monitor her progress in our follow-up appointments and reassess. For now, she can continue to take them daily before bed."

"Do you think I'm stuck like this?"

The attention shifts back to me, an air of discomfort settling over the room.

"You're not *stuck*, Alina," Dr. Meyer begins, setting his clipboard on his desk. "It's still very early. There's always room for improvement, and it's likely your recovery won't be linear."

A crow lands on a branch near the window, taking cover beneath the overhang as the rain begins to fall. My mother and sister remain silent.

"How does a brain just forget everything it knows, anyway?" My grip tightens around the thick fabric of the sweater I hold in my hands as I watch the bird.

"Your procedural memory is perfectly intact. Once you're back in your normal environment, I'm confident more things from your life, your past, will come back and be familiar." He sets the bottle on his desk then leans back in his seat. "The mind is a wondrous thing. It's not that your brain has forgotten everything it knows, rather, those memories are locked away, and you can no longer find the key. You may find that key again someday, or you may not. My goal is to give you the tools to cope with either outcome."

A wave of nausea builds in my belly, and I don't know if it's an aftereffect of smashing my head against a steering wheel, a reaction to his words, or a delightful mixture of both. Waking up to a life that feels brand new and being told you were in a deadly car accident you're lucky to have survived is harrowing. I don't feel lucky. I feel cursed.

The details of the accident were explained to me in simple terms: I was at a party. I left the party. I crashed my car into a tree. I was found by someone out on a run hours later, long after the sun had already risen, though the sounds I remember make it seem as though it all happened in a matter of seconds. Every time I hear it, it feels like nothing more than a story about a stranger, something tragic I might tell someone in passing, not something that belongs to me.

"I think we're finished here," he says. "Unless you have anything else you'd like to discuss."

Despite the fact that there are about a million burning questions on the tip of my tongue, I shake my head, and we all stand, heading for the door. I wander farther down the hall, drifting and ghostlike, while Sofia gets a final word in with Dr. Meyer, speaking in hushed timbres. Audrey stands next to them, shooting me concerned glances every few seconds.

Our physical resemblance reassures me that they truly are my family—we have the same intense brown eyes, dark hair, and tawny skin—but I have no recollection of our life before these hospital corridors and neurology appointments. I don't even know what they think of me.

After several moments of watching the rain fall outside the large windows of the hospital entrance, they join me, and we make our way outside.

A raindrop hits my nose, and Sofia does her best to cover us using her bag as a makeshift umbrella, but it doesn't provide much shelter. My hair is damp by the time we reach the car. As we roll through town, my eyes melt into the landscape of cookie-cutter houses backed by lush mountains and my fingers curl around the strap of my seat belt as I listen to the whir of tires gliding through rainwater. The sun hasn't shone in Pender Falls since I woke up.

Sofia tells me I've lived here all my life. Years of bouncing around British Columbia led her to settle down in a small town in the Interior, somewhere she deemed appropriate to raise a family.

"That's your elementary school," she says as we drive by a blue building with children's artwork pasted to the windows, rain battering the weathered jungle gym.

It continues on like this as she points out the shadowy park I used to frequent as a child and the church next to the cemetery we attend on special occasions. Audrey fills in the gaps from the backseat, accompanying every place with an amusing story. With each one we drive past, it feels like I'm seeing it for the first time. I have no doubt their intention is to help me become familiar with my surroundings, but it only makes me feel like more of an outsider.

After turning onto Seymour Avenue, we pull into the driveway of a house a little ways down the street. It's large, built of red bricks, with sprawling vines creeping up the front and wrapping around the white pillars on the porch like something out of a storybook. Sofia kills the engine and nobody moves for a second.

"This is home," she announces tentatively.

I've been dreading this. Even though Audrey and Sofia were constantly with me in the hospital, it's an entirely different thing to actually live with strangers who are supposed to be family. In reality, they feel about as familiar as the doctors and nurses who milled about the hallways during my stay, coming in and out of my room to bring me medication and rouse me from my sleep.

Sofia pushes open the front door, and I follow her inside.

Immediately as we enter, a barking dog bounds in my direction, and my pulse kicks into gear. The animal, a black and white border collie, jumps onto my legs, growling maliciously, and Audrey scrambles to grab its collar, easing it away.

"I'm sorry!" she exclaims. "Scout isn't your biggest fan but she's usually better than this."

"Audrey." Sofia chastises her. "I told you to take Scout outside before we left."

"Parker must have let her in."

Audrey looks at me apologetically as she struggles to wrangle the animal, expression sincere. She's older by a couple of years, but I've been told we were often mistaken for twins when we were young. Now, I seem to favor our mother more than she does, bearing the same slender nose and defined cheekbones.

Sofia takes hold of Scout's collar and pulls the dog to the French doors, releasing her into the backyard. A boy scrambles into the kitchen, looking flustered. His features are kind, and he has black hair a few shades darker than his skin cropped close to his head.

"This is my boyfriend," Audrey explains. "He's living with us for the time being, until he finds his own place."

He extends a hand toward me. "Parker. My apologies for the dog."

My shoulders melt in relief. He's the first person who hasn't been obviously uncomfortable about having to reintroduce themselves to me. "Nice to meet you," I say, shaking his hand, before adding, "again."

"It's good to have you back," Parker says.

I've heard a lot about him already—he was the subject Audrey gravitated toward to keep the flow of conversation going whenever we hit a lull, but he never came with her to the hospital. Parker watches me for a beat too long, and my face grows hot under his scrutiny.

Sofia touches my shoulder, oblivious to the exchange. "Come, I can show you around."

Leaving them behind, she gives me a brief tour of the house. It's cozy and lived in, family photos adorning the walls, throws draped over couches, and comforting tones of burgundy spread throughout the rooms. In a way, it feels a bit like a cabin, woodsy and warm. She saves my bedroom for last, stopping outside of a door at the end of the hall on the second floor. The short journey up the stairs is enough to make my body feel weary.

Subconsciously, my breath hitches as she twists the doorknob.

A string of fairy lights hangs on the wall above the bed, bright and twinkling, and a diffuser sits on the nightstand, emitting wafts of lavender, making me relax my shoulders. There's a desk in the corner, a surge of intrigue sparking in my chest at the sight of the laptop on the surface, as it's likely to be a treasure trove of valuable information. Across from the bed, a myriad of photos are stuck to the wall, snapshots of someone else's life.

The room is beautiful, but it doesn't feel like it's mine.

Any hope of my memory making a reappearance is rapidly snuffed out, and disappointment presses heavily against the backs of my eyelids. "It's nice."

"I'll let you have some privacy," she offers.

"Thanks, Sofia." It's the first time I've addressed her by name, and I don't realize the magnitude of my mistake until I see the look on her face. "I'm sorry."

"It's all right," she says, her voice wavering. "I'll be downstairs if you need anything."

She leaves the room in a rush. I gravitate to the wall of photos, trying to move past the interaction. The level of awkwardness has apparently been upped now that we're trapped in a house together, and it's hard to imagine a time when it won't feel this way.

There are so many pictures it's hard to focus on one at a time. The majority of them have been taken in crowded living rooms. I've usually got a red Solo cup in hand, surrounded by the same handful of people—a beautiful blond with a dazzling smile, a curly-haired boy most often showing me some form of affection, and a stocky guy wearing a letterman jacket and a goofy grin.

A slew of faces with no memories attached to them. I don't know if I can become the person in the pictures.

A knock sounds on my door, startling me.

"Come in," I call, taking a seat on the bed.

The door clicks open slowly, and Parker pokes his head inside. He sees the look on my face and hovers in the doorway, sticking his hands in his pockets.

"Hey." He greets me.

"Hey," I respond evenly.

He takes my greeting as an invitation to enter the room, then sits on the bed a short distance away. "How are you doing?"

"You know, I've been asked that question so many times, and I don't think I have an answer." A beat of silence hangs between us. "Even if I did, I don't think I'd be able to put it into words."

"I can't even imagine."

"Do we know each other well?"

"We do. You're one of my closest friends."

"Is that really me?" I gesture to the wall of photos with my chin.

"For the most part, yeah," he says. "You were always out. Always. Out with your boyfriend, out with your friends, out doing God knows what. I think you liked being unpredictable." I stare at a photo of me laughing, my arms thrown around the people on either side of me. "But you clashed with your family a fair bit. There were a lot of arguments around here before."

"Wow, I sound *great*," I say sarcastically, causing him to break out in a grin.

"You are," he reassures me.

"At least we get along. It's good to know I wasn't public enemy number one."

He ducks his head, coughing to cover a laugh. I can't explain it, but being around him is the most relaxed I've felt in the short amount of life that I can remember. I believe that we were close before everything happened. It makes him feel more familiar than anyone else. Maybe the relationship with my mother and sister truly was strained.

"What's it like?" he asks suddenly.

"The whole amnesia thing?"

He nods.

"Like I've stepped into somebody's life and now I'm picking up where they left off, except I have no idea what happened before I got here. Everyone is going to expect me to be *that* girl," I say, pointing at the photos on the wall, "but I don't even know her. All I'm going to do is disappoint everyone. I have this constant feeling of guilt—"

"Stop right there." Parker interrupts me, his hand on my arm. "You have absolutely *no* reason to feel guilty. This isn't your fault. You didn't choose this."

It's the first time I've heard the words, and I didn't realize how much I needed them until now. "I don't know why, but I feel like I can trust you. I trust that you'll tell me the truth."

"Of course," he says, reaching out to squeeze my hand. "You can always ask me anything."

"Thanks." I look down at our intertwined fingers.

"I'm so glad you're home," he murmurs, letting go of my hand.

In the next second, he's cupping my face. A jolt runs down my spine as he leans closer and I freeze, but it only takes a second for me to come to my senses.

Placing my hands on his chest, I hurriedly push him away and stand up. "What the hell are you doing?"

Parker looks equally shocked, mouth floundering to come up with an explanation. I wait for him to speak, and he runs a hand over his cropped hair, cursing under his breath. "I'm sorry—that wasn't supposed to happen."

"You're Audrey's boyfriend."

"I am," he confirms, his voice low.

"Then what was that?"

"Something that shouldn't have almost happened again, especially right now." He looks at me remorsefully. "I'm so sorry, Allie. I thought I had more self-control than that."

"*Again?*" The urge to vomit is suddenly sharp. "You've done this before?"

Parker is silent for a few beats. "No," he says finally. "Last time you kissed me. But—"

"This is so messed up!"

"It won't happen again."

"You're right, it won't," I say, gritting my teeth. "You should go."

Without another word, he heads out the door, closing it gently behind him. Once he's gone, my face crumples, and I press my fists against my forehead, mumbling a string of curses like a mantra. What kind of person would do this to their sister, to their boyfriend, to *anyone*?

Minutes ago, it had felt like I had someone in my corner. Now all I feel is the sting of betrayal.

Removing my hands from my face, I stare at the wall of pictures, automatically drawn to a photo of Parker, Audrey, and me. I wonder what other secrets lie behind the multitude of faces and how long it'll take before they all start coming to the surface.

02 | RETURN

With each day that passes, the fact that I likely won't be regaining my memory any time soon becomes more apparent.

Because of this, Dr. Meyer suggested that I try to make my return to school, though Sofia took it as less of a suggestion and more of an order. I think they're all hoping that everything will magically come back to me if my circumstances are exactly how they were before the accident.

The thought of having to spend the day with hundreds of people I don't know is terrifying. Dealing with three virtual strangers every day for the past two weeks since leaving the hospital has been more than enough. My time has been made up of stifled conversations, trips to the neurologist, and wandering around inside because anything beyond my front door is completely unknown, and therefore unwanted.

After extracting myself from under the bedsheets, I tiptoe to the downstairs bathroom, not wanting to wake anyone. The house is old, and the wood floors creak and groan with every step. Once I've finished and washed up, I look in the mirror, studying the face that stares back at me once more: the vacant, dark eyes and pink lips pressed into a firm line. I wonder how long it will take me to get used to my reflection. Tilting my chin, I turn my head, examining it from all angles.

I try out several smiles but all of them feel horribly fake and tight. The only way my expression looks okay is if I'm completely emotionless.

When I exit the bathroom, Parker is in the hallway, and I stop short.

"Okay," he teases, "that is definitely an Allie look. Are you sure you're not just pretending to forget everything?"

"Positive."

"Must be muscle memory. You were always the master of giving people looks that could kill."

The mood shifts and an uncomfortable tension settles over us, one that's becoming quite familiar. It doesn't help that this is the first time we've been alone together since he tried to kiss me. Up until now, I've pretended he's invisible. Audrey keeps asking me to do things with them—take a walk, sit in the car while they buy groceries, go out for coffee—and she'll only accept the "I think it'll give me a headache" excuse for so long. Being forced to acknowledge her boyfriend has me feeling cornered.

He lowers his voice. "I'm sorry about what happened."

"I am too," I say firmly.

"Don't be. It's my fault. Just… forget about it."

"Is that a joke? I already have amnesia."

He's silent for a few seconds before he processes my words, then laughs breathily. I feel my lips twitch. The motion draws his attention, and my pulse quickens.

"Bad word choice," he remarks.

He looks as though he wants to say more, but movement in the other room snaps us out of our trance. I push past him, moving toward the kitchen. Inside, Audrey slides a bagel into the toaster, glancing over her shoulder as I breeze into the room, Parker trailing slowly behind.

"Oh, you're both here," she says brightly. "Good morning."

I busy myself with making a cup of tea. "Morning."

"How are you feeling about going back to school today?"

"If I had to choose between going to school or launching myself into space, I'd pick space."

"Oh, come on," she remarks. "I'm sure it won't be *that* bad."

I give her a dubious look.

"Just think about it like starting at an entirely new school. That's exciting, right? You can make new friends."

"I'm a senior in my last semester of high school," I point out. "I'm sure everyone here has already made up their mind about me."

Audrey lifts a shoulder, looking at me sympathetically. "There's still time for things to change."

Parker hums his agreement over his mug of coffee.

"Maybe," I say, not truly believing her words.

Sofia seems deep in thought as we coast through our neighborhood on the way to school.

The houses are neat and polished here—character homes with lush, manicured lawns and expensive-looking cars parked out front. Sofia is a lawyer at a local law firm, which must be the reason we're able to afford to live in this part of town. She's been off work for the past month and a half taking care of me, and today is her first day back too.

A thin layer of fog hangs above the ground, a companion to the stark grey sky. Spring is supposed to be bright and colorful, but here, March is a palette of greys, blues, and deep greens. From what I've seen of it so far, Pender Falls is beautiful in a way that feels heavy and haunting. The promise of buried memories lingers around every corner, and I don't know if I'll ever be able to uncover them.

Maybe that's a good thing.

Sofia turns to me when we pull onto a main road and stop at a traffic light. "If you need anything, you can get the office to call me," she says. "I'll have my cell on me all day. Audrey will pick you up after school. Or earlier, if need be."

"I know." She's reassured me of this fact multiple times since last night, making it clear that I can reach out if the day becomes too overwhelming, but it doesn't make me feel any more at ease.

Whether I last the entire day or only five minutes, I'll feel the burning urge to vomit the entire time regardless.

"Are you eager to get back to work?"

Sofia seems caught off guard by the question and straightens in her seat. "I have a lot to catch up on. My boss has been very accommodating of me taking so much time off."

"That didn't really answer the question."

"I feel restless being away from work," she says. "But I'll also feel restless thinking about how it's going for you at school today."

The words soften me a bit, though the weight of being a burden on her is troubling.

We arrive at the Pender Falls High parking lot, and I take a deep breath, my knee bouncing. The sight of the plethora of students making their way to the entrance of the old brick building makes me want to disappear into the thick row of trees directly behind it. I wonder how many of them I'm supposed to know, how many of them are my friends. After consulting with Dr. Meyer, Sofia decided it would be best for anyone who isn't family to give me some space until I could return to school.

"Are you ready?" Sofia asks, straightening the collar of her charcoal blazer.

No.

"I guess so."

Her expression has been static over the last couple of weeks: impassive but with sadness and worry bubbling just beneath the exterior. She pushes her door open and exits the car. Her heels click on the pavement, and I work to even out my breathing, following her lead. Heads turn in our direction from the people standing in clusters in the parking lot, and each stare feels like fingers on my skin. Ignoring them, I focus on the school as we enter, looking up at the ceiling of the atrium that casts gloomy, blue light on everyone inside.

The whispering starts the minute the doors close behind us, sparking up in one place then spreading like wildfire. Sofia places a gentle hand on my arm to guide me to the front office, hesitating when she feels my rigid posture. Despite my best efforts to block out the background noise, I can't help but hear a snatch of conversation before the door closes behind us.

Apparently she lost her memory. Do you think she's faking it? Seems like something she'd do.

By the time we stand before the secretary, a plump woman with fiery red hair pulled back in a bun, my jaw is sore from clenching my teeth. The nameplate on her desk reads MRS. GALLAGHER.

"Allie," she says pleasantly, offering me the same kind of smile I've been receiving from everyone else, pitying and uncertain. "It's great to see you."

Sofia nudges my arm, prompting me to answer, "Thanks."

"We're going to do everything we can to make this transition easy for you," she promises. "We want you to feel safe here, and comfortable. Anytime you need anything at all, don't hesitate to ask. We'll be happy to help."

Her exaggerated, friendly demeanor makes me wonder how long every adult will be this overly nice and treat me like I'm made of glass. The purpose of all of this is to make me feel normal, but normal people don't get looked at as though they're about to fall to pieces at any second. As Mrs. Gallagher pulls out a class schedule, I'm drawn to the window facing the hallway, watching the students as they walk past, some of them attempting to be discreet as they peer inside the office to get a peek at me.

There's one face that catches my attention: a boy with inky brown hair and a strong jaw in the middle of grabbing something from his locker. He looks at me when he notices my stare, and his expression is a combination of stony and calculating, his eyes frigid, even from a distance.

My mind goes blank, and then he turns away as though nothing happened, disappearing down the hall. Something about the brief interaction makes my heart beat faster. Turning back to Mrs. Gallagher, I try to regain focus.

"Your English classroom is just around the corner," she says, and I take the copy of my schedule from her hands, along with a slip of paper with the combination to my locker. I adjust the strap of my backpack. "But don't worry, I'll get someone to show you around."

She gets up from her chair and shuffles to the door, then pokes her head out of it.

Sofia takes the opportunity to check in on me once again, her voice quiet. "Everything okay so far?"

"So far," I say, thinking about the boy in the hall. The day hasn't even truly begun yet, and it's already strange.

"Here she is," Mrs. Gallagher announces, gesturing for someone else to enter the cramped office.

A blond girl enters the room, wiggling her fingers in a wave. I instantly recognize her from the photos on my bedroom wall. She's tall and slim, wearing a plaid skirt and collared shirt paired with a matching headband. It's odd to see her in motion when I've grown used to seeing her frozen in time.

"This is Zoe Harris," Mrs. Gallagher explains. "She'll be your tour guide. She's also one of our brightest students."

"Oh, I don't know about that," she says, though there's a hint of pride in her voice. She addresses my mother. "It's good to see you, Ms. Castillo."

"Thanks for doing this, Zoe," Sofia says. She checks the watch on her wrist and looks at me apologetically. "I should really get going. I have an appointment with a client."

"Oh," I say, suddenly panicked by the thought of her departure. "Okay."

"Remember you can always call me," she says. "You're very brave."

It takes everything in me to resist scoffing at her last words, because they imply that this was *my* decision. If I had any say at all in the matter, I wouldn't be here right now.

Sofia calls out a parting word on her way out, and Zoe motions to the hallway, allowing me to exit first. An air of discomfort lingers between us.

She holds her arms out wide, gesturing to the linoleum floors and walls lined with navy blue lockers that stretch out ahead of us. "Welcome to Pender Falls High," she says unceremoniously. "Otherwise known as My Least Favorite Place in the World, population five hundred."

This earns a short laugh of amusement, and it's a slight reprieve from the tension I've been feeling this morning.

"We'll start the grand tour at your locker." She rounds the corner, and I hasten to keep up with her. "We can grab your stuff for English. It's actually a decent class. Ms. Warren is the best teacher here."

As we walk through the hallways, it's as though every pair of eyes is connected to me by a string, following my every move. Several strangers call out greetings and well wishes as I walk by, and I nod at them awkwardly, straightening the hem of the sweater I borrowed from Audrey. Somehow wearing one of her things felt less like stealing from a stranger than wearing the clothes in my own closet.

"We're good friends, right?" I blurt, and Zoe turns to me, looking surprised as she slows down. Heat rises to my cheeks, and I scramble to explain. "It's just—I have all these pictures on my bedroom walls of us together."

"Yeah," she says, voice subdued. "I didn't want to make you uncomfortable by bringing it up, but we've been best friends since middle school."

"It's okay," I say, internally reminding myself that none of this is my fault. "I'd rather know about everything than be kept in the dark."

"I guess that makes sense. This is yours." She brings us to a stop in front of a locker, and I pass her the combination from Mrs. Gallagher, watching as she twists it open. I'm greeted by another photo of us tacked to the inside, along with a few others I recognize from my room. "You'll need the red notebook and the copy of *Macbeth* for our first class."

In the picture of us, I've got my arms looped around her shoulders and we're laughing, oblivious to the other people around us. For a brief moment a scene flashes through my mind—a crowded living room, a throbbing bassline, a feeling of dread, faces that feel both familiar and nameless. But then it's gone before I can register any of the details, and a headache forms at my temple. I'm unsure if the images are from an actual memory or just something my brain conjured out of thin air.

"I'm sorry about . . . all this." I fiddle with the books in my hands.

"You don't need to apologize to me for something completely out of your control," she states. "Because I won't hear it."

"Okay."

"Besides, maybe your memory will come back once you see Damien," she teases. "Speak of the devil."

Turning around, I immediately recognize the boy approaching, the touchy one in all of the photos of us together. As he strides toward us eagerly, I register that his coffee-colored curls are longer than in the pictures, his skin golden and sun kissed. The boy next to him is bulky and intimidating, though the expression on his face looks more like a child's on Christmas morning.

"Allie!" Damien exclaims, pulling me into a bear hug. I freeze, my mouth falling open as he squeezes me tightly, lips grazing my ear, crushing my books into my chest. I'm too stunned to say anything or step out of his embrace. "Thank God, you're back."

"Damien!" Zoe admonishes him, placing a hand on his shoulder and pulling him back, allowing me to breathe again. "Slow down. You're practically a stranger to her right now."

"Shit, I'm sorry." His eyes widen, expression startled. "It's just so good to see you. After you woke up they didn't allow us to visit anymore. They said it might overwhelm you."

I can see why.

"It's all right," I say, tucking some hair behind my ear, though my pulse is racing. "I understand."

"Forgive him," the other boy says, laughing as he gives his friend a playful shove. "He's only got about two working brain cells."

Damien scowls and shoves him back. "Shut up."

I look to Zoe for help, and she gestures to the taller boy. "James," she explains, and he winks amicably. "Don't be fooled, his brain functions at about the same rate as Damien's."

"Hey!"

A bell rings overhead, and I'm grateful for something to save me from the rest of this conversation.

"We'll see you guys at lunch," she says, inching farther down the hall. "Hopefully you'll have learned to behave yourselves by then."

Damien places a hand over his heart and ducks his head. "I'll be counting down the minutes."

I stick close to Zoe's side as we make our way to the English classroom, not wanting anyone else to catch me by surprise.

"Are they always like that?"

"Unfortunately, yes." She pauses. "Damien is so in love with you that it makes him act like a complete idiot, as you just witnessed."

I already assumed we were romantically involved, but having it confirmed makes me feel worse, especially given the knowledge about my relationship with Parker. It's somewhat violating to know

I've been varying degrees of intimate with at least two boys I don't remember—through no fault of their own—and that I cheated on one with the other.

"Everything's going to be okay," she offers softly.

My feelings about the situation must be pretty easy to read.

"Thanks."

We enter the classroom and the room immediately goes silent. Zoe slides into a seat near the front, looking at me apologetically as she flips her poker straight hair over her shoulder.

"We have a seating chart," she explains, sounding reluctant. "You're back there."

"Right," I say, nodding stiffly before turning to head to the open seat at the back.

The boy from the hallway is sitting in the one next to it, his head down as he scribbles something in his notebook. All of the nervousness instantly returns to my body, and I fervently wish I could sit in any other seat apart from that one. He peers up at me when I get closer, pen stilling on the paper, and I shift into my seat carefully, pretending not to see.

As I set down my notebook and my copy of *Macbeth* in front of me, a young woman with rich brown skin strides into the room, pulling her multitude of braids into a bun.

"Good morning, everyone," she says, perching on the edge of her desk. "I'm sure you've noticed a familiar face has returned to us safe and sound. Let's all give Allie a warm welcome back."

Everyone in the room turns to look in my direction once more, awkwardly applauding me because of the mere fact that I didn't die. Ducking my head, waiting for it to be over, I imagine myself disappearing into the floor. The boy next to me doesn't clap.

"Now, we're going to pick up from where we last read, in act two."

The words send everyone into a slow frenzy, flipping through their books to find the right page. Except I have no idea where we last read from and when Ms. Warren begins to read aloud, everything sounds jumbled and confusing without any context.

The boy in the seat next to mine watches me fumble through the pages. Up close, it's clear that one of his eyes is green, the other blue, and the combination is striking, nearly impossible to look away from.

"Thirty-four," he says quietly, then returns his gaze to the paper.

I nod gratefully and flip to the correct page, feeling unfocused.

"Do you know me?" I finally ask in a whisper.

"Everyone knows you."

"That's not what I meant."

"I know."

Turning back to his book, he proceeds to ignore me for the remainder of the class.

03 | FALL

The end of the school day can't come quickly enough, but when it does, I'm hit with the realization that I have to come back here tomorrow and the day after that and the day after that. Dropping out and hiding in my room for all of eternity is becoming more appealing by the second. My body would certainly thank me for it. Miraculously, I walked away from the accident with minimal injuries—besides the whole amnesia thing, of course—but the effects of being in a temporarily comatose state linger, and I'm not as strong as I should be.

The sun decided to make an appearance in the late afternoon, banishing the clouds in order to bask the front lawn of the school in warm light. I wait for Audrey outside, keeping an eye out for her rusted Corolla, squinting as I lean against the brick of the raised garden.

It's an odd thing to be dropped into the middle of a life, like someone pushed me overboard and expected me to be able to keep myself afloat even though I never learned how to swim. For the most part, people kept their distance as I stumbled my way through my classes, trailing behind Zoe like a lost puppy. It's hard to imagine myself ever striding across campus with purpose and confidence, despite knowing I must have at one point.

Maybe tomorrow I'll at least be able to find the bathroom without having to ask someone for help. And maybe soon the shock waves of my return will fade away and people will stop looking at me like I just dropped down from another planet.

Damien approaches, bringing me back to the present as he steps into my line of vision.

"Hey."

He's wearing a varsity jacket and a sheepish smile as he settles in next to me. I haven't seen him since lunch, and even then he seemed to sense that I needed some space.

"I'm sorry about earlier," he says. "I know I already apologized, but I feel like I should do it again."

"Oh." I wave a hand dismissively, trying to appear casual even though I wish he hadn't brought it up. "Don't worry about it. Seriously."

"School has felt so empty without you." Damien reaches out, looking as though he wants to take my hand in his, so I adjust my backpack strap, shifting my weight between my feet. "I'm really glad you're here, Allie."

"Yeah," I say, unsure if I feel the same. Biting the inside of my lip, I debate with myself for a few moments. "Damien, you seem like a great guy. But I'm going to need some time. This all feels so new to me."

His face falls. "Of course."

"You're all right if we take things slow?" I persist, not sure what the protocol is for asking a boyfriend for space when you don't remember anything about the relationship.

"I'm willing to wait for you."

"Thanks," I say, a bit of tension leaving my body.

"Just don't make me wait forever."

My heart sinks. It's going to take at least forever to get used to the idea of dating him at all. Is it wrong to give him false hope?

Damien glances at the parking lot and gestures to it with his thumb, seemingly oblivious to my inner turmoil. "Hey, do you need a ride home?"

I shake my head quickly. "Audrey is coming to get me."

"Are you sure?"

"Positive."

"Okay. I guess I'll just see you tomorrow then," he says, sounding reluctant as he makes his way to the parking lot.

The thought of having to go through all of this again causes my headache to return, and I close my eyes, massaging my temples. It's going to take ages to settle into this new routine and relearn how to be myself. As if I even know who that is.

A vehicle rolls to a stop in front of me, and I straighten, opening my eyes and adjusting to the bright light once more. Audrey's silver Corolla is parked next to the curb, and relief washes over me knowing it won't be long until I'm back home and in relatively familiar territory.

I pull on the door handle and slide into the car, exhaling heavily as I set my backpack on my lap.

"Thanks for picking me up," I say, reaching over to buckle my seat belt.

"No problem."

That voice definitely does not belong to my sister. Much to my dismay, Parker, wearing a baseball cap, a red flannel, and an apologetic grimace, sits in the driver's seat.

"What are you doing here?" I demand. He's the last person I want to be alone with right now.

"Audrey got called in to cover a shift at the restaurant last minute," he explains. "I swear it wasn't my idea. But I'm the only one around."

I briefly consider getting out of the car, until I remember it's highly likely I would get lost on the way home, and it's too far to walk anyway. Sighing in defeat, I lean back against my seat, fidgeting with my fingers and glowering out the window.

"Fine."

He pulls away from the curb after gaining my reluctant approval.

Parker doesn't say anything until we're a fair distance from the school, and it dawns on me that we're heading in the opposite direction of the house. I sit up straight, feeling a shudder of unease.

"Where are we going?"

He peers at me out of the corner of his eye. "While we're at it, I thought I'd show you one of your favorite places," he explains softly. "It might help."

"Okay," I mumble, despite knowing that spending more time together is an incredibly stupid thing to do. "But make it quick."

"You're going to love it, trust me."

With our destination decided, Parker increases our speed, and I reach forward to turn on the radio as the scenery flies past in hues of green, brown, and blue. I suppose out of all the lives I could've woken up to, this one is pretty damn great in terms of location. Pender Falls is nestled in the mountains, an alcove of forests and lakes, and a hop, skip, and a jump away from the ocean. Everything else I could do without, but at least the town is nice to look at.

We drive through the downtown core, where rows of quaint, vintage-looking shops and restaurants line the streets. In an effort to distract myself from the discomfort of being stuck in a car with my sister's boyfriend, I try to envision myself having had a life here, walking along the sidewalk with the sunlight filtering through the branches of the oak trees, window shopping, grabbing a bite to eat. It's hard to picture, and I find myself wondering if I ever really felt like I belonged.

When I can't stand the silence anymore, I turn to Parker. "Have you lived in Pender Falls your whole life?"

"Yeah," he replies. "I grew up here. It's a nice little town. But, you know, it's small. People talk."

"I've noticed," I remark, unable to hide the bitterness from my voice as I think about all the conversations I failed to tune out today.

Parker cringes, then signals a left turn that leads us away from the main hub. I watch the people in my side mirror gradually disappear.

"I'm sorry," he says sincerely. "Can you blame them, though? It's not every day something like this happens. Your circumstances are very unique."

"I'm not an alien."

"You're right. But it'll get better. They'll find something new to talk about eventually," he says quietly, before returning to his normal volume. "For now, I have something that will take your mind off everything."

"You're really hyping this place up."

"You'll see soon enough."

Eventually, we reach the outskirts of Pender Falls, driving along a gravel path surrounded by trees that blot out the sun, making it feel closer to night than day. We arrive at a parking lot where a rickety sign reads BOULDER TRAIL. Parker turns the key in the ignition, sitting back to appraise my reaction.

"We're here," he announces.

I raise an eyebrow. "Hiking?"

"It's more of a leisurely walk, nothing too strenuous." He passes me a yellow raincoat, and I take it gingerly, peering at the sky. All the gloom from this morning has completely melted away and it's bright and clear now. His mouth twitches. "Just put it on and follow me."

We get out of the car, and I do as he says, sliding my arms through the sleeves and flipping my hair out of the collar, letting it fall across my shoulders. Parker sticks his hands into his pockets and gestures with his chin for me to follow him along the path leading to the forest.

As we walk through the woods, I focus on trying not to trip on the roots beneath my feet, grateful I chose to wear my Blundstones today. "Are you going to tell me where we're going?"

"Nope," he responds promptly, not seeming to mind matching my slow, unsteady pace.

It's quiet save for the sound of twigs snapping, the dirt crunching under our feet, and the occasional bird twittering in the trees above.

My nose is met with the smell of pine needles and fresh air, and I find myself unwinding from the day I had at school. There's something about being out in nature, away from it all, that makes me feel at ease, even if my body is a little wobbly.

"Are you doing okay?"

"Yeah." My cheeks warm. "Sorry I'm so slow."

He crouches slightly, ducking under a branch then holding it out of the way for me. "It's all right, nature is meant to be savored."

"So," I begin, trying to keep my voice light, "how long have you and Audrey worked together at Antonio's?"

The trail gets wider, and a man on a bike whizzes past, going in the opposite direction. It's wide enough for us to walk side by side now, so I fall into step beside Parker.

"It's been about seven months. That's where we met."

"How long have you been together?"

"We started dating after a month of knowing each other."

"When did you move in with us?"

"Is this an interrogation?"

"I have a very limited memory bank. Sorry for trying to learn literally *any* information I can."

Parker coughs out a laugh at the unimpressed tone of my voice. Some of my anxiety begins to uncoil itself when I realize he's not going to pull anything like he did when I came home from the hospital. "Touché," he says. "Just under two months ago."

"That's a while."

"Longer than I anticipated," he agrees.

Even though I'm badgering him with questions, I don't have enough answers quite yet. "Are you going to tell me what really happened between us?" I ask hesitantly. "I deserve to know."

"I didn't know if you'd want to hear it," he admits. Sighing, he gestures to a fallen log nearby then takes a seat, and I'm grateful for the opportunity to give my legs a break, making sure to leave some distance between us. "Audrey was just a co-worker at first. I always liked when we had shifts together, and it wasn't really anything more than that until she confessed she had a crush on me. I wasn't sure if I felt the same, but I thought it couldn't hurt to give it a try."

He falls silent as other tourists traipse in front of us, and it reminds me that we're still in public. Perhaps this isn't the best time to be talking about this stuff, but it's too late to stop.

"After a while, she introduced me to you," he remarks, lips quirking upward slightly, and he peers at me out of the corner of his eye. "We got along instantly. I don't know what it was, but I felt drawn to you. Then one night you went to this party and called me for a ride home. You were drunk out of your mind and you kissed me."

Squeezing my eyes shut, I listen to the nearby sounds of laughter and bike tires gliding over the dirt. A gust of wind blows my hair into my face, and I take a steadying breath, pushing it behind my ear.

"I didn't realize how I felt about you until then." Parker sighs. "You told me that it was a mistake and to pretend it never happened, and I tried at first, but I just couldn't let it go. It was all I could think about. I knew I couldn't continue to be with Audrey knowing what happened and the way I felt."

"But you're still with her."

He lets out a short, self-deprecating laugh. "I'm still with her," he repeats, and the words sound bitter. "Because I'm a coward. I was going to do it but then you got into your accident, and I saw how much it affected her and I couldn't. I wanted to be there for you too."

I bite the inside of my cheek, feeling tense. Even when I was on the brink of death I was finding ways to ruin my sister's life.

"When I heard what happened, heard that I might've lost you . . ." He trails off, shaking his head. "Though I suppose I lost you anyway."

"Did I feel the same?"

He considers the question for a long time. "I don't know," he admits finally. "I wanted you to. But at the same time, I knew it was incredibly selfish to want that."

This version of myself doesn't reciprocate his feelings, and likely never will, but maybe the old one did. I might never know. At the end of the day, it doesn't matter, because nothing will ever happen between us. The person I am now wouldn't do that to her sister.

"Anyway, I want you to know that before everything, I was your friend. And I'm still your friend."

When I look up, his face is kind.

"I'm here if you need me," he finishes.

"Thank you," I reply, my voice soft. His offer confirms the gut feeling I had about him the day I came home from the hospital—the belief that I had someone in my corner, someone I could trust. I haven't had that feeling with a lot of people since my return, and I wonder if I've always felt that way. Even so, he can't be that person anymore.

Before the awkwardness of the situation has a chance to fully sink in, he places his hands on his legs, preparing to stand. "Are you ready to keep going?"

I nod eagerly, wanting to put the conversation behind us, and he helps me back to my feet before we continue down the trail. The path begins to incline upward slightly, but I have no idea where it's leading. I glance at him again, catching the troubled look on his face.

"What are my interests?" I ask with a sigh.

"What?"

"What do I like to do?"

Parker's shoulders relax visibly and his face softens. "You're a great actress," he tells me.

"Really?"

"Oh yeah," he continues. "I've been told the school's theater program would be garbage without you. I think you've starred in nearly every production."

"Huh," I say.

When I think about it, it's really not that surprising. I must've been quite the actress if I could kiss my sister's boyfriend and get away with it. But I don't think that's something worth celebrating.

I stop short, noticing a faint rushing sound in the distance for the first time. "What is that?"

"We're almost there, come on."

The path narrows again as the sound grows louder, and I concentrate on my footsteps, ending up a few paces behind him. We walk this way for a while until he stops abruptly, and I nearly crash into his back.

The noise has reached its peak, and I look up slowly, locating the source. A waterfall stands proudly before us, and I feel foolish for not recognizing the sound earlier. The sight of the water descending is breathtaking, deep-green trees meshing with pale-blue water, and it's almost like an optical illusion.

Parker places his hand on my arm, ushering me out of the way of a couple trying to get onto the path, and the action brings me back to my senses. A climb up slippery rocks brings us closer to the natural wonder, and despite the danger, a large grin takes over my face. Water splashes up to meet us, and I understand the need for the raincoat.

I stick my hand out, letting it become submerged in the downpour, which splashes onto my face and hair, drenching both instantly. Parker watches me, his amusement clear. I'm confident I'm acting like a complete child right now, but I don't care. In this small, inconsequential pocket of time, I feel like I'm truly alive rather than just going through the motions.

It's only when we're back on the trail—me with dripping hair, him with a damp hat—that the adrenaline fades. The air has cooled down significantly, especially when we're in the forest without the help of the sun, and the fact that I'm soaked to the bone doesn't exactly help. But it was totally worth it.

"Did I come here a lot?" I ask, trying to keep from shivering, exhaustion beginning to weigh heavily in my bones.

"Sometimes people throw parties here in the clearing," he explains. "And I know your dad used to take you all the time, but I don't think you've been in a while."

"Where is he? No one has mentioned him."

He gives me a sympathetic look over his shoulder as he shrugs. "Don't know," he remarks. "They don't talk about him much. All I know is that he left a long time ago."

Parker is quiet for a while. "I'm sorry," he says. "I never should've come up to your room that night."

The words are sobering, causing any progress we might've made in the past hour to dissipate.

"We could have started over," he laments. "It would've worked out perfectly. You wouldn't have remembered me. Things would've been the way they're supposed to be."

I don't say anything for a while, wondering if I should respond at all. But the pain in his voice makes some of my anger melt away. It's an internal battle that feels familiar, like I've already fought and been defeated. "We can't change the past," I tell him. "But we can make sure it won't happen again."

"Yeah," he says, voice low as he sticks his hands deeper into his pockets before looking up. "We're almost to the car."

Just like that, the subject is dropped, and neither of us says a word the whole way home.

When we turn onto Seymour Avenue and pull over in front of the house, the first thing I notice is the cop car parked outside. The sight of it gives me a feeling of dread in my belly, and I share a nervous look with Parker.

After a moment of hesitation, I hop out of the car and walk up to the house with him trailing behind me. The front door is open, revealing a thoroughly unimpressed Sofia standing in the entrance with a man in uniform. When she sees me, I can't tell if she's happy or displeased by my arrival.

The policeman turns to look over his shoulder as we approach, offering me a smile beneath his thick moustache.

"What's going on?" I ask, looking between the two of them.

"Allie, welcome home," Sofia says briskly, and there's an awkward pause before she gestures to the man next to her. "This is Officer Edwards."

He's clearly trying to appear friendly, but I take a subconscious step closer to Parker. "Hello, Allie," he says. "It's nice to see you again."

Sofia purses her lips. "He has some questions about the night of your accident."

"I really don't remember much," I say, feeling like this is a use-less endeavor. I didn't even remember my own name when I woke up, what makes them think I'll suddenly be able to tell them exactly what happened?

"That's all right," Officer Edwards encourages, holding a hand out. "We can take it slow. We're just trying to piece together what happened. With your mother present, of course. Is that all right with you?"

I look to Sofia for guidance, but her face is unreadable. "I guess so."

My mother turns to the officer and gestures for him to enter the house. "Shall we?"

I move to follow them to the living room, before Parker catches my arm, leaning down to ask, "Do you want me to be there too?"

"No, it's okay," I reply, though the second the words leave my mouth, I'm not sure if I mean them.

He lets go, nodding, and I resume my path to the other room, taking a seat on the sofa across from Officer Edwards. Sofia sits beside me, clasping her hands in her lap. I watch as he flips open a notepad to a blank page, and it feels awfully similar to being assessed by Dr. Meyer.

"Now, you're aware you were at a party that night," he begins.

"Yes."

He flips back a few pages. "It took place at Iris Wen's house, correct?" The name is unfamiliar, but Sofia nods. "I'm going to take a wild guess and say that there was alcohol at this party."

"I don't know."

"She has amnesia, as I'm sure you're aware," Sofia interjects, her voice frosty, and I'm extremely grateful to have her with me.

Officer Edwards lifts his hands up innocently. "Of course," he says. "We're doing our best to paint a clear picture of the events that took place, and we hoped you might be ready to talk now. Allie, is there anything more you can tell me?"

I chew on the inside of my lip, thinking about the nonsensical images my brain has drummed up from that night, and the flashback I had in the hallway this morning. It's unlikely that any of it is helpful. I'm not sure if it's even real or if my mind is playing tricks on me.

"Whenever you're ready," he encourages.

"Sorry, I can't think of anything," I say, shaking my head. It's not a complete lie, I just don't want to waste his time.

"That's a shame," he says, disappointment darting across his features. "There are some things about that night that just aren't adding up, and even the tiniest bit of information could help. Open liquor was found in your car, yet none was in your system. What do you think about that?"

Heat floods my cheeks, and I shake my head again. "I—"

"I think that's enough for today," Sofia announces, rising to her feet.

"Ms. Castillo," he says, "we're just looking into every possibility—"

"And she already told you everything she knows. You can clearly see she's not mentally fit to be questioned."

Sofia's voice is chilling and firm, and the force behind her words makes the hair on the back of my neck rise. Officer Edwards stammers as she ushers him to the door, but she ignores him, locking it once he's outside. The sight of her scaring off a policeman as if he's nothing more than a pesky fly is bizarre—and, admittedly, pretty badass—but judging by her clear lack of discomfort, this isn't the first time. She sighs deeply, shaking her head.

"Useless," she mutters. "They have nothing better to do. Don't ever let them talk to you alone, you hear me?"

Feeling baffled, I nod. "Okay."

"The cops in this town have had it out for you for years," she admits. Clearly her irritation stretches far beyond today. "It's getting out of hand. Having a few strikes on your record doesn't give them the right to interrogate you when you're the victim of a life-altering accident. I've been holding them off, but they're obviously chomping at the bit."

"Strikes?"

She realizes she's said too much. "Don't worry about that now. You've had a long day. Let's go have some dinner, I'll order us something to eat."

With that, she heads into the kitchen, and I wonder whether Officer Edwards's visit was simply a cop doing his job or if his presence was meant to be a threat.

04 | ELICIT

A few nights after the police visit, I have my first vivid dream.

I'm standing at the base of a playground, surrounded by never-ending trees, an icy breeze grazing my skin. It's quiet and empty, and at first I think I'm alone, until I notice a little boy sitting on the swing set. He watches me solemnly as I approach, eyes striking—one blue, one green—and using one foot in the mulch to push himself back and forth.

The sky is a thick, hazy grey, and something about the stillness makes me wonder if the boy needs any help. Trying to appear friendly, I plaster a smile on my face and crouch down to his level. "How's it going?"

He doesn't speak, the swing creaking with each sway.

"Where are your parents? Are you here by yourself?"

Again, I receive no response, and I straighten up, glancing around the barren park. The sky rapidly grows darker, becoming nightfall at an unnatural pace, and I take a step back, suddenly feeling unsafe.

Like we're being watched.

"Hey, I think we should get out of here," I tell him, reaching out a hand. "Do you want to come with me?"

He blinks, his face remaining stoic. But this time he speaks. "Are you awake?"

"What?"

"Are you awake?"

He looks at something over my shoulder as the playground is lit up in a flash of white. He points, and I turn around just in time to see a pair of glaring headlights barreling in my direction.

Gasping, I dive out of the way, but before I hit the ground, I come to with a start, grabbing hold of my comforter and breathing heavily.

There's a knock on my door, and I squint at the sunlight coming in through the window, pulse racing. It takes a few moments for me to register reality and shake off the dream. Dr. Meyer told me this might happen—that my brain is working double time to try to right itself, and bizarre, semitruthful dreams could be the result. I try to grasp the details before they fade away. Surely it has to mean *something*.

"Allie." I hear Audrey's voice on the other side of the door, startling me again. "Are you awake?"

"Yeah." My voice is hoarse.

"I made breakfast. You should eat soon if you don't want to be late for school."

As her footsteps retreat down the hallway, I catch sight of the clock, realizing I slept through my alarm. After getting dressed and settling my heart rate, I head downstairs, hit instantly with the smell of something sweet.

Audrey uses a spatula to place a pancake on a plate, then sets it down on the island, and I take a seat in front of it, mouth watering.

"Thank you," I say sincerely, digging into the meal as she takes the stool next to me.

We eat in silence for a while, until I think back to my conversation with Parker at Boulder Trail, about our family. It's most likely a touchy subject to bring up with her, but I decide to do it anyway.

"So," I start hesitantly. "Parker mentioned something the other day."

She tilts her head, taking a sip of orange juice.

"About our father."

Her hand visibly stiffens.

"I noticed you guys don't talk about him."

Audrey takes a deep breath, and it's the most solemn I've seen her. "I figured you would ask eventually," she admits. "We don't talk about him because he's a scumbag. He ditched us years ago."

"Why?"

"He cheated," she says simply, and my breakfast suddenly feels like a massive rock in my gut. "And then he left when Mom said he couldn't have both of them and completely forgot we existed."

"That's awful."

"No kidding," she agrees. "The worst part is, it was one of Mom's clients. It's not like this lady thought he was single, she knew."

Shaking her head, Audrey stands up and clears her plate, and I offer her mine, too, having lost my appetite. "It's fucked," she says, dumping the dishes in the sink. "I don't understand how anyone can do that."

"Me neither," I say, trying not to think about Parker but unable to think of anything else.

"The three of us should've stuck together after he left. Instead it just drove us apart, and we never really recovered," she says. "Your accident made me realize how much time we wasted fighting with each other. I don't want to do that anymore."

I muster a distracted smile, sweat forming on my palms.

"Anyway." She sighs. "This conversation is way too heavy for breakfast. Let me change and then I'll be ready to drive you to school."

"Sure."

As she heads to her room, I find myself wishing I skipped breakfast altogether.

Even hours into the school day, I can't stop thinking about my dad, Sofia, and my own mistakes. Why would I have an affair when that was the very thing that destroyed my family and made me resent my father? Maybe it was a ploy to get his attention. Maybe it felt like revenge. Regardless of how I spin it, it's a terrible, terrible thing.

I'm exchanging my books at my locker when a pair of hands cover my eyes abruptly, making me flinch, panic rising in my chest.

"Guess who," a low voice whispers, breath tickling my ear.

"Not the best thing to ask an amnesiac."

Damien laughs, dropping his hands. "You have me there," he says. "Good morning, beautiful."

"Hi," I mumble, wondering if he's already forgotten our talk from the other day.

"Let me walk you to class." He sidles up next to me, greeting several people who pass by, while I keep my head down, making my way to the biology classroom.

We've only made it a short distance down the hallway when I spot the boy from my English class. I didn't know he was here today; he must've ditched this morning. He glances up, looking over at me, and my heart constricts.

His eyes. They're the same ones as the little boy's in my dream—somber and heterochromatic. The images filter through my mind again, of him on the swing set, giving a silent warning about the danger behind me.

But he doesn't linger, ducking his head and stalking in the opposite direction, and I watch him disappear over my shoulder.

"Damien," I blurt, gesturing to the boy before he completely vanishes. "Who is that?"

"Mason Byrne." He frowns. "Why?"

"No reason," I lie.

He sticks his hands into the pockets of his letterman jacket. "Weird guy. He doesn't really talk to anyone."

I wonder if I'm reading into things too deeply or if there really is a connection between the boy in my dreams and Mason. There has to be—the eyes are a dead giveaway. But Damien doesn't notice my stewing and continues to trudge down the hall.

"Anyway, I was thinking . . ." he begins, trailing off. "We should go out tonight."

"I thought we agreed to take things slow."

"Oh I know," he says eagerly. "Consider this a get to know each other date."

"But you already know me."

"Okay, then consider it a get to know Damien Sanchez date."

"How exciting," I tease, as we stop outside of the classroom. "All right, Sanchez. Show me what you've got."

"I'll pick you up at six," he tells me with a grin before sauntering to his own class.

True to his word, Damien arrives at my house right at six, telling me our destination is a surprise. I'm growing pretty damn tired of surprises, but I figure it's best to just humor him. He takes the time to greet Sofia and present me with a bouquet of flowers before offering his arm to walk me to the car. We drive past lush green trees, and they look vibrant against the overcast sky. My mind wanders to the forest, imagining what it's like to stand in the middle of it, surrounded by nothing but nature.

When we pass a playground, I think of the dream again, barely noticing Damien tapping his fingers on the wheel in time to the song on the radio. There's a part of me that's fearful every time I climb into a car, knowing it was the thing that ruined my life, but I try not to dwell on it too much.

"So, what do you wanna know?" he asks, breaking the silence. "Ask me anything."

"Where are we going?"

"Ask me something about *me*."

"Well, *you* know where we're going."

He chuckles, keeping his focus on the road. "It's a surprise. Next question."

"How long have we been dating?"

"Two years," he says. "I know. A long time, right?"

"How did we get together?"

"Hooked up at a party. I'd liked you for a while and finally wore you down."

"How romantic," I remark sarcastically, though I'm not all that surprised. There were loads of photos of us intoxicated and all over each other hung up in my bedroom. The scene isn't that hard to picture—I can easily conjure blurry images of a high school party and the sixteen-year-old versions of Damien and me falling over each other. I wonder what it was that made me give in.

"Modern love," he agrees, and I laugh.

"Right."

"As far as I'm concerned, I'm the luckiest guy in the world."

He pulls the car into a parking lot, and I realize I've forgotten to pay attention to where we were going. Light catches my eye in the side mirror, and I look over my shoulder to see a Ferris wheel across the street, placed in the middle of a bustling fair. Music, laughter, and shouts reach my ears, and I'm sure it's going to feel like sensory overload once we get closer, but from here, it's easy to appreciate the spectacle.

I look at Damien to find that he's watching me expectantly, gauging my reaction.

"Pretty good surprise?" he asks.

I nod. "Pretty good surprise."

"They have this festival every year to help with the seasonal depression," he quips, stepping onto the pavement.

Minutes later, we're in the middle of it all, strolling alongside the carnival booths. Kids with painted faces are running around, followed by frantic parents bringing up the rear, while middle schoolers laugh about it to their friends. I have a ball of pink cotton candy in my hand, and Damien is working on a candy apple. The ghost of a headache forming pulses in my temple, but I ignore it.

We pass by a dart-throwing game and Damien stops, turning to me.

"Can I win you a teddy bear?"

"You can play, but I don't want the bear."

"Aw, come on," he protests, dropping his shoulders. "I thought it would be cute."

"If I want something, I'll try to win it myself. The game is the fun part."

As I begin to meander down the aisle, he walks close enough that our arms brush, and I'm a bit surprised by how numb I am to the gesture. Damien is an attractive, sweet guy who's clearly very into me, and we've been together before, so I don't know why being with him doesn't stir up anything inside of me. Not a single butterfly.

I wish I could catch a glimpse of the old Allie, just for a moment, long enough to see how she acted, how she talked, what she truly thought about everything. But even if I could study my old life for hours on end, it would never be enough to make me the same person I was back then. My circumstances and experiences must have been a large part of what made me who I was, and now that all of that has been stripped away, it's impossible to replicate. If only everyone else understood that.

"Fair enough," he says, after a pause. "We'll go back to our other game. Any more questions?"

"Hm," I hum, gently pulling apart a piece of cotton candy and placing it in my mouth, feeling it dissolve. "The letterman jacket." I gesture to it. "Are you a jock or something?"

He smirks, puffing out his chest proudly. "Captain of the soccer team."

"Of course. Am I a cheerleader?"

Laughing boisterously, he throws his head back. "Not even close."

Damien grins as he throws the stick from his candy apple in a nearby trash can. "Exercise isn't really your thing. You're actually a theater kid. It's super dorky."

"Hey, watch it!" I give him a playful shove, prompting him to laugh again. "Theater seems sophisticated, you ass."

"I didn't say it was a bad thing. I'm very much into dorky."

"Damien," I start, "how do you feel about all of this?"

"You being a dork?"

"Me not remembering you," I say softly.

Damien's face becomes solemn. "Crushed," he admits. "It's kind of like you died in the accident but you're still here. I don't like that I'm a stranger to you now."

I never expected Damien to be the one to accurately describe the way I've been feeling—like I really did die that day and now I'm a ghost inhabiting someone else's body.

"But I'm telling myself it's just a temporary setback," he finishes. "I'm not losing hope yet."

"Temporary?"

"There's a good chance you'll get your memory back, right? And even if you don't, I'm confident we can get back to the way things were."

He reaches for my hand, intertwining our fingers, and I stop myself from pulling out of his grasp. Just like Audrey, it's clear he's clueless about my relationship with Parker. Because of my near-death experience, they both treat me like I'm a saint. I don't deserve it.

Desperate to change the subject, I'm drawn to the neon lights ahead of us. "Can we ride the Ferris wheel?" I blurt, less than subtle.

"Oh," he says. "Yeah, if you want to."

As we wait in line, Damien sticks close to my side. The day turns to twilight, and the temperature drops. I shove my hands in my pockets to keep my fingers warm, bouncing on my heels. Eventually, it's our turn to board, and I regret my decision as soon as I step into the rickety cart, grabbing the railing for balance. It swings beneath my weight, and my heart hammers in my chest.

Damien sits next to me, and we slowly ascend, the twinkling lights of Pender Falls visible from the top. In the distance, I can see the outline of mountains and the first stars that poke holes in the darkness. The air is cooler up here, and my breath comes out in a swirl of fog, dissipating into the atmosphere.

I take it all in, tucking my palms under my legs, feeling content. "It's beautiful," I breathe.

"It is," Damien echoes, staring at me. A groan tries to escape my throat, and I have to work to suppress it.

He slides closer, and I pray for the ride to move faster. Distantly, I hear screaming coming from the livelier rides, but our gondola feels secluded.

"This will be over soon, right?" I ask.

"Why? Scared of heights?" he teases, leaning into my side.

I peer down at the ground far below us, my stomach dipping. It feels a lot farther than the last time I looked. "Maybe."

"Don't worry, we're totally safe." He stretches his arm out behind me.

I take a deep breath as we come to a stop at the highest point of the wheel.

"You know, I'll be honest," Damien begins. "There's a part of me that's jealous of you."

"Why would you be jealous?"

His gaze is on the festival below before it flickers back to me. Light and shadow dance across his face, sober once more, as the gondola sways. He plays with my hair, and I'm stiff as a board. "I have a few things I would kill to forget."

It all begins to feel like too much: the lights, the shouting, the height. Damien. I close my eyes as my head starts spinning, fire exploding in my temple. A cool sheen of sweat forms on my forehead, and my hair sticks to my skin. Despite the temperature, my jacket feels too hot, making me squirm in my seat.

"Allie?"

I peek at him.

"Are you okay?"

Swallowing, I shake my head. "I think I need to get off."

He watches me for a few beats, as if trying to decide if I'm being sincere, before nodding. "It's almost done. We can get off soon."

Another wave of nausea passes over me and I ball my hands into fists. I lean forward, tempted to sit on the floor of the cart and put my head between my knees, skull pounding. Every time it moves, I have to fight to keep from spilling my guts onto the floor.

When I look up, the sight of the world moving in a blur beneath us causes me to slump forward, gripping the railing for balance.

"Here," Damien offers, reaching out.

Instantly, an image of another hand jolting toward me flashes through my mind, filling my chest with an immediate sense of dread. I hear another scream, but it's an echo, coming from somewhere inside of me. Blanching, I shove Damien's arm abruptly as the world turns black.

"Don't touch me!"

He holds his hands up in surrender, and my vision wavers between a dark forest and the bright lights of the fair, unable to process either sight. "Sorry," he says quickly. "I was just trying to help."

It takes a few seconds for what just happened to sink in, embarrassment flooding my cheeks. We've attracted the attention of everyone within earshot. "Oh my God." I place a hand to my lips. "I don't know what came over me. I'm so sorry."

He breathes out a laugh, running a hand through his hair and looking nervous. "It's okay." He pauses. "Are you all right, though?"

"I—I think so."

"You sure?"

"I'm sure. Let's go back to having a good time."

Clasping my hands in a white-knuckled grip, I resist the urge to flinch at every shout in the distance and banish all thoughts of shadowy woods and malice from my brain. We don't say anything for the rest of the ride, and when we step off, Damien has to grab my arm to keep me from collapsing to the ground.

He walks me over to a bench, and I shiver, my legs shaking even as I'm sitting down.

"I don't think you're all right, Allie."

"I am, I just need a minute."

The headache rattles around in my skull, and I can't stop myself from wincing.

"Come on," he says, gesturing to the entrance with his chin. "I'll take you home."

Begrudgingly, I drag myself to my feet, feeling embarrassed. Dr. Meyer told me I would have flashbacks, strange dreams, and tiny whispers of memory, but he failed to mention the possibility of reality-altering hallucinations.

The night has grown completely dark by the time Damien drops me off. As we approach the house, the motion light flickers on, feeling like a glow of warmth and safety in the middle of the black.

I'm unnerved by the image I saw. It feels like another frame in the short slide show of pictures that I remember from the night of the accident, one of the many puzzle pieces scattered throughout my subconscious.

We reach the front door and I place my hand on the doorknob, pausing.

"I'm sorry for freaking out on you," I say sincerely, face contorting in an apologetic frown.

"It's nothing," he remarks, though I know he's just trying to be nice. "Don't worry about it."

"Okay," I concede. "Well, I was having fun before all that happened."

"Me too. I'm glad you said yes."

Silence falls over us, and he watches me intently. I know this is probably the point where he would kiss me good night, but he most likely doesn't think he's allowed to. It's a strange territory to be in, not knowing what the boundaries should be. I can't think of a single thing to say.

Acting on impulse, I stand on my tiptoes, reach over, and press my lips against his cheek briefly. When I pull away, I see the look of shock on his face before it turns into a smile, spreading from ear to ear.

"Good night, Damien," I say faintly.

"Night," he says.

He turns away, heading for his car, and I open the door to the house, entering and closing it behind me. Leaning against the door with a heavy sigh, I'm left to wonder why his reaction to the kiss makes me feel like I just made a colossal mistake.

05 | BEND

The sound of quick footsteps coming from behind reaches my ears, followed by a pair of arms encircling my shoulders gently, causing me to stumble. Damien plants a delicate kiss in my hair as he rights us, and I find my footing again. Laughing uncomfortably, I subtly disentangle myself from him, reaching up to pat down my hair.

"Hey." He greets me.

My heart sighs wearily when it registers the hopeful look on his face. "Hi," I say as we walk to the cafeteria. The hallway is bustling with activity as usual, though I still draw attention as I pass by. "I don't mean to sound like a broken record, but I thought we were going to take things slow?" Taking things slow does not equate to overbearing public displays of affection in my mind, but maybe it does in his.

He laughs shortly. "Well, we said that before you kissed me."

"Damien," I say, disappointment coloring my tone. "It was a kiss on the cheek. To say thank you. It didn't really mean anything else. I'm sorry."

He only lets his devastation show for a split second before recovering. "Regardless, it was a great night, and we should do it again sometime."

The idea of going out with Damien again is not the worst thing in the world, considering I actually did have a decent time yesterday, but if this is the result, it doesn't seem wise. Being with someone I have zero memory of loving proves to be more difficult every day. There's a voice in the back of my mind telling me I should end the relationship and avoid stringing him along, but I don't know if that would be fair. It hasn't been that long yet.

"Maybe we can invite Zoe and James too," I suggest.

"Allie," he begins, "that's not what I meant—"

"You called?"

We're abruptly joined by James as he throws open the cafeteria doors and slings an arm around each of our shoulders, dragging us along with him. I'm thankful for the distraction that saves me from our conversation, but Damien looks annoyed, side-eyeing his best friend as we stumble through the room.

"What are you talking about?" Damien asks.

"I heard my name," James says simply, oblivious to what he interrupted. "I'm starving. You guys hungry?"

"I am," I say, ignoring Damien.

After making our way through the lunch line, we join Zoe at our usual table, and I slide into the seat next to her. She reaches out an arm to give me a squeeze.

"Just the gal I wanted to see," she says brightly.

I peel back the plastic on my container of salad. "Oh?"

"What would you say to getting out of this place for a while this afternoon?"

"I would be intrigued," I reply, remaining cautious. "But I would also say that I probably shouldn't miss any more classes."

Zoe pouts, slouching her shoulders. "Oh, come on," she protests. "You deserve a break, and you have the world's most valid excuse. Just say you have a headache or something."

"Excuse me," James interjects, raising a hand. "What about us?"

"What about you?"

He gestures as if it should be obvious. "Aren't we invited?"

"Absolutely not."

James scoffs, looking affronted, but she doesn't seem to spare him another thought. Damien is sulking, pushing his food around on his plate, and I stifle a smile at the dramatics, turning to Zoe.

"What do you have in mind?" I ask.

"Retail therapy, of course," she explains. "There are some amazing shops about an hour out of town. We could grab dinner too."

I take a deep breath, debating, as Zoe clasps her hands in a pleading gesture, batting her eyelashes. Getting out of Pender Falls and away from school for an extended period of time does sound rather appealing. It would be a chance to get to know my supposed best friend a bit better too.

"Are you sure it's okay to ditch?" I persist.

Zoe huffs. "Ugh, the new version of you is such a goody two-shoes. Usually I'm the only one who cares about school."

James barks out a laugh. "For real. You used to ditch all the time."

Realistically, an afternoon of school isn't that much in the grand scheme of things. "All right, fine." I point an accusatory finger in Zoe's direction. "But if Sofia murders me, my blood is on your hands."

Zoe crosses her heart with feigned seriousness. "I accept full responsibility."

When the lunch bell rings, I stand and bring my tray over to the garbage bin. After I've dumped the contents inside, I turn around to find Damien behind me. He takes great interest in the cafeteria floor, looking sheepish. A nudge of apprehension builds in my chest.

"Excited to hang out with Zo?"

"Yeah," I say. "It'll be nice to spend some time together."

"Allie," he starts, immediately dropping the small talk. "I really did have a good time last night. I know everything is crazy for you right now, and you feel like you don't know me. I get that. But I can't just turn off my feelings." He takes a deep breath. "I love you. And I want you to know I'm going to do whatever I can to make you feel the same way again. No matter how long it takes, okay?"

Discomfort prickles on my skin. "Damien, I can't promise you anything. I don't want you to get your hopes up. I might never—"

"I know. But I won't give up."

There are a few beats of charged silence before another voice breaks in, bursting through the tension. I take a subconscious step backward.

"Allie," Zoe calls as she hurries in our direction. "We're wasting precious daylight. There's a very small window of opportunity to sneak away before anyone notices us."

I hesitate, stuck in my conversation with Damien, tempted to tell him not to waste his time on me. As far as I'm concerned, it's a lost cause. But he remains stonefaced and stubborn. Instead, I turn to Zoe, nodding. "Okay."

"Have fun," Damien calls, making an effort to lighten his voice as Zoe tugs me out of the cafeteria.

Out in the parking lot, she instructs me to keep my head down as we make a beeline for her car. Despite my initial reservations, I feel a thrill of adrenaline over breaking the rules. I'm sure I'll regret it later if Sofia finds out, but for now, it's nice to have a change of pace.

"If any teachers see us, I'll say I have period cramps and have to go home," she whispers, keeping an eye out for any bystanders. "Works every time."

It takes great difficulty for me to suppress my snort of amusement, until Zoe curses under her breath, grabs my arm, and ducks behind an old truck. I follow her lead, struggling to keep my balance, bracing myself against the rusty metal.

"Incoming." She nods in the direction of the school doors.

Ms. Warren exits, fiddling with her bag as she makes her way to her car, and we remain hidden. I hold my breath, legs beginning to ache from crouching. Zoe peers through the window of the truck, watching as Ms. Warren reaches her vehicle and places a hand on the door handle.

At the last second before getting in, the woman pauses, glancing in our direction, and Zoe frantically ducks down again as we share a panicked look. For a few moments, everything is still, until we hear the sound of Ms. Warren's car start up and pull out of the parking lot.

Zoe exhales, leaning against me, and I finally release the laughter I've been holding in. "Close call," she quips, grinning, before standing and reaching for my hand.

We arrive at a sleek, silver car that looks like it costs more than most of the other ones in this parking lot combined. Zoe unlocks it, and the car makes a melodic beeping sound as she slides inside, gesturing for me to do the same. I sit down on the plush leather seat, feeling the material beneath my fingers. Definitely expensive.

She turns the key in the ignition, blond hair shining over her shoulder, and the engine hums to life, a pop song floating from the speakers. It's strikingly familiar, conjuring images of driving in the summertime with the windows down, Zoe in the driver's seat, laughter echoing between the lyrics, and I can't tell if they're real or fake.

"All right, let's get the hell out of here," she announces after we buckle our seat belts.

Reaching down, she shifts gears, glances behind her, and prepares to back out. But when she presses the gas, the car lurches forward until she slams on the brakes, causing the two of us to jerk, straining against our seat belts.

"Shit," she hisses after we've come to a stop, inches from the fence surrounding the lot.

My heart thunders, black creeping around the edges of my vision as my head throbs with phantom pain. I blink rapidly until the cracks in the windshield disappear and the branches recede into the forest.

Not real.

Zoe is staring at the fence, wide eyed. My hand shakes as I reach out to touch her arm gently, wanting something to ground me in reality. Her muscles are rigid. "Are you okay?" I ask. "That was just an accident."

She swallows, letting out a breathy laugh. "Sorry." She runs a hand over her skirt, looking at me apologetically. "New car. Let me try that again."

This time, she smoothly backs out of the space, and I can feel her relax. It takes me longer to calm down, seeing flashes of blood every time I close my eyes, but eventually my heart rate returns to normal and I'm able to lean back against the seat. We don't talk much as she drives, listening to the peppy songs on the radio instead, and I watch the scenery pass by the window. The sun is out in full force today, filtering through the trees and creating intricate patterns on the pavement.

It gives the town a lighter feel than usual, as people emerge from their homes to enjoy the sunshine, strolling the shopping strip and taking advantage of the parks scattered throughout the neighborhood. But it doesn't take long until we're going past the town limits and heading onto the highway, weaving a path through the mountains.

Zoe rolls the windows down, and I reach a hand out, letting the cool breeze glide between my fingers. Eventually, the mountains give way to a lush valley where people have set up their homes in the fields below. As usual, the sights are breathtaking. It's crazy to think that I've lived in this area all my life and looked at this view every day growing up.

"Almost there," Zoe announces, turning the music down.

I turn to her, trying to push my hair back as it blows into my face. "Do we always come this far out to go shopping?"

"At least once a month," she explains. "Pender Falls is cute and all, but there is absolutely jack shit to do there."

Pender Falls is beautiful, and there's something alluring about it, but I can imagine it must feel small and secluded to someone like Zoe, who seems like she has the world at her manicured fingertips. "What are you going to do after high school?"

"It's weird to hear you ask me that when we've had so many conversations about it in the past," she admits, looking a bit uncomfortable. "I'm going to McGill University in Montreal. If everything goes to plan, you'll be calling me Dr. Zoe Harris in, like, ten years."

"Impressive."

"My parents are thrilled," she says, not bothering to hide the boredom in her voice.

"Did I ever talk about what I wanted to do?" I ask, and she softens a bit, seemingly relieved she's no longer the subject of conversation.

"College wasn't really your thing. You were determined to become a star someday," she says, sounding wistful. "If anything, you would've studied acting, I guess. But most of all, you just wanted to leave this place far behind you."

"Where did I want to go?"

She laughs once without humor. "Anywhere."

We arrive at a sprawling shopping center on the outskirts of a city that I miss the name of, and Zoe parks the car, killing the engine. She straightens out the lapels of her blazer before stepping out onto the pavement, and I follow her inside.

"This place is a hidden gem," she tells me, pride in her voice.

Once inside, it's as if Zoe develops a laser focus, heading straight for a store called Plaisir, and I hurry to keep up. She immediately spots a form-fitting, lacy black dress and lifts it off the rack, holding it up to her body.

"What do you think? Is this me?"

"Beautiful. You should try it on."

She perks up, draping the dress over her arm and continuing to leaf through the racks. "I will."

I do the same, eyeing a forest-green dress, until I take one look at the price tag and put it back. Window shopping it is.

After a while of looking through the clothes, I notice Zoe watching me out of the corner of her eye.

"How have you been doing with everything?" she asks, keeping her voice low.

Her question catches me off guard. "I kind of feel like I'm waiting to wake up again, if that makes sense. Like this is all a dream, and I'm just riding it out."

"Mm," she hums.

I think for a beat longer, trying to form my thoughts into words. "And it feels like I'm playing catch-up on someone else's life. It doesn't feel like it's mine. I don't know if that will go away."

"It will," she tells me gently, and my throat becomes thick. "Everything doesn't have to go back to the way it was. You can choose what you want. It *is* your life, even if it doesn't feel like it. You get to decide."

I hadn't realized how much I wanted to talk about it with someone who wasn't my mother or Dr. Meyer. "Thanks, Zoe," I say, working to keep my voice steady and letting the fabric of a soft sweater slip from my fingers as I move to the next rack, not really paying attention to the clothes anymore.

"Anytime. You know, just because the old you wanted to run away after high school and become famous, that doesn't mean the new you has to do the same. You could totally hate acting now."

"That's true," I agree, even though there have been times that it's clear she expects me to act a certain way. "I needed to hear that."

"Any other problems you want me to solve?" she teases.

"Well," my voice falters. "I've also been having these weird flashbacks."

She pauses, tilting her head. "Flashbacks?"

"I think that's what they are," I explain. "But they're really fragmented, and they don't make any sense. Kind of like a bunch of random puzzle pieces that might not even go together."

"What do you mean?"

I purse my lips, unsure of how much I want to reveal. "For example, today in your car. When you accidentally went forward, I saw these images of broken glass and blood. I think I'm seeing tiny moments of what happened that night."

Zoe watches my face intently, looking somber. "Spooky."

"Yeah."

"That's all you can see?"

"Mostly. But I did have a weird dream the other night."

"Oh?" she asks, looking intrigued.

"I saw this little boy at a playground." I pause, certain that I probably sound insane. "I don't know why, but I'm pretty sure it was Mason. They had the same eyes."

Zoe stops again, pausing in her search, and looking at me as though I've grown another head, the atmosphere rapidly changing. "Mason Byrne? Why the hell were you dreaming about him?"

"I don't know!" I protest, my cheeks flaming at her instant judgment.

"Mason Byrne," she repeats, shaking her head, amused. "Now that's the bottom of the barrel."

"What makes you say that?"

She gives me another look. "Allie, have you ever even seen him talk to anyone? He's just some weird social pariah who lurks in the hallways. It's creepy."

I feel strangely defensive, and let go of the clothes, crossing my arms over my chest. I've noticed that he keeps to himself, and he certainly hasn't said anything to me since my first day back, despite us sitting right next to each other, but that doesn't mean anything is *wrong* with him. "Right now, I'm the exact same thing."

"That's completely different," she remarks, waving a hand. "You went through something traumatic."

"Maybe Mason did too."

"Allie, this"—Zoe holds her hand up high—"is where we are. Mason is *all* the way down here." She brings her hand to a spot just inches above the ground.

"Why?"

"We've worked hard to get where we are," she explains. "I've made my way to the top of every class I'm in by any means necessary, you're the most talented actress in the school, Damien is captain of the soccer team, and James is, well, he's got charm. And he's Damien's right-hand man."

I can't suppress my scoff as I focus on the racks again. "That all sounds very superficial."

"That's high school. We have the talent and the connections and the money, so people like us rise to the top."

"And people like Mason end up at the bottom. That's what you're trying to say."

Zoe shrugs again, holding a blouse up to her frame and glancing in the mirror before putting it back. "Don't blame me, I didn't invent the system. But it's the natural balance of things."

"Whatever." I sigh.

"Anyway, don't tell Damien you're dreaming about other boys," she chirps, nudging me with her elbow. "He'll get jealous."

He doesn't even know the half of it.

"I won't."

With that, she brushes off the conversation, and I decide not to tell her about the rest—the car barreling toward me and the hand reaching out to grab me at the festival.

"I'm going to try this on." She holds up the black dress. "Come to the dressing room with me? I need your opinion."

"Sure," I say, smiling halfheartedly.

We make our way to the fitting room, and I sit on a plush cushion in the waiting area as Zoe changes into the dress. Shortly after, she emerges, lifts her hair into a ponytail, and does a twirl as she stands before me, assessing her reflection in the mirror from all angles.

"Thoughts?"

"It looks gorgeous on you," I say. Watching her makes my self-esteem plummet. I don't necessarily have a problem with the way I look, but I'm envious of how comfortable she seems to be in her skin. It's clear she feels at home in her body, whereas I feel like I'm a guest in mine.

"Something isn't right," she remarks, placing her hands on her hips, and frowning. "I think it's the waist. Boo. I really liked it."

"No, Zoe, it looks perfect." I encourage her, but her expression doesn't budge. "Seriously."

A fitting room attendant folding clothes nearby looks between the two of us, before returning to her task. "Your friend should try it on," she says simply.

"Me?"

"Yes, you."

Zoe turns to me slowly. "Do you want to?"

"Um . . . sure," I say. "Why not?"

She heads back into the change room and comes out a couple of minutes later in her regular clothes, then hands me the dress with a wooden smile. "Here you go."

After taking it from her delicately, I slip through the door. I take off my jeans and the turtleneck I borrowed from Audrey, then slide the dress over my head. It fits my body like a glove, and I smooth my hand down over the lacy skirt.

Feeling exposed, I step out of the change room. The attendant instantly lets out a delighted gasp, and Zoe's lips part. Laughing uncomfortably, I peer at my reflection, fiddling with a loose thread.

Both of them come up behind me, and the attendant beams. "That dress was *made* for you."

"She's right," Zoe says quietly, seeming a lot more reserved than before. "You should definitely get it."

A pensive expression takes hold of my features. Despite the fact that I'm staring at myself in the mirror, and what Zoe told me about my life still being mine, it doesn't stop me from feeling as though I'm watching a stranger, and the real me is hidden somewhere underneath. Putting on a pretty dress doesn't make me feel any more at ease.

Instead, it makes me feel like the girl Zoe was describing, the one in the photos in my bedroom, at the top of the high school food chain, looking down on everyone else.

"Maybe another time," I say finally, and Zoe straightens her posture, expression unreadable.

"Are you sure?"

"Yeah." I nod, taking one last lingering look at myself before heading back into the change room to take the dress off.

When I come out, Zoe's gaze is riveted on the dress, burning a hole in the fabric as the attendant hangs it on the rack, and it's not until long after she's dropped me off that I recognize the look in her eyes as raging jealousy.

06 | SUBMERGE

The next morning, I have an appointment with Dr. Meyer.

Sofia takes the day off work, and it gives me a valid reason to skip out on school this time. I get ready in my room, selecting one of my many black blouses and running a brush through my hair. It isn't long before I hear a tap on my door and look over in time to see Sofia entering the room.

"Almost ready?" she asks, eyes raking over my appearance.

"Yeah," I say, reaching for my bag.

"I have something for you," she announces, and it's only then I notice the box in her hands. She offers it to me.

It's a brand-new smartphone. I lift the lid off the box and pluck the sleek device from the packaging, turning it over in my fingers.

"Since they couldn't find your phone anywhere after the accident," she explains, clasping her fingers, "I wanted you to have an easier way to contact us. Anytime you need. We can set it up after your appointment."

I study her for a few beats, touched by the gesture. Her body language is stiff and uncertain, but this is clearly her way of showing that she cares. Our relationship has been the most difficult to navigate, and it's hard to get a read on the way things were before. But I suppose all that matters now is the both of us trying to make the best of it.

"Thank you," I say, voice warm.

Sofia takes a seat on my bed, smoothing out the duvet cover, before looking at me squarely. "Allie," she starts. "I know you skipped school yesterday. Your teacher called."

"Oh." I try not to cringe.

She raises an eyebrow to give me a stern look, though her features are soft. "You're not in trouble," she tells me. "But you should be taking your classes seriously. The school has been very accommodating despite everything that's happened in the past."

I toy with the phone in my hands. "I know. I'm sorry."

"Were you feeling overwhelmed?" she asks gently. "You could've called me."

"I guess I just needed a break."

She sighs, rising to her feet. "Next time, tell me, and we can figure something out. I don't want you falling back into your old patterns. This used to be a regular thing for you, and I'd hate to see it happen again." I mumble my assent and she nods briefly, placing a hand on my back. "All right, let's go."

Dr. Meyer's office is unchanged, everything in the exact same spot it was the last time I was here—the potted *Monstera* in the corner, the framed photo of his family on his desk, the clock that ticks persistently in the silence. Being back at the hospital in general gives me a feeling of dread. It's impossible not to think about how horrifying it was to wake up here for the very first time, even if it's starting to feel like a lifetime ago.

I sit in an armchair across from the man himself, gripping the arms with white-knuckled hands, my knee bouncing impatiently. I haven't been able to sit still since we arrived, and it very clearly annoyed the nurse who checked my vitals and tested my memory. Dr. Meyer assesses my anxious movements, noting something on his clipboard before setting it aside.

"Tell me," he begins, folding his hands neatly. "How have you been adjusting to life at home?"

"Okay, I think," I say, glancing out the window into the courtyard. The world outside always seems to feel more dim when I'm in this room. "Still figuring out how to navigate this."

"Of course. That will take quite some time." He checks the clipboard. "How are you finding your classes?"

"In most of them, I can catch on pretty quickly. The information feels new and familiar at the same time."

"That's wonderful," he says. "It's like I told you before, a lot of things are stored in your brain. You just need to learn how to access them."

"But that's not the stuff I want to access." Knowing how to divide fractions and decode figurative language is hardly useful.

"Have you experienced any other changes regarding your memory?"

I take a moment to consider, wondering where to start. There's the image of a party I saw on my first day back at school, the dark hand that had me freaking out on the Ferris wheel, the strange dream involving Mason, and the hallucinations in Zoe's car.

And then there's the matter of whether any of it is even relevant at all.

"I keep seeing these pictures," I explain. "I'll see something in reality, and then these things will flash through my mind, kind of like the ones I first told you about. But they're like fragments in time. I can only see them for a second, and then they're gone, and I have no idea if they were even real to begin with."

"What kind of pictures?" he asks, leaning forward.

"The first one was a snapshot of a party," I say. "I think it might be the party I went to that night. Or maybe that's just what my brain wants me to think."

"There's a very strong possibility it could be real," he reassures me. "What about the others?"

"I had this dream. I was trying to talk to a little boy in the park, but he wouldn't answer me. He pointed over my shoulder and a car came out of nowhere, heading straight for me. I barely got out of the way in time, and then I woke up."

The doctor takes a moment to consider my words as the clock on his desk ticks in the background. "It could very well be a tilted reflection of what you witnessed the night you got into the accident. Trauma, when repressed, can reveal itself to you in different ways."

"Tilted?"

The notion that the gut-wrenching sight of bright headlights barreling in my direction might've been what I actually saw that night is harrowing.

"That's right. Sometimes our brain shifts what we remember about traumatic events, so some pieces of what you saw may be real, and others may be completely fictional."

I contemplate what this new information might mean for my memory. Does it make what I've been seeing more real or less so? And how am I supposed to tell the difference between what's real and what's not?

"Allie," he says, leveling a serious look at me. "We're going to try something different today. Are you familiar with hypnotherapy?"

An uneasy feeling settles in my chest. "Vaguely."

"You're perfectly safe here," he remarks, holding his hands out. "We're just going to ease you into a state that might make it easier to retrieve some of your memories. You'll still be totally in control."

"I don't know ... A lot of what I've seen so far has been frightening."

"It may be scary at first, but remember, you're in my office," he says. "Nothing is actually happening to you. This is a safe space."

"And you really think this will help?"

"It's worth trying."

I bite the inside of my lip. "Okay."

"Excellent!" he exclaims, standing from his seat and walking over to mine.

He pushes a button that makes my chair recline slowly until I'm staring at the tiled ceiling, feeling like I'm splayed out on an examination table. I fold my hands over my stomach, trying not to let them tremble. Dr. Meyer's footsteps retreat, and I hear the crinkle of the leather as he sits in his chair once more.

"Now," he says, his tone a lot softer and melodic than it was before. "All I need you to do is relax. Close your eyes whenever you're ready."

Once I've taken another beat to consider, I do as he says, letting my eyelids flutter shut as I adjust my position.

"Slow down your breathing and let the tension leave your body. That's it. Nice, deep breaths."

I force my shoulders to relax and my limbs to become loose, trying to empty my brain of all coherent thoughts.

Dr. Meyer taps my knee gently to stop my leg from bouncing.

"I want you to imagine that you're completely weightless," he murmurs. "Drifting, floating, but safe."

After a while of deep breathing and concentration, the material of the chair beneath me slowly fades away, and I feel as though I'm suspended in the air, but the thought is calming. My eyelids are fastened shut, like I couldn't open them even if I tried. Dr. Meyer's voice continues to float toward me gently, though it becomes further and further away the longer he speaks, until I'm underwater, alone.

I exhale, and the air releases in a stream of bubbles in front of me. I imagine myself reaching forward to touch one, but the scenery changes, and now I'm in a room, a man with bronze skin and a familiar smile crouching down with outstretched arms.

"Darling," he says, mouth spreading in a grin, and a feeling of comfort melts through my body.

The image ripples away before I can reach him, superimposed with different moments in time—peals of laughter around a dinner table, the heat of a fireplace lapping against my skin, pages of a storybook being flipped seen through drooping eyelids—until the man disappears completely, and I feel a chill in his absence.

The boy from my dream emerges, but there's a grin in place of his solemn expression as he runs through a field of flowers, looking back at me over his shoulder, and I float along behind him, butterflies dancing between us, a flicker of excitement in my chest.

He laughs, and I graze his shirt with my fingers, causing him to come to an abrupt halt, digging his shoes into the grass to stop himself.

"Aw," he groans. "Not fair! I'm gonna get you back."

The boy turns on his heel, hands outstretched toward me, and then the world tilts on its axis again.

I'm dropped in the middle of a party, surrounded by people I know only on a surface level. The corners of my vision are hazy, and this scene has a significantly darker feeling than the other ones I just witnessed. They made me feel warm and safe, but this one is cold, teeming with bad intentions.

I stumble through the living room, weaving my way between different partygoers, trying to get to the exit. Someone shouts for me to stay, but it only makes me move faster, giving in to the distinct urge to get as far away as possible.

"Leave me alone!" I hear, and the voice sounds like mine.

They call for me again, hot on my heels as I stalk through the house.

Finally, I reach the front door and fling it open, but all I see is darkness, the world shattering into tiny pieces beneath my feet. I hear the screech of tires, see the glare of headlights fast approaching, and this time, I'm unable to move out of the way before it strikes me. I brace for impact.

But I feel nothing, a slideshow of memories fluttering through my mind too quickly to latch onto any of them, until I'm plunged into the deep dark of the forest.

A guttural feeling of terror takes over my chest, and I want to scream, each shadow a menace. My chest heaves, and when I look down, my fingers are covered with blood, my vision swaying.

"At the sound of my voice, you'll come back to the present."

Dr. Meyer's voice breaks through the noise, and I follow the thread desperately. The trees slip into oblivion one by one, and I begin to feel the chair beneath me again, tethering me to the present.

"That's it," he coaxes. "Open your eyes whenever you're ready."

I inhale sharply, eyes snapping open, and instantly I register that my cheeks are wet with tears. My body feels numb as I gaze at the ceiling, trying to even out my breathing. I focus on the sound of the clock ticking, settling my heart rate.

Dr. Meyer waits until I've calmed down. "How are you feeling, Allie?"

"I . . ." I stammer, doing my best to remember everything I saw before it disappears too. I hold my hands up, half expecting to still see blood staining my skin.

Not real.

"Take your time."

The weight of what just happened settles heavily on my chest, and I take a shuddering breath. "I don't want to do that again."

"Can you tell me about what you saw?"

I push myself into a sitting position, my head spinning as I fumble for the button to make the chair sit upright again. "I'm done," I tell him. "I want to go home."

"But we need to discuss—"

"I'm done," I repeat, forceful this time, though my voice shakes. He falls silent.

"Of course," he says somberly. "We'll only do as much as you're comfortable with. Remember you're safe here."

"Yeah? Well, what just happened didn't make me feel very safe."

All I want is to get out of this office.

"My sincerest apologies, Allie," he remarks. "That wasn't the intention of this exercise."

I stand, wrapping my arms around my torso, and he walks with me to the door, where Sofia waits in the hallway. Before either of them can say anything, I storm toward the exit, and Sofia scurries to follow me.

"What happened in there?" she asks when she matches my pace.

I shake my head as we reach the doors. "I don't know."

"Allie."

Sofia catches my arm, forcing me to stop and look at her once we're outside the building. My lip trembles, and I bite down on it stubbornly.

"Talk to me."

"He tried to help me access old memories," I admit, moving toward the car at a slower rate than before, allowing her to walk beside me. "It was traumatizing."

She's quiet as we slide into the car, waiting a beat to turn on the ignition, and it's long enough that scattered raindrops begin to fall, landing on the windshield before gliding into a full-on downpour.

"You haven't even told me what all happened that night," I say.

Sofia looks caught off guard, and I watch her face carefully. "I didn't want to overwhelm you. I thought the simple details would be enough. You're already taking in a lot of information every day," she reasons.

"I want—I need to know everything."

She sighs, leaning back against the seat and turning down the radio. "I have a lot of regrets about that night," she confesses, voice low. "And everything that came before it. We were arguing— we always argued."

"About what?" I adjust my position, turning toward her.

"That night in particular, it was that I didn't want you to go to the party," she says, lips curling upward. "You were always getting into trouble—shoplifting, skipping school, drinking, picking fights with the other kids. I often felt like my only job was cleaning up after you. Even when you were grounded, you found ways to do whatever you wanted.

"I'd told you I didn't want you spending time with your friends anymore, but you didn't care. Unfortunately, you get your stubbornness and temper from me." She chuckles quietly before sobering. "It was explosive. We both said a lot of things we didn't mean. And when you didn't come back that night, I thought it was just because you were angry at me. It certainly wouldn't have been the first time."

Her voice breaks on the last sentence, and my throat becomes thick. I want to reach out to comfort her, but I don't know how.

"You were found in the morning by a runner," she finishes, clearing her throat. "Thank God for them. I haven't always been the best mother, and I'm trying to change that." She sniffs, straightening up in her seat and buckling her seat belt. "We need to get better at comunication. I want you to know you can talk to me about anything."

"Thank you," I whisper, taking one of her hands in mine. The gesture seems to surprise her, but she squeezes it gently in return. "And I'm sorry. For everything I put you through."

"I'm sorry too," she says. "What you went through was horrifying, even if you don't remember it all. But it might be a blessing if you never do."

As she pulls out of the parking lot, I stew over what she just told me and what I witnessed in my session with Dr. Meyer, a headache pulsing in my temple. The vision at the end, in the forest, is extremely similar to what I first remembered about the accident. But it doesn't make sense.

The story of that night is that I crashed into a tree and hit my head on the steering wheel, immediately losing consciousness. So why do I keep seeing myself in a forest, wandering around with bloody hands?

Blinking back tears, I wish for all of this to go away. I didn't ask for any of it. But going back in time and reversing the accident and the amnesia means being in a timeline where I'm actively cheating on my boyfriend with my sister's partner, constantly at odds with my mother, and thinking I'm better than everyone else when I might've actually been the worst of them all. That's not a reality I'd prefer either.

Before I know it, we're back at the house, pulling into the driveway.

"Sofia," I say, once she shuts the car off. "Do we have any old photo albums?"

"I have some buried in a box somewhere."

"Can I look at them?"

To my relief, she doesn't press the issue, instead she simply nods as I follow her inside. I wait in the kitchen while she searches her bedroom, and minutes later she emerges with her arms full of worn albums then passes them off to me. After thanking her, I retreat up to my bedroom, sitting on the wooden floor and spreading them out in front of me. They all have different years and names scrawled on the side, and I select one with mine.

I flip over the cover, leafing through the pages slowly, looking at photos of me as a newborn in the hospital, cradled in Sofia's arms while a pint-sized Audrey beams proudly at her new baby sister. I slide my thumb over the plastic cover.

Turning to the next page, I'm instantly met with the man from the flashback I saw earlier, confirming my suspicions. My father. *Darling,* I hear his voice again in my brain, a hint of the warmth returning as I look at a picture of me perched on his shoulders. A lump forms in my throat, and I feel overcome with emotion, but I can't tell whether it's sadness or betrayal.

Going through the album, I move through time, watching myself grow up through a stranger's lens, witnessing an entire life I can't recall. Though I know we're the same person, I can't help but feel as though something went wrong and the old Allie split in two, and now I'm hijacking her life without putting in any of the work to make it what it is. It's odd to see the familiar faces, different versions of the people I know now.

There are so many moments, conversations, and experiences that have been swept away in the blink of an eye. I don't know whether I should feel cheated, or if, like Sofia said, forgetting my old life might be an undercover blessing.

I close the album. As I move to set it aside, a loose picture flutters to the floor, stopping me in my tracks.

My heart stops when I register the face that stares back at me.

The boy from my dream, beaming brightly with his arm slung around the shoulders of a younger version of myself. I pick up the photo and flip it over to see the words scrawled on the back:

Mason and Allie, 2007

07 | IGNITE

Several days pass before I start to feel normal again.

The images I saw in my session with Dr. Meyer proceed to haunt my dreams, but eventually they fade, feeling even more surreal and hazy than they already did, and I question whether the whole encounter happened at all.

At lunch, I skip out on going to the cafeteria to eat with my friends. Instead, I slip into the computer lab and try to remain unnoticed as I zero in on a seat in the back corner of the room, away from the few other people catching up on homework or playing games.

After signing in with my school ID, I open up an internet browser, fingers hovering over the keyboard. Until now, my accident hasn't been something I've truly wanted to explore. But the longer time goes on, the more it becomes apparent that whatever happened that night isn't as simple as it seems, and any information I find could be the key to unlocking the truth. Considering the fact that I'm a minor, it might be hard to find a lot of information about it. At the same time, a teenage girl getting into a collision and waking up with amnesia is big news for a small town.

Tapping my foot on the linoleum floor impatiently, I peer around the room, listening to the click of other keyboards and the music coming from the computer of the kid who forgot to bring head-phones. An idea dawns on me, and I quickly go to the web version of Instagram, searching for one person in particular as soon as I remember her name.

Iris Wen.

I have yet to meet the girl herself, and I don't even know what she looks like, but it seems like a good place to start. Her feed is a collection of homemade baking, digital art, a fluffy white dog, and a slew of photos from parties, awfully reminiscent of the ones hanging in my room. Her latest post is one of her art pieces, a picture of two faces spliced together to make one, a jagged line in the middle. The eyes of both girls—one brunet, one blond—are full of emotion, though I'm unable to discern whether it's sadness or anger. The caption simply says *The End of an Era*.

It doesn't take much scrolling to get back to the middle of January—the night it all happened. After looking through her profile, I can easily tell which one is Iris in the group photos she posted from the party; her hair is cut into a sleek, black bob, and round frames perch on her nose as she lifts up a red Solo cup as if to propose a toast.

The lighting of the pictures is dim, and it's hard to make out much besides the girls in the foreground, but it feels odd to swipe through them knowing I was there and that they were taken during the last few hours before I lost myself completely. When I get to the last slide, a wide shot of the living room, I stiffen, breath catching. There's no denying it's the room I've been seeing in my flashbacks.

Zooming in doesn't bring any more clarity; the people in the photo don't look familiar beyond being nameless faces I pass by in the hallway. Unwilling to give up yet, I type *Pender Falls accident* into the Google search bar, and check out the results. One by one, I read through the headlines that range from workplace mishaps to deadly car crashes until I see something that piques my interest.

Teen hospitalized after nearly fatal allergic reaction

I click on the article that was posted six months ago. There's a photo attached of a brunet boy smiling brightly.

Jacob Griffin, 17, a student at Pender Falls High, was sent to the hospital on Wednesday afternoon after going into anaphylactic shock at school. Griffin is described as being extremely cautious because of his severe allergy to peanuts, and his mother believes his food was tampered with. His EpiPen, which he reportedly never leaves home without, was nowhere to be found at the time—

"So, this is where you're hiding out?"

The sound of Zoe's voice causes me to flinch and jerk away from the computer screen as she takes the seat next to mine. She sets her container of salad on the desk, leaning closer to my screen with a frown.

"Geez, you scared the shit out of me," I breathe.

An indecipherable emotion darts across her face. "What are you reading?"

Suddenly I'm hit with how odd I must seem and exit out of the article. "I don't even know how I got here," I say. "Fell down a rabbit hole I guess."

Zoe makes a noise of amusement, though it sounds distant.

"Did you know him?" I ask, gesturing to the screen.

"Not really. He never came back to school after that."

"Damn," I say.

"Anyway," she says, flipping her hair over her shoulder and refocusing on me. "I've been looking everywhere for you. Why didn't you tell us where you were going?"

"I didn't think it would matter," I admit. It's a more diplomatic way of saying *I didn't know I had to ask for permission.* "What's up?"

"Your eighteenth birthday is next week. We need to celebrate."

My shoulders immediately tense. I already knew my birthday was coming, it's scrawled on the calendar in the kitchen—March 21—though it seems my family is afraid to broach the subject. They can probably sense it's the last thing I care about right now, and I doubt I'll like whatever Zoe has in mind.

"Celebrate how?" I ask warily.

"With a party. Duh."

"Do we have to? I'd rather just hang out with you guys."

"But it'll be so much fun!" she persists. "I'll plan the whole thing. You won't even have to lift a finger."

"That's not what I'm worried about," I say, lowering my voice and glancing around the computer lab. "Who would we even invite? Everyone here looks at me like I came from outer space."

"They just don't know how to handle this situation," Zoe reasons, softening. "They're not used to seeing you like . . . this." She gestures to my body, and I look down at it, wondering if I should feel offended.

"Why doesn't anyone else sit with us in the cafeteria? I don't think they like me."

"We're exclusive. I already explained how the system works. We can't let just *anyone* join the group." Zoe blinks, as if that should be obvious. "Besides, I am excellent at throwing parties. Trust me, people will come."

I weigh my options, squirming in my seat as Zoe watches me. On the one hand, a party could be a chance to relax and get to know some more people from school. But on the other hand, it could also be a chance to feel even more alienated than I already do.

"An evening of socializing kind of sounds like a nightmare," I admit.

"Allie," she scolds. "Turning eighteen is a milestone. This is not negotiable. You'd do the same for me."

Taking a deep breath of defeat, I realize I don't actually seem to have a choice in the matter. "Apparently I can't say no."

Zoe reaches over to give me a squeeze. "You won't regret this."

I wince, waiting until she lets go to mutter, "Don't make promises you can't keep."

The lunch bell rings soon after, and we stand, collecting our things and preparing to go to our separate classes. After I part ways with Zoe, Damien spots me in the hallway, stopping short.

"Allie!" he exclaims with a grin, striding over to me in a few quick steps and sliding his hand into mine. "There you are. I missed you at lunch."

"I needed to get some stuff done," I say.

"Can I walk you to class?" he asks, and I stare at our intertwined fingers, feeling uncomfortable.

"Actually," I say, reaching up with my free hand to scratch my head. "I need to talk to Ms. Warren before my next class." I've been meaning to ask the English teacher if she'll let me stay after school to catch up on my ever-growing pile of assignments. Judging by what I've heard from Sofia, my grades weren't all that great pre-accident, and I doubt they'll be improving much now. School feels like a useless endeavor, but I suppose it's nice to have some semblance of normalcy.

"Oh," he says, face falling. He lets go of my hand. "Well, do you want a ride home today?"

"Audrey is picking me up, same as usual."

"Of course." He nods, and it's clear he's trying to mask his hurt, keeping his voice light. "I'll see you later, then."

"Bye, Damien."

Not wanting to wait around in the awkward atmosphere, I quickly head to the English classroom. The conversation Damien and I had last week has stuck with me, taking what little brain space I have left after all of the other things that keep me up at night. I already assumed he loved me, but having him state his intentions so plainly made me feel like I was suffocating.

There's too much on my plate right now for me to be trying to fight for a relationship that might not have even been great to begin with. It's hard to imagine myself ever being happy with Damien. It's not that there's anything inherently wrong with him. We just don't seem to go together as well as he thinks we do. The old me evidently wasn't that interested, either, if she was busy going after Parker.

Glancing over my shoulder before turning the corner, I see that he's hovering in the hall a distance away, watching me wistfully. When he catches me looking, he snaps out of his trance, nodding and turning on his heel.

I need to tell him that it's over.

It won't be much longer before I break his heart.

When the final bell rings at the end of the day, it feels like I can breathe easier.

My friends stop by my locker to say good-bye before heading home, and I text Audrey to let her know I'm staying late. As I make my way back to the English classroom, the halls steadily clear out, until it's only me and a few stragglers left, our footsteps echoing on the tiled floor.

Ms. Warren is speaking into a cell phone when I enter the room, but she gestures for me to sit down, and I do so, taking a desk near the front. I deposit my books on the surface, starting with my stuff for English.

While Ms. Warren finishes up her call, I read about Macbeth's mind completely unraveling at the sight of the ghost of his best friend turned murder victim. When she's done, she stands from her desk and comes to look over my shoulder.

"Is it making sense?" she asks.

"Surprisingly, yes," I tell her. "It kind of feels like second nature."

"That's wonderful," she says. "You always were a fan of Shakespeare. Let me know if you have any questions."

She takes a seat once more, and silence falls over the room as we both work on our respective tasks, rain pattering gently on the window outside the classroom. Once I'm done with the reading, I tuck my copy of *Macbeth* into my backpack, mind swirling with thoughts of guilt, murder, and power struggles as I reach for my math books.

"You know," Ms. Warren begins, and I glance in her direction. "I was happy you wanted to stay late today. I've been meaning to have a chat with you."

I set the books on the surface of my desk slowly.

"I'm the head of the drama department," she says. "We used to spend a lot of time together."

"Really?"

Ms. Warren nods, pushing her braids over her shoulder. "Oh yeah," she remarks. "Ever since you entered high school, you've been in the majority of our school's productions. Last spring we did *Romeo and Juliet*. You were Juliet."

It's hard to imagine myself on a stage, basking in the glow of the lights, when all I want now is for everyone to stop paying so much attention to me. Though I suppose the whole pretending to be some-one else part must have been nice.

"Do you have any photos?"

"Of course. My partner makes all our costumes. She was very proud of this one."

She grabs her phone, pulling something up before passing it to me. I take the device gingerly and see a photo of myself on stage in the gymnasium, my expression one of longing, as I stand in a white dress, angel wings strapped to my back. I swipe through the pictures, feeling disoriented.

"I look like I'm having fun," I say, staring at a photo of myself holding hands with the boy who played Romeo. I think he's in my history class.

Ms. Warren smiles at the photos. "You were," she agrees. "You're a very talented actress, Allie. You have a lot of potential. You'll go very far if you can learn to stay out of trouble."

I frown as I hand the phone back to her, and she tucks it to her chest, looking as though she regrets her last sentence. "What kind of trouble?"

"Normal teenager things," she says lightly. "To be honest, you had a rocky relationship with the other students here and less than stellar attendance. The school is very familiar with your mother; she's had to deal with some unpleasant phone calls."

"Oh," I say, deflating.

"What happened last fall was the worst of it—" Ms. Warren stops herself, shaking her head. "You don't need to hear about that."

"It's okay. I should know these things."

"No, it's not my place," she says firmly. "Allie, don't worry about your past. All that matters is right now. Your future is bright."

She gives me an encouraging smile, and I return it feebly. "Can we take a break? I'm going to get a drink from the vending machine."

"Of course."

I stand from the desk and hurry out of the room, wondering why the interaction leaves a bad taste in my mouth. I haven't had a clear picture of how the adults at school saw me, but I'm starting to get it now. Though I have to wonder what she meant by "rocky relationship." Zoe told me in as many words that the exclusivity of our friend group meant we actively worked to keep people out of it. Does it all come down to a high school clique, or is there more that I'm missing?

Sighing, I move through the empty hallway to the vending machines. I fish some coins out of my pocket, put them through the slot, and select a water. Seconds later, the water bottle slides down, landing at the bottom with a loud thump, and I reach for it.

When I turn around, I realize I'm not alone.

Mason Byrne stands on the other side of the hallway, digging through his backpack with a frown of concentration as his dark hair falls over his forehead. He looks up as I approach, my heart hammering a little faster. Even though we sit next to each other in English, he's barely looked my way since my first day back, ignoring me whenever possible and leaving the second bell rings. Sometimes he doesn't show up at all.

The photograph of us together flashes through my mind, as well as the scene from my dream and the one from my session with Dr. Meyer.

"Hey," I start timidly, tucking a strand of hair behind my ear.

He moves slowly, sliding his backpack over his shoulder and regarding me with cautious eyes. Up close, the colors are even more brilliant. "Hi."

"Mason, right?" I say, as if I don't already know.

"That's me."

"Do you . . . do you hate me or something?" I blurt.

Mason shakes his head, looking bewildered. "What?"

"Did something happen between us?" There has to be something that led to us growing apart. Taking into account both the telltale photo and the fact that he keeps popping up in my brain, I assume he's a very significant part of my past. "Were we, like, involved?"

He barks out a laugh, increasing the heat in my face. "Please don't flatter yourself."

"That's not what I meant," I say, glaring at him indignantly. "I just thought—never mind."

He studies me clinically. "You just thought what?"

I hold his stare, feeling like there's more hidden underneath but not wanting to press the issue. Besides, it's far too embarrassing to say, *I've been dreaming about you.* "Pretend I never said anything."

"If you say so," he says, adjusting the strap of his backpack.

Zoe's voice comes back to me. *Have you ever even seen him talk to anyone?* The memory of myself playing tag with a younger version of Mason flashes through my mind. He obviously used to talk to me.

I can't explain it, but something inside of me has the desire to rekindle whatever friendship we may have had in the past, even if he doesn't feel the same.

"Hey," I say again, feeling a bout of nerves in my belly. "It's my birthday next week, and Zoe thinks it's necessary to throw me a party. I don't even know what we're doing, but . . ." I pause. "You should come."

"Are you inviting me?"

"I'm inviting you."

Mason reaches up to scratch the back of his neck. "I don't really do parties."

"Right now, I don't think I do either," I admit. "We can not do parties together." I reach into my pocket and pull out my new cell phone. "I can text you the details. When I figure out what they are, that is. You can make your mind up then."

"Are you sure having me there won't ruin your reputation?" he asks, sarcasm evident in his voice, raising an eyebrow.

"What do you mean?"

"I'm gonna go out on a limb and say Zoe wouldn't like me hanging around."

"Well, it's *my* birthday," I say simply. "I should at least have a say in the guest list. And I don't care about maintaining a reputation I don't even remember earning."

He hesitates a few beats longer, as if trying to decide whether or not I'm being sincere, before accepting the phone, adding his information, and passing it back to me. Our fingers brush, and I feel my pulse quicken in my throat.

"Okay."

"Okay, as in, you're coming?"

"Okay, as in, I'll make my mind up later," he remarks, amusement dancing around his mouth.

"I can live with that."

Mason takes a step back, making to leave, but his gaze lingers on me, footsteps faltering. "Alina, wait."

I tilt my head, curious.

"I—"

"Allie!"

We both turn at the sound of Audrey entering the hallway, looking out of breath. Mason presses his lips together, swallowing the rest of his words.

"Audrey, I thought I told you I was staying late," I say, confused.

"Yeah, and then I told you I have plans tonight, so I would have to pick you up earlier," she says breezily, not seeming to realize she interrupted anything. It felt like I was finally getting somewhere. She notices Mason and does a less than subtle double take. "But apparently you were too busy to see it."

"Sorry," I sigh. "I'll go get my things."

When I turn around again, Mason is already making for the exit. I wonder if I'll ever hear what he was about to say. Audrey watches him leave, interest evident in her features as she looks between the two of us.

"Was that Mason Byrne?" she asks, nudging my elbow.

"Yeah, why?"

"You guys used to be attached at the hip when you were kids, but I haven't seen him in ages. He's all grown up now." She hums in thought before inclining her head toward me, and I try to fathom how Mason and I went from being integral parts of each other's lives to complete strangers. "What were you talking about?"

"Nothing really, I just had a question about the homework," I lie.

"It looked intense, if you know what I mean."

"Audrey." I chastise her, cheeks warming.

She bites back a smile and ushers me in the direction of the classroom. "I'm just saying, he could end up giving Damien a run for his money," she teases. "Anyway, grab your stuff so we can get out of here."

I hurry down the hallway, trying to put my embarrassment behind me, but my mind lingers on the moment Mason's fingers grazed mine, a sensation that felt familiar and foreign at the same time.

08 | UNCOVER

Torrential rain arrives in Pender Falls on the same night as my party. It comes down in sheets, soaking everything in sight, making for low visibility and blurred headlights, especially with the added cover of nightfall. I get ready in Zoe's lavish bedroom, holding still while she swipes glitter across my cheeks.

Her house is stunning. It's a three-story character home with a wraparound porch and Victorian references everywhere you look. Both the exterior and interior are beautiful, although extremely intimidating. I thought my house was nice, but it feels like nothing compared to this.

"Excited?" she asks, concentrating as she puts on the final touches. She's beautiful as always, her winged eyeliner making her eyes look sharp, but they're softened by the glitter on her own cheeks. Her blond hair has been styled in loose curls, a thin, gold headband nestled into her hairline.

"Sure."

She gives me an unimpressed look. "It's your birthday. Can you at least smile?"

I do my best to obey her orders, but I have a feeling it comes off as more of a grimace.

Zoe laughs, turning to the mirror to fluff up her hair, and I peer at my own reflection, feeling like a doll she's primped and polished, entirely unlike myself. My features are more defined thanks to Zoe's makeup expertise, and my hair frames my face nicely, but my expression is somber. It reminds me of how I looked when I tried on the dress in Plaisir—a skewed reflection of the old Allie. She pulls out her phone, loops an arm around my shoulder, and brings me to her side as she takes a mirror selfie. Standing side by side like this, we're reminiscent of an angel and a demon. After snapping a few more in which I try not to look miserable, she seems satisfied and tosses the phone into her purse.

"I'm just nervous," I admit, fiddling with my skirt. "And you haven't even told me where we're going yet."

"You have nothing to worry about. I'll be with you all night," she promises. "Pinkie swear."

I reach up to lock our pinkies together. "Okay."

The door to her bedroom bursts open, and Mrs. Harris enters. Zoe is practically the spitting image of her mother, but with younger, rounder features. The way the woman carries herself reminds me of Sofia: poised and dignified, seeming to be above everything else.

"Is that what you're choosing to wear?" she asks, directing the question at her daughter.

Zoe stiffens, looking down at the white dress she's selected for tonight. It makes her look like she belongs on a runway instead of at a high school birthday party, but apparently her mother thinks otherwise. "What's wrong with it?"

"If you want to wear a dress from last season that looks three sizes too small, by all means, go right ahead. But I'm sure you could find something more flattering," she comments offhandedly. Zoe purses her lips, features darkening, and I feel uncomfortable, like I shouldn't be present for this conversation. "The choice is yours, darling."

The words make me shift in my seat, and I wonder if Mrs. Harris has even noticed I'm in the room or if I've suddenly become invisible. Zoe looks as though she's struggling to maintain her composure.

"I think she looks amazing," I blurt, immediately regretting the words once her mother's cutting stare lands on me for the first time.

"Ah yes," she says politely, gesturing at my outfit. "As we all know, Sofia Castillo's daughter is the pinnacle of fashion in Pender Falls. Allie's opinion is the only one that matters."

Her lips curl upward as if she's laughing at some private joke, and my skin prickles. It's the first time I can recall ever seeing the woman, but she certainly doesn't seem interested in treating me with the same delicacy as the other adults I know.

Mrs. Harris turns back to her daughter, dismissing my presence. "Graduation isn't that far away," she remarks, crossing her arms over her chest. "You have a lot of eyes on you right now, and I don't want you to lose focus by throwing useless, juvenile parties like this. It's a waste of potential."

"I won't, Mom," Zoe replies woodenly.

The older woman accepts her answer, breezing to the door just as quickly as she bulldozed into the room, leaving a trail of destruction in her wake.

Zoe stalks into the en suite the moment her mother is gone. I watch as she washes her hands, scrubbing at her skin furiously even though her hands weren't all that dirty to begin with. She mumbles some words under her breath, but it's hard to hear over the rushing of the water from the tap.

After finishing up, she dries her hands, then takes some time to assess her reflection once more, making sure everything is where it should be. She turns to me as though nothing happened. "Let's go."

Outside, we huddle together beneath an umbrella, laughing as we make a mad dash down the sprawling driveway to her car. She cranks up the music as we glide through the wet streets, though I notice her fingers tremble on the steering wheel, similar to when we went shopping. An uneasy feeling tugs at my chest. The bad weather and uncomfortable tension in the car make me feel as though more flash-backs are imminent.

I turn the music down, trying to latch onto a distraction, and Zoe looks at me quizzically.

"Do you want to talk about what just happened?" I ask gently.

"Are you referring to my mother?" She scoffs. "Please, that's a typical day in the Harris household."

"I'm sorry."

"Stop that."

"No, really," I persist. "I am. No one deserves to be talked to like that."

"Damn," she says. "The old Allie would've just called my mom a bitch and moved on."

"Zoe."

She shifts in her seat as we reach a stoplight, the windshield wipers furiously doing their best to manage the flow of water outside. "I've learned that the universe doesn't actually care what people deserve," she murmurs. "If it did, things would be a lot different."

I might've agreed with her at one point, but the more I learn about myself, the more I wonder if the universe actually does dole out punishment to those who deserve it.

"Has it always been like that for you at home?"

"Pretty much." Her voice is flat but it's clear she's trying not to let me hear the hurt behind her words. "It's definitely gotten worse as I've grown up. They're so focused on building this perfect, artificial, robot daughter that I don't think they've taken the time to actually learn anything about me. Or they just don't give a shit."

"Would you ever talk to them about it?"

She laughs shortly. "Don't be stupid. They don't listen to a word I say. There's no hope of fixing that."

I frown as the light turns green and we glide forward again. "Things will get better someday."

"A word of advice," she remarks. "You can't spend time waiting for things to get better on their own, because they won't. Sometimes you have no choice but to take matters into your own hands and make them better yourself."

We drive in silence for the remainder of the ride until we pull up to a large building, and I squint through the rain at the neon sign. ROCKWELL'S, it reads, accompanied by two sets of roller skates that light up alternately to look as though they're moving.

Zoe puts the car into Park.

"We're roller skating?"

A bad feeling creeps into my chest at the thought, and I take note of the packed parking lot. Apparently, the weather didn't deter what seems like the entire high school population from showing up. People hurry to the doors, trying to get out of the rain before it does too much damage.

She doesn't answer, looking smug as she clicks her door open. "Come on," she says. "I don't want to get my hair wet."

The closer we get to the door, the louder the music becomes, and the rate of my pulse increases with each beat. I lean closer to Zoe, grabbing her arm as we head inside. The place is decked out in balloons, several of them shaped to spell out Happy Birthday, and a whole lot of glitter as far as the eye can see. From the vases filled with flowers on the food table to the bowls filled with party snacks, everything sparkles.

"This looks incredible," I say, raising my voice in order to be heard. "I'm kind of supposed to avoid flashing lights, though. And loud noises."

Zoe turns to me, an apologetic expression immediately taking hold of her features. "Oh no," she says. "I didn't think about that."

Surveying the room, I'm unsure of what I'm supposed to do now. The party swirls in front of us, pulsing with energy, and everyone else looks happy. Zoe spent so much time planning this thing, and I've already complained.

"I'm sure you can find ways to have a good time, though," she offers generously. "Mingle, eat food, enjoy the show. You can always go outside if it gets to be too much."

"Wait—"

After giving my arm a squeeze, she weaves her way through the crowd, greeting people as she passes, and I'm left standing alone. So much for pinkie promises.

My head is already pounding. I spot several faces I recognize— Damien and James are doing laps in their roller skates, and across the room Audrey and Parker share a laugh by the food table.

Somehow, I immediately catch Parker's attention. I've been doing my best to avoid him ever since he took me to Boulder Trail, so I quickly look away, pretending not to see him. A few people I don't know pass by, shouting birthday greetings, and I move to take a seat on one of the chairs along the wall where it's quieter.

Much to my dismay, I'm joined by Audrey and Parker, the former plopping down on the seat next to me. Parker remains standing, hovering awkwardly with his drink in his hand.

"*Well*, this is something," Audrey remarks.

Slouching in my chair, I say, "It's something, all right."

"How are you feeling? This must be a sensory overload for you."

"Did you know this was what she had planned?"

"No! I mean, we figured it out when she finally gave us the address, but by then it was too late." She pauses. "I'm sorry, Allie. This probably isn't how you thought your birthday would turn out."

Shrugging, I straighten up, then glance at Parker, who dutifully refrains from looking at me. "I don't really care that it's my birthday. But I don't know why Zoe threw me a party just to ditch me at the door."

"You two have a unique friendship," Audrey muses. "Best friends one moment and at each other's throats the next."

I look out at the partygoers, watching Zoe as she skates with a boy, smirking as he twirls her around. A spark of jealousy ignites in my chest. Despite the balloon letters and the photographs of me scattered throughout the room, it's jarringly clear that this party wasn't thrown for me at all. It's been Zoe's party since the beginning. I doubt people would even notice if I left.

"Let me get you something to drink," Audrey says, touching my arm gently. "Wait here. Parker, keep her company."

She pecks him on the cheek and squeezes his shoulder before leaving the two of us alone. As if this night couldn't get any worse.

Parker sinks into the chair my sister left open, and I bite down on the inside of my cheek, my knee bouncing. "It's been a while since we've talked," he says.

"We should probably keep it that way."

"I agree," he says. "That's why I wanted to tell you that I'm leaving."

"What?"

"I'm moving out. I should've left a long time ago."

Parker's face is impassive, revealing nothing, and I don't know how to react. It's obvious that this is the right decision, and he's not wrong when he says it should've happened long before now. Calling our circumstances complicated would be the understatement of the century. He's the first person who felt like a friend—even if he wasn't allowed to be. But there's no way for any kind of relationship between us to exist without stabbing the knife further into my sister's back. Too much damage has already been done.

"Does that mean . . . ?"

He nods. "I'm going to end things with Audrey."

Across the room, my sister fills a cup with punch, oblivious. When she turns to look back at us, innocence written all over her face, the intensity of my guilt is like a sucker punch to the gut. The downfall of her relationship is entirely my fault.

"I'm sorry." I don't know what else to say.

"It's for the best. But God, I'm going to break her heart." His voice falters, before he clears his throat, swallowing.

"Are you going to tell her?"

"I don't know," he admits. "Do you think I should?"

As she begins to make her way back to us, I spring up from my chair, anxiety building in my chest. My palms are suddenly clammy and I feel like I can't breathe.

"Allie?"

"I just—I can't do this right now," I say.

As I weave through the crowd, a tangled mess of emotions forms a vortex inside of me: shame, remorse, jealousy, anger. I don't understand where they're all coming from—some are closer to the surface while others feel deeply ingrained, like they've been carved into my skin. All I want is a rewind button, a way to turn back time and erase the night I kissed Parker and everything that came after it. I would kill to be anywhere but this stupid party that's claiming to be something it's not.

Someone steps in front of me, effectively blocking my path. "Hey, it's the birthday girl!"

A boy who looks vaguely familiar stands in front of me, hands stuck into his pockets. I want him to move out of my way.

When his greeting receives no response, he continues. "You remember me, right?" *No.* "I'm Travis. I sit behind you in biology."

"Oh," I say. "Hi."

"Crazy about your accident, huh? You almost *died*."

"I know." I remain deadpan. "I was there."

He knocks me on the shoulder with his fist amicably. "You survived, though. That's badass. Anyway, I don't know if you recall the deal you made with me—"

"I promise you I don't."

"—but in freshman year, you said we could make out on your eighteenth birthday. Seeing as that's today. . . I think you know where this is going."

My mouth falls open in disgust. "*Seriously?*"

His hands shoot up in a show of surrender. "I swear I'm not lying."

"Travis, was it?"

He puffs out his chest proudly. "That's me."

"I'll make out with you when hell freezes over," I say, smiling sweetly.

"So, next time, then?" he calls as I brush past him.

A wave of irritation pulls me under, and I storm over to the counter, facing off with the bored employee who leans against it in his checkered polo. Fuck sitting on the sidelines. Clearly that's where all the creeps hang out.

I place my palms on the surface. "Can I get a pair of skates?"

He sighs, begrudgingly straightening his posture. "What size?"

I tell him, and he fetches the skates, holding them out. After snatching them from his grasp, I march to the edge of the rink and sit down on the ground to slide them on. Tying up the laces, I ignore the pounding in my skull. I'll be damned if I can't enjoy my own birthday. Once I've got the skates fastened to my feet, I use the railing to pull myself into a standing position, feeling a little wobbly. I prepare to step inside the rink, determined, before fingers encircle my arm gently, stopping me in my tracks.

"I wouldn't do that if I were you."

Mason Byrne stands next to me, maintaining his grip as he raises a dubious eyebrow.

"You came," I say, unable to hide the awe in my voice.

He releases me. "Kind of a weird party for a girl with a head injury."

"No kidding."

"And yet . . ." he trails off meaningfully, looking down at the skates on my feet.

Embarrassment floods my cheeks at my apparent stupidity, and I shake my head as I back away from the railing. "I don't know what I was thinking." I pause. "I wanted to participate in my party, but I don't think it was ever mine to begin with."

"Everyone in this town has ulterior motives," he says, laughing bitterly. "I'm sure you're catching onto that very quickly."

Reaching down, I untie my skates, slide them off, and tuck them under my arm. Mason follows me back to the counter, and a jolt of adrenaline accompanies me. I'm happier than I should be about the fact that he was even willing to come tonight. And that he hasn't left yet. After our talk in the hallway, my expectations were low.

"Still," I say as the strobe lights dance across his features. "I'm glad you're here. Misery loves company."

Silence filled by the overbearing thrum of the music falls over us as we stand next to the counter at the edge of the room, watching everyone else have the time of their lives. In the middle of the rink, Parker holds Audrey's hands as she skates with uncertainty, keeping her upright. James schmoozes a group of girls as Damien looks on, unimpressed. Zoe is with the boy from earlier.

It's like we're invisible, nothing more than ghosts hovering on the outskirts. I wonder if it's just the hazy lighting of the rink or if I always felt like no one ever truly saw me. Maybe that's why I liked being on stage. It would've forced people to acknowledge me.

After a while of random people from school coming up to give me their insincere birthday greetings, Mason turns to me, bending closer to my ear. "Do you want to go outside?"

"Definitely."

He leads the way through the crowd until we reach the main entrance and step into the chill of nightfall. The rain pounds on the pavement, but beneath the overhang of the roof, it's dry. Immediately, I feel relaxed by the sound of the rain mixing with the buzz of the neon sign, watching as cars whir past.

There's a bar across the street, the lights on the sign flickering as they debate whether or not to completely burn out, and something about it is comforting. Today I got a glimpse into what my life before might have been like—getting ready with Zoe to go out to places where I don't feel like I truly exist. But the sign feels authentic somehow, tethering me to the present.

"So," Mason begins, breaking through the white noise yet somehow managing to not disturb the peace. "You invited me here for a reason."

"What do you mean?"

"I'm pretty sure it wasn't out of the goodness of your heart," he says, not bothering to hide his cynicism. "We've barely spoken all through high school."

The accusation catches me off guard. I didn't expect him to read my intentions so easily, and I don't think it's wise to tell him about the dream, but a partial truth might be okay. Sighing, I reach up to tuck a section of hair behind my ear.

"I saw a photo of us," I confess. "As kids."

"Ah," he says. Something flickers on his face as he studies me.

"We looked close. I just wanted to know what happened," I explain, nervous all of a sudden.

"We used to be friends," he admits simply, expression unreadable. "But that was years ago. It doesn't matter anymore."

"Why aren't we friends now?"

"I don't know, we just grew apart." He shrugs. "People change, Alina."

"Are you sure that's it?"

He meets my gaze levelly. "Positive."

I turn away, unable to shake the feeling that there's more he's not telling me. Kids drifting apart as they grow up is a natural phenomenon, but our history feels tangible, on the tip of my tongue yet always out of reach.

"Is that all you wanted to know?"

"What?"

"You got your answer. That's all you needed me here for, right?"

"No," I say slowly. "I wanted—"

But I stop short, unsure of how to finish that sentence. In all honesty, I think I was just intrigued by the idea of spending more time with him.

"That's what I thought," he concludes, edging toward the sidewalk.

"Don't go," I reply, somehow feeling like if I let him leave now, he won't ever speak to me again. "You just got here."

"I told you, it's not really my scene."

"It's not mine either."

After a few more moments during which he seems to war with himself, he gives in, pulling the door open and gesturing for me to go ahead. We don't make it very far before Damien appears, blocking our path.

"Allie!" he exclaims. "I've been looking for you all night!"

His eyes dart between me and my companion, and then he reaches forward to pull me to his side and press a kiss into my hair. I put my hand on his chest, trying to widen the gap between us.

"Happy birthday, baby," he says.

"Thanks," I reply, sharing an uncomfortable look with Mason. "Where are Zoe and James?"

Damien shrugs, unconcerned, brushing some of my hair out of my face, and it takes all of my willpower to not shrink away. "No idea. I just wanted to spend time with my beautiful girlfriend."

My stare must be burning a hole in the side of his face, but he ignores it, nodding at Mason.

"Oh hey," he says. "Didn't see you there. How's it going, man?"

"Great," Mason replies sarcastically, before turning to me. "Look, I think I'm gonna head out. Enjoy the rest of your party."

His last lingering look feels charged with words left unsaid as he turns on his heel and heads for the exit. Disappointment stirs in my chest as I watch him leave, and I want to ask him to stay, but I don't think he would at this point anyway. Feeling a surge of frustration, I turn to Damien.

"What the hell was that?"

"Huh?"

"You were being totally possessive," I accuse. "I was just hanging out with a friend."

Damien scoffs, affronted. "Since when are you friends with that guy? I didn't think he *had* friends."

"Since now. Damien, we're taking things slow, remember? You can't treat me like that. I'm not an object."

He gives me a wounded look. "Sorry for showing that I care."

"Come on," I say. "You know that's not what I mean."

"Do I?" he says. "Every time I try to get close to you, you push me away."

"Damien," I say, my tone sounding as tired as I feel. "Stop."

"I wanna know why you won't give me a chance."

"That's not fair."

"How is it not fair?" he protests.

"Because you're putting so much pressure on me," I say, pointing a finger at his chest. "And you have *zero* understanding of how I feel. Being with you is—"

I stop short, exhaling. The pain in my head throbs obnoxiously as the party continues on around us. My unfinished sentence hangs in the air, and I have the desire to either swallow the words and take them back or vomit everything onto the floor.

I think we should break up is on the tip of my tongue, but this would be the worst possible time to say it. Instead, I sigh, forcing the tension to leave my body, and he avoids looking at me directly. "Can we not do this now?" I plead, my voice gentle, suddenly aware of a few pairs of eyes watching us. "This is a party. We're supposed to be having fun."

"Fine. I hope you enjoy yourself."

Without another word he strides away from me, clearly upset. It must be hard for him to give up on our long-time relationship, but what we have right now isn't healthy for either of us. It's exhausting, and nobody is happy. He should understand that now is not a good time for us to be together.

Relatively speaking, he's only a few steps above feeling like a total stranger to me, meanwhile, he's hung up on a version of a girl who no longer exists. In any other circumstance his childish behavior would've been the last straw. However, watching Damien have an even bigger public meltdown is definitely not something I'm in the mood for tonight.

Just when I'm about to wallow in a pit of self-pity, I spot my so-called friends all the way across the room, making them hard to see through the crowd. They're in the corner of the room, like they want to be out of sight, gathered in a tight circle to keep others out. Creeping closer to the edge of the rink, I try to get a better look. Damien appears to be doing most of the talking, gesturing wildly as the others listen. James's bulky arms are crossed over his chest, and Zoe stands next to them, closing out the huddle.

Finally, she holds up a hand, bringing Damien's ranting to an abrupt halt. She says something forcefully, and the boys are silent. I inch closer to their hiding spot, my curiosity burning brightly.

They notice me approach, and their body language rapidly changes. Zoe straightens, clearing her expression and fixing me with a large smile. Damien gives me a forlorn look before storming off, and James winks, following him.

I head over to Zoe, and she keeps the grin plastered on her face.

"Hey, babe." She greets me. "Having fun?"

"What were you guys talking about?"

Zoe tilts her head, looking at me confused. "I don't know what you mean."

"Just now," I push.

"Oh," she says. "Damien was just being dramatic about something. But don't worry, I took care of it."

"How?'

She laughs shortly. "God, Allie. What's with the interrogation? Not everything we do has to involve you."

We maintain eye contact for several beats, and it's as if we're waiting to see which one of us will concede and give the other one the victory.

"Anything else you want to ask me?"

My face clouds over for a moment before I match her expression, my lips curling upward. "What's the point of asking if I won't get a straight answer?"

"So dramatic," she scolds patronizingly. "I guess that's why you're the actress of the group."

Once again, she slips away into the crowd, and I watch her disappear. For whatever reason, that's my tipping point. I refuse to waste any more time waiting for Zoe to be a good friend. I find Audrey sitting on a bench in the process of removing her skates.

"Hey," I breathe when I reach her.

"My feet are killing me," she whines.

"Can we go home?" I ask bluntly. "Like, now?"

Audrey looks at me in surprise. "Really? But the party isn't over."

"It is to me."

Much to my relief, she doesn't question me, and after catching up with Parker, we leave Rockwell's far behind us.

09 | INTEND

I have trouble sleeping all weekend. By the time Monday morning rolls around, I give up on sleep entirely well before it's time to get up for school despite how much both my body and mind are begging for rest.

The events of Friday night have been festering more and more each day until it's all that I'm able to think about, and the image of my friends hiding in the corner of the room has branded itself into my mind.

I knew adjusting to my life would be hard, but I didn't think everything would be so damn *complicated*.

On Saturday, Sofia took Audrey, Parker, and me out for dinner to have a proper birthday celebration. Nobody explicitly told her, but she seemed to sense that things at the party had gone awry and that I needed something to make up for it. Even though my cell phone was practically an early birthday present, Sofia made sure to shower me with a ton of smaller gifts. While I may not be comfortable enough to truly consider them family yet, it's clear they're trying, and the whole day left me with a tender feeling in my chest.

Yesterday, Audrey helped me set up a new Instagram account. She assumed I wanted one to keep in touch with everyone from school, but really, I wanted a way to look at Zoe's private account. After opening the app on my phone, I scroll through my timeline, seeing a slew of photos from the party. Zoe posted the one of us in her bedroom mirror, along with a deceivingly heartfelt birthday message, and I glower at the screen, teeth gritting. I don't want to see her today or put any amount of effort into pretending that I do.

The drama department's account pops up, and I quickly tap on it, eager to see more. Their most recent post is my yearbook photo, with a caption mentioning my accident and wishing me a speedy recovery. The rest of their feed is pictures from various productions, similar to the ones Ms. Warren showed me. I see myself on stage, deep in the middle of an emotional scene, then posing with my cast mates afterward, the glow of excitement fresh in my cheeks.

There's a link on their profile leading to a website, and I follow it, navigating until I find a section with past performances. *Romeo and Juliet* is the first one to capture my attention, and I watch the video, skipping through it until I see myself appear. As soon as I set foot on the stage, my chest constricts. It's me, but it's someone else. She speaks with my voice and moves with my body, even though I've never met her. It almost feels violating. I watch until I can't stomach it anymore.

Throwing my phone to the side, I crawl out of bed and slink down the stairs to make a cup of tea. To my surprise, Audrey is already awake, too, sitting at the counter, huddled over a mug of coffee. She looks up as I enter, clearing her throat, and I don't miss the dark circles under her eyes.

"Morning," she says, voice hoarse.

"Are you okay?"

It takes her a while to answer, lip trembling violently. "Parker left."

"Seriously?"

Audrey shrugs helplessly. "He's gone. He broke up with me."

"I'm so sorry." Guilt instantly wraps around the words, and I hope it passes for sympathy.

At that, her face crumples. "I didn't see it coming at all. I don't know what I'm supposed to do now."

Putting aside my discomfort, I loop my arms around her shoulders. Without hesitation, she latches onto me tightly, doing her best to stifle her sobs. I squeeze my eyes shut, feeling light headed.

Parker told me at the party that he was going to leave, but I didn't think he would do it so soon. I thought I had more time to mentally prepare myself for Audrey's heartbreak, more time to brace myself for the influx of self-hatred I'm about to experience.

"You don't deserve this," I say, struggling to keep my voice steady.

She whimpers in response before releasing me, and I take a step back as she wipes her cheeks. "Sorry, I'm a mess," she apologizes, voice thick. "I can still take you to school today, I just need a second."

"Take your time," I say. "Is there anything I can do?"

"No," Audrey says. "Thanks, though."

After giving her a fleeting smile, I hurry to the bathroom, feeling as though I'm going to vomit, but everything stays bottled up inside, the way it always does.

Upon entering the English classroom, I greet Ms. Warren timidly, staring at the floor to keep from looking in Zoe's direction as I pass her desk.

"Allie," Zoe says softly, reaching out a hand, and her fingertips graze my arm.

I don't acknowledge her. Maybe I'm being overly dramatic by hanging on to what happened at the party, but I can't help the way I feel. Friday night gave me a better indication about the true nature of our friendship, and it's hard to pretend things are normal.

Setting my books down on my desk, I make eye contact with Mason, sitting in the seat next to mine as usual. I feel a wave of embarrassment as I'm reminded of the way Damien treated him. In my periphery, I see him peer at me before he quickly looks away.

I take a pen out of my pencil case, fiddling with it between my fingers, then take a deep breath and turn to face him. "I'm sorry about the other night."

"What are you sorry for?"

"The way Damien acted was obnoxious," I say, grimacing. "I feel bad that you left right away." I'm confident the rest of the night would've gone a lot better if he'd stayed.

"You don't have to apologize for him," he says. "He's not you."

"But I asked you to come, and you didn't have a good time," I persist.

At that, his lips curve upward ever so slightly, and I wonder if it's the first time he's actually smiled at me. "It wasn't all that bad until that point," he says.

"Really?"

Ms. Warren shuffles papers at the front of the room, humming under her breath, and a low roar of chatter floats around the room. I can sense Zoe watching us from her desk, needles of irritation pricking at my skin.

"Alina," he continues, lowering his voice, face somber once more. "I need to talk to you about something."

Of course, Ms. Warren decides that now is the time to start class, cutting off all external conversation. Mason's dark eyebrows draw together, and he doesn't look at me anymore.

We dive back into our study of *Macbeth*, and when the bell rings at the end, Mason only casts me a fleeting, unreadable glance before exiting the room. I feel a sting of disappointment, gathering my books from my desk as I prepare to try to avoid Zoe once more. This time, she springs up from her seat, following me out of the room.

"Allie, wait up," she says, sounding exasperated, struggling to maintain my hurried pace.

I ignore her, reaching my locker and pulling it open after twisting the dial on the combination lock. After I've traded out my books, she reaches forward and snaps the door shut. I flinch, looking at her for the first time. Her lips are pressed into a firm line as she assesses my expression. She looks perfectly put together as usual, from her pin-straight hair to the matching plaid of her skirt and headband, and it irritates me.

"Are you mad at me?" she asks finally. "I'll take that look as a yes." I move to walk away before she catches my arm. "Is this about Friday?"

"What do you think?"

"Allie, I'm sorry." She continues when she sees my skepticism. "Really, I am. I was being selfish."

There isn't long before our next class, and there's a large part of me that's tempted to walk away and ignore her apology. But I decide to be the bigger person. The least I can do is allow her a conversation.

"You could've just thrown a party without pretending it was for my birthday," I point out, hugging my notebook to my chest, feeling tense. "Maybe stuff like that was normal for us before, but things are different now."

"I know," she admits. "I really did want to do something nice for you, but I guess I got carried away. And I broke my promise. I kind of ditched you, huh?"

"Kind of?"

"Okay, I totally ditched you. That was wrong of me. I'm not winning Friend of the Year anytime soon," she says. "Come on, will you let me make it up to you?"

Despite my best efforts, I feel my resolve wearing down. "How?"

"Anything you want. Say the word and we'll do it."

I hum, tapping a finger to my chin and pretending to consider. "Give me some time to think of an appropriate punishment."

She breaks into a grin, looping her arm through mine as we prepare to walk down the hall. "I can't wait to hear it."

We head to our next classes only to stop abruptly at the sight of two unfamiliar girls blocking our path. My smile fades as I take in the anger etched into their expressions, seemingly directed at me, before sharing a worried look with Zoe. She places a hand on her hip, looking thoroughly unimpressed.

"Um, hi," I say cautiously. "Can we help you with something?"

"I see you're continuing to play pretend," one of them says. She's a tall brunet with thick-rimmed glasses, and her voice drips with malice. In a way, she looks familiar, but I can't place her.

"What are you talking about?"

"Oh, come *on*," she continues, and her companion scoffs. "You don't seriously expect us all to believe you really lost your memory. It seems terribly convenient. We were giving you space to recover from your little 'accident,' but clearly you're doing well, judging by your party last weekend."

"You think I'm faking?" I ask incredulously.

The words bring me back to my return to school, to the snippets of conversation I overheard against my best wishes. Trepidation twists in my gut.

"Of course," the second girl breaks in, mouth curling into a sneer. "How else could you get out of paying for all the awful shit you've done?"

"Jesus, Whitney," Zoe says. "Take it down several notches."

"Well, you two have certainly made up," she points out, laughing shortly. Beside me, Zoe stiffens. "Do we have Allie's *amnesia* to thank for that too?"

"Zoe, what is she talking about?"

"Nothing," she says, the word clipped.

Even Whitney looks confused by Zoe's behavior, and the brunet speaks again, bringing the attention back to me. "Anyway," she says. "Just because you've magically forgotten the fact that you're an evil bitch, that doesn't mean the rest of us have. My family certainly hasn't."

Overhead, the bell rings, and I'm late to my next class, but I can't make myself move. In my head, I hear Ms. Warren's voice telling me how I used to clash with other students.

"Did you lose your hearing too?" she presses.

"For God's sake, give it a rest," Zoe snaps, taking a step toward them. "This is getting ridiculous. Allie doesn't even remember either of you, so you can take the sticks out of your asses now."

"But—"

"Shove it, Amber," Zoe says simply, grasping my wrist and pulling me down the hallway in the opposite direction of the biology classroom.

I stumble along behind her, grateful to have her support, but still feeling shaken from the conversation. My mind races as I try to process what just happened, and Zoe guides us out the back door of the school, letting it fall closed behind us with a sigh. I shiver absentmindedly, rattled by the late March breeze, and wrap my arms around my torso.

Zoe sweeps her hair over her shoulder, appearing agitated as she leans against the brick wall. We're sheltered by the overhang of the roof, and beyond it, a light flow of raindrops trickles to the ground, watering the rose bushes lining the building.

"What the hell was that about?" I ask finally, my voice not as strong as I'd have liked it to be.

"They were just trying to start shit," she says firmly. "Ignore them."

"Zoe, I want to know," I push. "Tell me what I did to them to make them hate me so much."

Zoe drops her gaze to the pavement beneath us and scrapes her oxfords against it, expression unreadable. "It's not like they didn't deserve it," she mumbles, before taking a deep breath, straightening out to look at me. "Amber is always trying to get a reaction out of people. She lies. And Whitney just follows her blindly."

"Ms. Warren made it seem like I had a problem getting along with people."

She considers this for a few beats, visibly shifting her weight between her feet. "When you have something other people want, they hate you for it," she remarks.

"What do I have that other people want?"

"Seriously, Allie," Zoe says, laughing without humor. "Look around. Things might have changed since you came back, but it wasn't always like this. People are constantly staring at you, and it's not just because you nearly died." My frown deepens. She sighs again, sounding frustrated. "You have this . . . magnetism. Everyone wants to be around you or be you."

The words make heat rush to my face, but I shake my head. "I don't believe that's true."

"It is true," she says. "A talented actress, dating the captain of the soccer team, charming, drop-dead gorgeous. It's like a superpower. You've even got Mason Byrne wrapped around your finger now. Throughout all of high school, I've barely seen him hang out with anyone, and suddenly he's following you around like a lost puppy."

A stray raindrop makes its way onto my cheek, but I barely notice it, feeling hot with embarrassment. Her description of me hasn't been the impression I've gotten from all that I've learned about myself. It feels inaccurate and misguided—like she's projecting.

"That doesn't explain why they hate me," I protest, and her expression changes again.

"That was Amber Griffin."

I shake my head, not recognizing the name.

"You remember that article you were reading in the computer lab? That's her brother."

It takes a minute, but then the photo from the article flashes through my mind, and I realize why she looked so familiar. She and Jacob have a striking resemblance. "The kid who had the allergic reaction? What does that have to do with me?"

"She's convinced you did it."

My blood immediately runs cold.

How else could you get out of paying for all the awful shit you've done?

"Why?" I breathe, blinking rapidly.

"He was your competition," she says simply. "Another rising actor who was stealing your spotlight. She's so eager to see your downfall that she's told herself you tried to get rid of him by messing with his food and stealing his EpiPen. It's crazy."

"I didn't, though," I stammer. "There's no way I did something like that. Right?"

"If you did, they were never able to prove it."

"What the hell does that mean, Zoe?" I feel desperate now, panic welling in my chest. "Did I do it or not?"

She pauses. "I don't know."

A rush of nausea crashes into me with full force, nearly causing my knees to buckle. Zoe looks as though she wants to say more, but she refrains. Even if she did, I probably wouldn't have heard her. My mind reels with this new information, and I don't understand how any version of me could be okay with intentionally endangering someone's life.

"Oh my God."

"Maybe you got angry and did it before you could really think about it," Zoe breaks in quickly, reaching out a hand. "One of those things that happen in the heat of the moment."

"Impulsively booking a flight to Europe is a heat of the moment thing, this is on an entirely different level, Zoe," I emphasize, panic creeping into my voice. "This is—this sounds premeditated."

Her posture has become stiff again, her face solemn, though her eyes look like they've been lit by a flame. "People do what they have to in order to get what they want. It doesn't define them."

I can't help the humorless laugh that escapes me. Swallowing, I try to force myself to calm down. "What happened? Why didn't Jacob come back to school?"

Zoe looks away. "He recovered but . . . they were probably worried something like this would happen again."

"God, no wonder they hate me. I feel sick."

"Allie, I never said you actually did it," she says, her fingertips grazing my arm again, but I move past her, not wanting to hear anymore. The fact that she doesn't know for sure is indication enough of my character. "It's just a dumb theory."

Pulling the heavy door open, I storm back into the school. I don't know where I'm going, but I know I need to get out of here as soon as possible. Being at school, knowing what I know now, makes me feel like I'm itching to get out of my skin. All the attention I've gotten, the constant stares and awareness of my presence, the way no one genuinely cared about my birthday, it's all beginning to make sense.

There's no getting around it: I was a *bad* person. Maybe I still am. I've done a lot of terrible things. How is it that someone like me was able to push the reset button and start over? Where's the justice in that?

I pass by the bathrooms, debating whether or not I should hide in there for the remainder of the day, but I think now might be a time to use my "get out of school free" card. Sniffling, I head toward the entrance, stepping out into the rain and pulling my cell phone out of my pocket.

I haven't gotten much use out of it yet, but I suppose now is as good a time as any.

"Allie?"

The familiar voice comes from behind me, and I turn to see Damien exiting the school. He's so not a person I want to see right now.

He steps outside slowly, letting the door fall shut. When he sees the first tear trail down my cheek, he hastens his pace, placing his hands on my arms. "Hey, what's going on?" he asks worriedly. "What are you doing out here?"

"I need to go home," I tell him, trying to step out of his grasp.

"Let's go together," he presses, smoothly stepping in front of me.

"I'm just going to call Sofia and—"

Damien takes the phone from my fingers, looking at me intently. "I'll drive you," he insists, his voice soft. "Come on, let me help."

"Don't you have class?"

"This is more important," he says, looping an arm around my shoulder and guiding me in the direction of the parking lot. "I'll take you."

It's the first time we've spoken since our argument at my birthday party. Though I don't particularly want to spend more time with him, I can't find it in me to be bothered about getting another ride home. The sooner I leave Pender Falls High behind, the better. Maybe if I ask nicely, Sofia will let me drop out.

I allow Damien to usher me to his car, nodding meekly when he opens my door, then duck inside, grateful to get out of the rain.

Once he's settled into the driver's side, he immediately turns on the heat, and I stretch my fingers toward the warmth coming from the vents. He pulls away from the school, and though I'm beginning to calm down, there's a ball of emotion in my chest that's threatening to detonate at the slightest misstep. Damien turns on the radio to a station that plays gentle, calming music, and it makes a lump form in my throat.

"Damien," I ask, after a while of driving in silence, watching the wipers dart back and forth over the windshield. "Why do you like me?"

He looks between me and the road, surprise coloring his features. "What?"

Without warning, Damien pulls over, puts the car into Park, and turns to face me squarely.

"Why are you asking me that?"

"Because it doesn't make sense."

"Allie," he remarks, reaching over to take my hand in his, intertwining our fingers. "Of course it does. You're the best person I know."

"That doesn't answer my question."

He studies my face for several beats, obviously trying to understand where all of this is coming from and failing. "You're . . . you're beautiful," he starts. When he sees my annoyed expression, he continues. "I wasn't finished. You're funny and you're smart and you're self-assured. You know how to get what you want."

The last part reminds me of the way Zoe described us—the top of the food chain, the ones who worked hard to get where we are. Apparently, making it to the top means devouring everyone beneath us.

"I think I've done a lot of bad things," I whisper.

Damien reaches out and tucks my hair behind my ear, and the genuine look on his face only makes me feel worse. "That doesn't matter to me," he says. He places his hands on either side of my face, and my body goes rigid beneath his touch. "If I believed all that stuff mattered, I would hate myself too. We all do bad things."

"But—"

"You're not the bad things you've done. You're mine. And I love you just the way you are."

When he leans in to kiss me, I turn, pulling away. The moment hangs in the air, suspended, and my breath catches when I realize what I've done.

"Damien," I start.

He looks flustered, cheeks burning brightly. The car feels like it shrunk in size.

"It's fine." His voice is low, wounded.

Without another word, he pulls back onto the street, and my knee bounces anxiously. I should've called Sofia instead. The ride from the school to Seymour Avenue feels as though it lasts for an eternity, and

I take great interest in the world outside my window. Finally, we slide into the driveway, slowing to a stop.

I place my hand on the door handle, looking at him for the first time. "Thanks for the ride."

Damien doesn't respond.

Feeling incredibly uncomfortable, I slip out of the car and into the rain. The second the door slams shut behind me, he reverses out of the driveway without looking back. Tension weighs heavily on my shoulders, and it's starting to feel like being both tired and on edge is my default lately.

I don't want to be his; I want to be mine. But the Allie that he thinks I am does belong to him. She belongs to Damien and Zoe and everyone else at school.

And as long as I look like her, I'll always belong to them too.

10 | BETRAY

The following Friday, I skip out on my morning classes to go see Dr. Meyer.

My progress has been stagnant lately, and there are times when it seems like the amnesia itself is put on the back burner because of all the other drama happening concurrently. The appointments are little more than routine checkups, and after the disastrous hypnotherapy attempt, I think it will be a long time before we try anything like that again.

Audrey drops me off at the school in time for lunch. She's reserved and gloomy, distant even when she's right next to me. I don't feel like I'm allowed to try to make her talk to me about what she's going through. And even if I was, I don't know if I'd be able to handle hearing it.

In the cafeteria, I'm distracted as I sit with my friends at our usual table. The rest of them are going on about some soccer game happening tonight, and I can't find it in me to pretend that I'm interested. Sitting here is starting to feel like more of a chore than a choice, but I don't think I belong anywhere else. When people see me, do they think about what happened to Jacob?

Looking up, I find Damien watching me thoughtfully. Things have been tense between us since I rejected him. He seems to have a better grasp on how unhappy with our relationship I really am, and he's done well to keep his distance.

"Hey sleepyhead," he says, amusement in his voice despite its soft tone. "Are you still with us?"

"Sorry," I say, smiling apologetically for the sake of the others at the table. "School is kicking my ass. I've been up late these past few nights doing homework."

"Are you coming to the game tonight?" Damien asks, sounding a mix of hopeful and hesitant. "You could take a break from studying. Breathe in some fresh air."

"I don't know, I'm already so behind . . ." I trail off, and his face falls. "But I'll try to make it."

"The captain of the soccer team should definitely have his girl-friend there to support him," Zoe says. "Schoolwork can wait. Plus, if you're not there, who am I supposed to sit with?"

Anyone else, I want to say.

"You don't wanna miss it. After all, *I'll* be playing." James winks, and amusement pulls at my lips. At least we have someone to provide comic relief.

"Yeah, we'll see how much longer that lasts," Damien says. "You're about one more skipped practice away from being kicked off the team."

"I've been a little busy."

"Screwing all the cheerleaders," Damien mutters under his breath, looking away.

"Gross," I comment, setting down the spoon and losing my appetite.

"A couple of teammates too. I don't discriminate." James smirks at me, leaning back and folding his arms behind his head. "But don't worry, I'll always make time for you, doll."

I'm about to tell him to leave me out of his dirty schedule when Damien presses his palm to the surface of the table aggressively, causing our trays to jump. He gives James a dirty look, his jaw tight.

"Can you stop being such a pervert?" he snarls. "She's my girl-friend, for God's sake. Fuck off."

A thick fog of tension envelops the table, and anger radiates from Damien's body, but James seems immune. I don't really need defending, and I'm not a fan of being labeled as his girlfriend when our relationship is currently on life support, but I swallow those sentiments, trying to think of something to calm him down.

"It's all right, Damien," I say nervously. "He's only joking."

"It's not funny to me," he spits out, standing from the table. He gives James another vicious glare before looking back at me, soften-ing slightly. "I'll see you at the game, yeah?"

I nod quickly, not wanting to worsen the situation. "Sure."

Turning on his heel, he vacates the cafeteria as if the room is on fire, and the three of us who remain at the table watch him leave wordlessly. If James feels any remorse about what just happened, it doesn't show on his face. Zoe lingers on the spot Damien last stood for a beat longer before she straightens out, reverting back to her usual self.

"Well, that was dramatic," she says breezily, uncapping her water bottle and taking a sip.

"Maybe you should apologize," I suggest, looking at James.

He lifts a shoulder. "It's kind of fun to piss him off."

The lunch bell rings after that, and I head to my next class with a frown. The dynamic of our whole friend group seems to be fundamentally flawed, a fact I become more aware of every day. Zoe and I have a strange, underlying tension, and Damien seems to be harboring some unaddressed anger toward his best friend. From afar, we look polished and perfect. But upon closer inspection, it's easy to see that everything is tangled and broken, and nothing functions the way it should.

I'm starting to think it never did to begin with.

Hours later, on the way to the infamous soccer game, I can't shake the dirty feeling I get from the idea of spending a whole evening with my friends. I have to wonder if I always felt this way, even before my accident, or if nearly dying and forgetting everything I've ever known has just given me a new perspective.

When I was in the middle of the hurricane, it must've been easy to get swept up in the excitement of the storm. But now that I'm on the edge of it, I find myself wanting to stay as far away from the epicenter as possible.

The air is cool as we arrive back at the school, cramped in James's car. The boys have been silent; I don't think I've seen them speak since the confrontation at lunch, and the awkwardness in the atmosphere is hard to think through. James pulls into a parking space, and we all file out of the car.

"James and I have to go get ready," Damien explains, turning to me, markedly calmer than he was in the cafeteria. "We'll see you guys after the game."

He pauses before shrugging out of his varsity jacket and passing it to me. I reach for it, my fingers clasping the material slowly, a frown of confusion on my face. "It's kind of tradition for the girlfriends of the players to wear them," he explains.

"Oh." I'm thrown off by his constant use of the word *girlfriend*. Three times in one day feels like far too many. Soon, he won't be able to call me that at all. "I don't know if I should."

Damien shrugs, looking at me imploringly. "It's just a jacket, Allie. Besides, it's chilly tonight."

After debating with myself, I accept the jacket, slipping my arms through the large sleeves and feeling my cheeks burn slightly.

A wistful smile stays on his face as he observes me in the jacket before he reaches out and lifts my dark hair out of the collar, letting it fan across my shoulders. "I've missed seeing you wear it," he admits.

"Damien," I begin, my voice low. "Can we talk? After the game?"

His expression immediately becomes guarded. "Yeah," he forces out. "I'll see you later."

"Good luck," I call weakly as he turns away, James in tow. I need to break up with him, and I need to do it tonight. I can't let this go on anymore.

Zoe smirks at me, her hand encircling my wrist. "Come on, let's go stake our claim."

She tugs me along behind her, trailing toward the bleachers. The smell of freshly cut grass permeates the air as Zoe leads me into the stands, waving at a couple of people I don't recognize. We end up in a spot near the middle, where she sits down after wiping off the seat.

I take the one next to her, burrowing into the jacket to keep warm and looking out at the field below us. All of it feels vaguely nostalgic. I've most likely sat in this exact spot many times, observing this same scene—the waning sunlight, the shadows from the nets stretching across the green, the electric atmosphere. It makes my heart ache. Like the old Allie is here, but she's just out of my reach.

As we wait for the game to start, a familiar figure makes its way up the aisle of the bleachers. Mason Byrne's blue-green gaze is steady on me for a breath, tousled dark hair falling over his forehead, and warmth blooms in my cheeks as he takes in the letterman jacket draped around my shoulders.

Two and a half hours later, Damien is down for the count.

He tumbled with a player from the other team during the third quarter, and it seemed the Pender Falls Lions couldn't function as well without their beloved captain, resulting in a crushing loss.

The four of us make our way to the Sanchez house, Damien next to me in the backseat this time, face contorted in pain as he clutches his throbbing knee, his free hand clinging to mine. The whole thing feels a tad overdramatic, but I play along anyway, trying to be supportive, knowing it's only a matter of time before I rip out his heart and stomp all over it. Zoe seems to think it's serious, what with the way she held her breath, her fingers balling into fists as Damien collapsed to the ground, writhing in pain.

James pulls into the driveway, and between the two of us, we help Damien to his feet. He keeps an arm around each of our shoulders as we maneuver him to the front door. It's a struggle to keep him upright, and my body feels weak beneath his weight. Zoe scurries ahead of us, punching in the code to unlock the door, and we awkwardly make our way through the entrance.

Damien's parents are on their way home from some fancy work dinner his father had to attend a couple of hours out of town. They rushed to leave as soon as they heard what happened, but for now, we have the house to ourselves.

"Well, we got through the door," James remarks, taking a deep breath, clearly exhausted. "Now for the stairs."

I can't suppress the groan that escapes my lips when I spot the stairway at the end of the hall.

"Oh, come on," Damien laments, muttering under his breath, "I'm not that heavy."

"Have you ever carried yourself?" James asks.

"Yes," Damien responds haughtily. "I do it every day."

"My hero," I say, my voice flat as I move with them to the bottom of the stairs.

"I'll go get some ice," Zoe calls, before disappearing to another part of the house. She and James are able to navigate here easily; it reminds me that I'm the outsider.

It takes a lot of effort, but we finally succeed in getting Damien up the stairs and to his bedroom, and he gratefully falls onto his bed. The school nurse said he should be back to normal in about a week, and I sincerely hope that's true, because there's no way I'm going to be able to put up with his glorified pity party any longer than that.

After he's set up among his pillows, James and I exit the room. Casting a glance over my shoulder, I take James by the elbow and usher him away from the open door and out of earshot. He looks at me in confusion.

"Can you and Zoe stay downstairs for a while?" I ask. "I want to talk to Damien, alone."

He studies me for a second before his look of bemusement is replaced by a smirk. "Ah, I see how it is," he remarks. "You're turned on by injured dudes? Maybe I'll have to twist an ankle."

"You're disgusting," I say, causing him to grin wickedly. "Just go downstairs. Please."

He holds his hands up in surrender, backing away. "Whatever you say, doll."

I swallow, gazing at the door to Damien's bedroom. Every part of me wants to just leave, go downstairs, walk home, and avoid everyone for the next five to seven business days, but I know I can't.

Taking another deep breath, I reenter the room and Damien looks up from the bed. I must have been in this room a million times before, but to this version of me, it feels brand new.

"Sorry for making you and James carry me around," he apologizes as I take a seat on the edge of the bed.

"Don't worry about it," I advise. "How's your knee?"

"You don't have to beat around the bush," he says with a sigh. "I know why you're here."

He's more perceptive than I thought.

It's quiet for a long time, and when he speaks again, his voice sounds tortured. "Please don't do this," he begs, face clouded with oncoming tears.

"Damien," I mumble, looking away.

He pushes himself up from the pillows, edging closer to me, his expression desperate. "Your doctor told you going back to your regular routine would help you regain your memory, right?" he asks, his words urgent, and I nod reluctantly. "Well, this isn't routine. This isn't how we *are*."

"What are you saying?"

His brown eyes light up with something dangerous, intense on mine. "All of this distance . . . it's not right. Please, just let me show you the way we're supposed to be."

He reaches forward to cup my cheek, his stare falling to my lips, but I flinch away, backing up. "We're not supposed to *be* anything," I say firmly, not bothering to hide my irritation anymore. "I can't do this anymore, Damien. I'm sorry. I need space."

"Don't—"

The air in the room is static for a moment before I break the spell, feeling the desperate urge to leave. I stand, setting the letterman jacket on his bed. He grabs my wrist forcefully, causing me to freeze. Glancing down at him, I see he's laced his fingers through his hair now, his gaze on the floor as he leans on his elbow. He doesn't say anything, grip tightening, and my heart thunders, trying to leap out of my chest. I've never seen him act like this before.

"I'm sorry," he grinds out, voice cracking. "I'm sorry about everything. All of it. Please don't leave. I should've never—I wish I could take it back."

I don't know what he's apologizing for. "Take what back?"

He keeps his head down, and I find myself holding my breath. There's something very disturbing about his silence.

"Damien," I say, louder this time. "What did you do?"

Damien chokes out a sob, and a feeling of dread tightens in my chest, but he doesn't answer, and I grow tired of waiting.

"Let go of me."

"Two years," he says, after a pause, low and haunting. "We've been together for two years. Don't throw that down the drain."

My heart sinks, plummeting into my stomach. But as soon as the next words come to me, I know I have to say them, no matter how much they'll hurt him. I need to sever our ties. "I don't remember either of them," I say.

When the sting of my words hits him, he releases me slowly, not even bothering to look up. His rigid posture sends a chill skittering down my spine.

"I'm sorry, Damien," I say, my voice as sincere as I can manage, and then I leave the room, feeling like I can breathe again once I'm out in the hallway.

I hurry down the stairs, unsure of what I'm supposed to do now. Voices carry from the living room. By ending things with Damien, I'm certain I probably just ruined my relationship with Zoe and James too.

"What are they doing up there?" I hear Zoe mutter. "It's taking forever."

"Jealous, are we?"

"Give it a rest, James."

For a few moments, I stare at the front door, tempted to walk through it without another word, but I'm scared of what the aftermath of that would look like. Swallowing both my pride and my anxiety, I square my shoulders and head into the living room.

They both look up as I enter, watching my face carefully.

"There she is," James remarks. "How's the patient?"

"I'm going to walk home," I say, working to keep my voice steady.

"What's going on?" Zoe asks.

"Damien and I aren't together anymore. I just broke up with him."

James lets out a low whistle, dragging a hand over his face. "Shit."

Zoe's eyes have gone wide, limbs frozen. "Are you serious?"

"Yeah." I clear my throat, palms sweaty as I take a step backward. "He didn't take it well. And I understand that he needs you guys, so I'll just keep my distance from now on."

"Allie, wait—"

Without giving her a chance to finish, I leave the house, letting the door fall closed behind me. Thankfully, Damien's house is in the same neighborhood as mine, and I don't have too much trouble finding my way home.

As I shiver in the brisk, night air, I'm unable to decide whether I feel devastated or relieved.

11 | ALLUDE

Over the weekend, I'm tormented by recurring nightmares about my breakup with Damien. They're all the same—I'm always trapped inside his room, rooted to the floor, my wrist enclosed within his viselike grip, and no matter how much I pull and struggle, I can't get away.

But in the worst of them, Zoe and James are there, too, blocking the door, watching me with blacked-out eyes and blank expressions as I try to get myself free. My breathing is frantic, and Damien weeps, inky tears trailing down his cheeks. I plead for him to let me go, but it's as though he can't even hear my voice.

"Damien," I grind out desperately. "You're hurting me!"

Branches burst through the floorboards beneath us, splinters of wood scattering on the floor as jagged trees grow in the middle of his bedroom. All of a sudden, Damien releases my arm, and the momentum sends me flying backward, slamming me into a tree trunk. He stands from the bed, and slowly, the three of them descend toward me.

The bedroom door swings open, blasting the room with a burst of piercing white light, and it's the last thing I see before I jolt awake.

My brain is foggy, and my cheek is pressed to the cool floorboards of my own room. I push myself into a sitting position, unsure of how I made it down here in my sleep, heart racing. The clock shows it's nearly noon.

The fallout of my relationship with Damien was absolutely inevitable, though I can't help but wonder if I went about it in the correct way, or if there was something more I could've done to soften the blow.

I think of the low timbre of his voice as he asked me to reconsider, the specific words he used: *I wish I could take it back.*

I'm not surprised by him letting something nonsensical slip out in the midst of everything. But I can't seem to move on from that one sentence in particular.

A knock sounds on my door, and I snap out of my reverie. Clearing my throat, I stand up, feeling stiff. A glance in the mirror shows me the glaring, red spot on my cheek where it was pressed to the floor, and I try to shield it with my hair. After pulling the door open, I'm faced with Audrey, looking more fresh faced than I've seen her in a while.

"Hey." She sweeps over my appearance. "Were you sleeping?"

"Kind of. What's up?"

"I'm going downtown—shocking, I know. But I need to get out of this house for a while, and I won't do it unless I have a purpose. Do you want me to pick up anything?"

Guilt tugs on my heartstrings, and I bite the inside of my lip. "Downtown?" I repeat, and she nods. "Would you mind having some company?"

Surprise flickers across her features, though she works to mask it. Audrey and I haven't exactly spent a whole lot of time together since I came home from the hospital. Sure, she's given me rides to and from school most days, but outside of that, we never seem to have a proper chance to talk. I know we fought a lot in the past, and she's had to be the bigger person and set that all aside. I wonder if there are still things she resents me for.

Maybe I'm offering to go with her for selfish reasons, as if being kind to her will wash away my sins.

"Oh," she says, after a pause. "I mean, if you want to come with."

"I wouldn't mind getting out of the house too."

Audrey backs away from my bedroom door, and I quickly change and make myself look more presentable. I find myself thinking again how strange this all must be for her. For everyone. When they look at me, they see the same face they've always seen, but there's a different person behind it now. At least, I tell myself I'm a different person.

There's no other way for me to reconcile what I've done in the past.

After I've thrown on my woolen peacoat and Audrey has donned her wide-brimmed hat, we file out of the house and into her car. She flicks on the radio then turns it down, gentle coffee shop tunes filling in the gap between us. The sky is a pale grey, as it most often is, but there are no rain clouds in sight. It's actually starting to feel more like spring, despite the overcast weather. As I look out the window, I sense Audrey peering at me out of the corner of her eye.

"Thanks for coming," she says when I turn to face her. "I guess I didn't really want to go alone."

"Anytime." Silence falls over us again, and I work to push past my feelings of shame in order to be supportive. "Do you want to talk about it?"

Audrey instantly understands what I'm referring to, straightening out in her seat as we pull up to an intersection. "No. Yes." She sighs. "I don't know."

The light turns green and we lurch forward.

"Everything just feels, like, *lonely*," she confesses, leaning her elbow beneath the window, and my heart sinks. "We were always together. I feel like I've lost a limb."

"I'm sorry," I say. Even though I know their relationship was never solid, it hurts to hear how different they felt about each other. I don't know if Parker ever actually loved her, but she thinks the world of him, even after he broke her heart.

"God, listen to me. Complaining about my breakup when you're going through shit that actually matters."

"You're allowed to feel what you need to feel."

"I shouldn't complain," she says, lowering her voice. "I just . . . I really thought we had a future together. I didn't think it would end like this. And I don't even understand why it ended at all."

I purse my lips, discomfort stirring in my belly. "There wasn't anything that hinted this might happen?"

"No!" she says emphatically, making a left turn and bringing us closer to the downtown core. "I was totally blindsided. Things were fine, and then all of a sudden they weren't. Anyway, enough about that."

Despite my supposed history of acting, I'm having a really hard time pretending I don't know the precise reason her relationship crashed and burned. Instead, I think of ways to change the subject.

"I broke up with Damien."

She turns to look at me. "Really? Are you okay?"

"I think so. I haven't decided yet," I say. "Being with him was starting to feel very suffocating."

"Then it's a good thing," she concludes firmly.

"Maybe." I recall the brief, unburdened feeling I had after leaving his bedroom, but the slew of nightmares I've had since that night makes me uneasy. "I'm not looking forward to seeing him at school tomorrow."

"I'm actually surprised you didn't do it a lot sooner, considering the circumstances," she admits, scanning the street for a parking spot. I keep an eye out, too, watching people stroll along the sidewalk.

"He had a way of making it really hard to turn him down," I mutter, rubbing at my wrist.

We turn the corner, and she slides into a spot, shifting the car into Park. "I never liked him. Something always rubbed me the wrong way."

"Really?" I frown as I click my door open and step onto the pavement.

"He *worshipped* you."

"That's a bad thing?"

Her lips twitch, and she gives me a wry look as she rounds the car, falling into line with me on the sidewalk. "Very funny. It wasn't in a cute way, though. It was obsessive."

My good humor fades, and I stick my hands into my pockets, sidestepping a couple looking in the window of a hat shop. Damien's voice comes back to me. *You're mine.* "I thought it was all in my head," I admit.

"Definitely not," she says seriously. "It's normal to be crazy about the person you're with, but that boy took things to new heights. One time you had to block his number because he was calling you too much. It wouldn't surprise me if he had a lock of your hair in his bedroom somewhere."

Audrey shudders, and there's a part of me that feels relieved that my gut instincts weren't misguided. However, the rest of me is deeply disturbed.

"Ugh, I don't want to talk about him anymore," I say.

Trying to distract myself from all thoughts of lovesick obsession, I take in all the stores lining the street, able to read their titles better up close. I've driven through downtown many times since leaving the hospital, but it's my first time actually checking everything out. The smell of espresso hits my nose as we pass the open door of a coffeehouse next to a kitschy furniture store, and I peer at the colorful items inside.

"Where should we go first?" Audrey asks.

I squint, scanning the options. Across the street, movement catches my eye, and I look over in time to see Officer Edwards heading down the concrete steps of the post office. I haven't forgotten about his visit, when Sofia was quick to usher him out the door, and I doubt he has either. I've been wondering when we would cross paths again.

He glances in my direction, and I duck my head.

"Let's go in here." Without taking the time to look at the name of the store, I veer into the nearest shop, and Audrey scrambles to follow me.

A bell jingles overhead as we enter, and I quickly realize we're inside a secondhand bookstore. The lighting is dim, the room filled with bookcases that are practically overflowing, stacks of extra books piled on the floor. A clerk nods as I walk past, wanting to get as far away from the window as possible. On the off chance Officer Edwards didn't see me, I want to stay off his radar.

Audrey trails behind me, taking in the multitude of titles we pass as we head to the back corner of the store. We come to a stop, and I look over my shoulder, but the shop remains quiet, and we appear to be the only ones inside.

"Well," Audrey says, picking up the nearest book and flipping to a page. "I never knew you were a fan of bodice rippers."

"Excuse me?"

I look down at the book in her hands to see the photograph of a scantily clad woman clinging to a shirtless man on the front cover, and I realize what section I've brought us to. Cheeks burning, I snatch it out of her hands and shove it back on the shelf as she laughs.

"Hey, no judgment," she quips.

"I wasn't paying attention," I insist.

"At least it's private," she says, sinking down and sitting cross-legged on the floor. "You could hide away in here for hours."

Mimicking her, I take a seat on the hardwood, feeling safer the more out of sight we are. I pick at a scuff mark on the floor, listening to the classical music floating down from overhead.

"Audrey, I wanted to ask you something."

"Yeah?"

I swallow. "Do you know Jacob Griffin?"

She instantly looks uncomfortable, and lowers her gaze. "Everyone in town does," she murmurs. "Why do you ask?"

"Did I do that to him?" My voice falters.

"Allie," she says, sympathetic as she scoots closer to me and places a hand on my back. "I never believed it was you. I know his sister thinks otherwise, but you've always vehemently denied it."

"I could've lied."

"I genuinely don't believe you were capable of doing something like that, even at your worst. Slipping an extra dress into your bag at Plaisir and drinking under the bleachers during class were more your style." Audrey pauses. "How did you find out about all of this?"

I lift a shoulder, unmoved by her words. "I saw an article about it. And then the other day at school, Amber confronted me, so I got Zoe to tell me the whole story."

"What happened to Jacob was tragic," she says. "He's lucky to have survived. I think his family is trying to find the truth."

Even if Audrey doesn't believe it was me, that doesn't change the fact that *someone* did that to Jacob. Someone at school.

After a few beats of silence, Audrey bumps my knee with hers. "Hey, the purpose of this trip isn't to sulk in the back of a dusty bookstore," she teases gently. "Let's do something fun. What if we try to pick out a book for each other?"

"Sure. Be serious, though," I warn. "No bodice rippers."

"You're so lame."

After rising to our feet, we part ways, and I read the names of the sections, trying to forget about Jacob Griffin and wondering what kind of books Audrey likes to read based on what I know about her. Judging by her thoughts on her relationship with Parker, I get the feeling she's a hopeless romantic. But, considering the breakup, maybe she doesn't want to read about that. Something the polar opposite might be better, with lots of action and excitement.

I wander over to the section that includes the staff's favorite books. Most of them are classic books that sound familiar, and after reading all the summaries, I decide on *Gone Girl*. Maybe a captivating thriller will be enough to take her mind off everything.

Tucking the book to my chest, I meander through the store, trying to locate my sister again. I'm rounding the corner of the cookbook section when I nearly ram into someone else, causing me to stop short.

"Hello, Allie."

Officer Edwards stands before me, a placid look on his face. His demeanor feels different than it was the last time we spoke, as if some of his friendliness has melted off the surface, revealing an uglier side lingering just beneath.

The bookstore is stuffy, suddenly a lot smaller than it was only minutes ago, and I listen for Audrey, trying to summon her.

"Hi," I return, taking a slow, subtle step back.

"It's nice to see you again," he continues, voice light. "We didn't get a proper chance to talk last time."

"I should probably find my sister."

Edwards tilts his head, ignoring my apprehension. "How's school going? Are you keeping up with your classes?"

"Yes," I say shortly, looking over his shoulder. Sofia's stern warning comes to me all at once. *Don't ever talk to them alone.* In this part of the store, I can't even see the clerk anymore, and it makes me feel like the towering bookcases are steadily creeping closer.

"I heard you had a birthday recently," he continues, placing his hands on his hips, and his badge gleams in the sliver of sunlight that creeps into the building. "It seems like you're doing well."

"I'm okay."

"You know, you and I used to see a lot of each other." His tone shifts again, sharper now, and goose bumps rise on my arms. I say nothing, keeping my mouth firmly clamped shut. "You and your friends had a penchant for getting into all kinds of trouble. Somehow your mother was always able to get you out of it." He pauses. "But she's not here now, is she?"

I stiffen at the thinly veiled threat and clutch the book tighter. "I'm not sure what you're saying, Officer," I tell him, working to keep my voice steady.

"You were building quite the track record for yourself," he says, raising his bushy eyebrows. "A nice string of theft, vandalism, underage drinking . . . Of course, you don't remember any of that. Lucky for you, forgetting everything is the perfect alibi."

Distantly, the door chimes again, and I hear the sounds of laughter as other customers enter the shop, but Edwards pays them no mind, steadfast. I'm not sure what he's trying to imply with his intimidation tactics, but they're a waste of time.

"It may be fun for now, but eventually, this little act is going to have to come to an end." The words are low, yet somehow he manages to inject his false friendly disposition into them.

"It's not an act," I manage. I don't know whether I should be flattered or offended that multiple people think I have enough talent and determination to *fake* amnesia for such an extended period of time.

"There are things about that night that aren't adding up, Allie," he continues. "Things that you may be hiding. Accidents are random and unpredictable, but yours feels calculated. You've always loved performing, isn't that right?"

"I don't think I should be talking to you."

"I know it's probably thrilling to play pretend, but things will only get harder for you as time goes on. Don't get me wrong, I don't believe you're capable of pulling off something like this on your own. If you're trying to protect someone—"

"I need to go now." My voice has a hard edge, sharp enough to cut anyone who comes close.

"What's going on here?"

At the sound of a new voice, I exhale, relief leaving my body in a rush of breath, and Audrey appears beside me. She instantly spots the agitation on my face and takes a step closer, partially blocking me from the policeman's view.

"Why are you talking to her?" she demands.

Edwards is unruffled, apparently not as intimidated by Audrey as he is by Sofia. "I was just saying hello," he says innocently, setting my teeth on edge. "I'm sure you're aware Allie and I go way back."

Audrey doesn't respond, looking at him levelly before placing a hand on my back and ushering me down the aisle.

"Until next time!" Edwards calls, tipping his hat in my direction as he saunters to the exit.

I don't breathe easier until I hear the chimes announcing his departure. Audrey reaches out and loops an arm around my shoulders, watching me with concern.

"What was that about?" she asks.

"He seems to think I'm faking everything," I mumble.

"I'm sorry, *what*?"

"He fits right in with the other people at school who think my amnesia is some sort of elaborate long con."

"That's ridiculous," she scoffs.

"I don't really want to talk about it," I say, nodding my chin in the direction of the book clutched in her hands. "What'd you pick out?"

Audrey gives me a tiny smile, revealing a copy of *The Shining*. "It's one of your favorite movies. But as far as I know, you haven't read the book."

"That sounds perfect." I pass her the novel in my own hands. "I thought you might like a suspenseful distraction."

Her face lights up in excitement. "You thought right."

After buying the books and exiting back into the April day that's steadily growing warmer, I see the police cruiser is still parked across the street. My guard goes up again, and I brace myself in case Officer Edwards is nearby, waiting to approach us again.

"Audrey," I say. "Would it be okay if we went home now?"

"Oh sure."

The shrill squeal of a siren pierces the air as the police car pulls away from the curb, speeding down the street, and I stumble on the sidewalk. I'm instantly plunged inward, to a scene of murky flashing lights, red and blue, battling against the dawn behind my eyelids. My head is heavy, barely able to process the voices shouting, calling out directions to each other. The scene flickers to something darker, and I have the sensation of extracting myself from a car and staggering to the ground.

But this time, I don't feel as though I'm alone. My own voice comes back to me, panicked and strained, bogged down with thick emotion.

What did you do to me?

And then, in the next instant, the flashback is over, and I'm standing on the sidewalk in front of the shops again, gripping the railing of the front steps of a boutique, blinking rapidly. Audrey is next to me, grabbing my arm, looking panicked.

"Allie, can you hear me?" she asks. "Are you okay?"

I give my head a shake, fingers trembling. "Sorry."

Audrey looks frightened and refuses to let go of me. "You weren't responding to me," she says, and I wonder how much time has passed. "Where did you go?"

"I don't know," I say slowly.

"I'm worried about you, Allie." Her eyes are shiny. "You look like you just saw a ghost. Or, like, twenty ghosts."

I move out of her grasp, swallowing. "I promise I'm fine. Let's just go. Please."

Reluctantly, she nods, only releasing me when I'm safely inside the car.

It's been a while since I've been struck with an image so vivid and visceral, and it leaves me with a hollow feeling in my gut, especially after my conversation with Officer Edwards.

The ride home is stifling, and I'm eager to get out of the car and be alone. We don't speak until Audrey pulls into our driveway, turns the ignition off, and sits back against her seat.

"I have to tell Mom about this," she says gently. "I'm sorry."

"Audrey," I protest.

She grabs our books from the backseat, pursing her lips. "That wasn't normal."

"Nothing about any of this is normal," I remind her.

"It's better to be safe than sorry, okay?" She gets out of the car and heads into the house, and I sigh in defeat.

There's no doubt my brain is trying to show me images of the night everything changed, but it's harrowing to only receive tiny fragments at a time. In every story I've been told of what took place, there's never been mention of anyone else being there. I was driving alone. I hit a tree. Nobody found me until the morning.

But the question I heard was undoubtedly directed at someone else. And, paired with Officer Edwards's accusation, it's becoming clear I'm not the only one involved in what happened that night.

12 | ISOLATE

On Monday morning, I make my way to the English classroom feeling as though I have some sort of identifying mark that lets everyone know all of their attention should be focused on me.

I know it's mostly in my head, as I'm not receiving any more looks than a typical day at school, but walking alone after what happened on Friday makes it feel vastly different. I haven't heard from Zoe or James since I left Damien's house.

There's no doubt that the ending of my relationship with Damien has thrown a wrench in our dynamic. It was a far cry from an amicable split, and he's had plenty of time to tell them about how I broke his heart.

As if I accidentally summoned him, I catch a glimpse of the boy himself at the opposite end of the hallway, propped up by crutches as James fetches his books from his locker and Zoe rubs his back soothingly. The sight causes me to stiffen, feeling like the lines have been drawn. I fully anticipated James sticking with his best friend, but there was a part of me that thought Zoe would have at least reached out.

Damien spots me, his expression desperate and forlorn, and I'm quick to look away, hurrying toward my first class. The seat next to mine is noticeably empty, and I feel a tug of disappointment. I was hoping to see at least one friendly face today.

Zoe slides into the classroom right before the final bell rings; I can tell she looks at me, but I pretend not to notice. Class begins, and the room fills with different voices as we come to the end of *Macbeth*. My mind is elsewhere. Ever since my conversation with Officer Edwards and the resulting vision, it's been hard to focus on anything for longer than a couple of seconds.

Audrey was quick to tell Sofia about my episode, and I know they're both eager to ship me off to Dr. Meyer again.

"Allie?"

Ms. Warren's voice cuts through my trance, and I snap to attention, feeling everyone shift in my direction. She looks at me imploringly, nodding her head. "Would you like to share your thoughts?"

"Oh," I stammer, mouth falling open. "Uh . . ."

Zoe is turned around in her seat, one arm leaning languidly on the back of her chair as she watches me with pursed lips.

"I'm sorry, I wasn't really—"

"I think Lady Macbeth is redeemable," Zoe cuts in, facing the front, and I blink in confusion. Is this her way of trying to help me out or showing off my incompetence?

Ms. Warren only looks slightly miffed that I'm not the one answering but nods for Zoe to continue.

"Throughout the play, we hear her suggest all of these wicked things, and it was her idea to take out King Duncan in the first place," she says, her tone firm and sure of itself. "But when it came down to it, she wasn't the one to follow through. And while Macbeth was on his killing spree, she was left to suffer in her guilt."

A hush has fallen over the room, and I stare at the back of Zoe's head at her sleek, blond hair that never seems to look anything less than perfect and the pressed blazer that frames her shoulders.

"In the end, her guilt consumed her," she finishes, softer now. "She made a mistake, and it ruined her life. But I don't think she's as bad as everyone says she is."

Her statement reminds me of what she said to me during our conversation about Jacob Griffin. *People do what they have to in order to get what they want. It doesn't define them.* I wonder if she's trying to comfort me again.

Ms. Warren nods thoughtfully, considering the words. "Very interesting perspective, Zoe."

Class continues on, and when it's over, I'm quick to rise from my seat, gathering my things and heading straight for my locker. After tucking away my English books, I find myself drawn to the photo of Zoe and me taped to the inside of the door.

Closing the locker with a sigh, I step back, preparing to head to calculus.

"Alina."

I startle slightly, turning to see Mason Byrne standing next to me, a look of urgency on his face.

"Hey," I greet him, unable to hide the surprise in my voice. He glances around the hallway, seeming distracted. "You weren't in class."

"Slept in," he says, his voice low, before taking a step closer. "Listen, I need to talk to you."

"Okay," I say slowly, laughing with uncertainty. "Talk to me."

He shakes his head, solemn. "Not here."

For whatever reason, those are the two words that allow me to clue in that something isn't right. I take in the way his eyes are darting in every direction, even though no one is paying attention to us.

"Mason," I murmur. "Is everything okay?"

His frown deepens. "I don't know. That's what I need to talk to you about."

"But you can't talk about it here," I clarify.

A look of irritation flashes across his features. "Meet me later tonight."

My heartbeat stutters. "Where?"

Mason opens his mouth to speak again, but we're joined by someone else, causing him to stand up straight, clamping it shut. I reluctantly look away in time to see Zoe sidling up next to us, looking determined.

"Allie," she says, placing a gentle hand on my arm, and I'm instantly uncomfortable. "Are you free after school?"

"Um, I don't know."

"I'd really like to talk about what happened on Friday."

At that, Mason looks my way curiously. Zoe seems to notice him for the first time, sizing him up with a calculated expression.

"Is that necessary?" I ask.

"Please?" She clasps her hands, attention returning to me. "Let's go for coffee."

The warning bell rings overhead, but Zoe doesn't seem to mind, continuing to bat her eyelashes. Mason gives me one last meaningful look before turning to head down the hallway. It seems every time we're about to have an actual conversation, we get interrupted some-how, and it's starting to get on my nerves.

"Fine," I give in, shoulders slumping.

"I'll see you later," Zoe says, touching my arm softly again, and I nod, hugging my books to my chest and watching as she walks away.

The end of the school day comes too quickly.

My classes didn't prove to be enough of a distraction, and I ate lunch outside in the courtyard to avoid seeing Damien and the others. I wait for Zoe in the parking lot, standing next to her car. I already texted Audrey and told her I don't need a ride today, but I really wish I hadn't.

Sprinkles of rain land on my shoulders, and I pull the hood of my coat over my head, bouncing on the balls of my feet. Across the lot, Mason is heading to his car, and I think of his words to me this morning and the troubled look on his face.

Despite knowing whatever he wants to talk to me about must be something serious, the prospect of meeting him outside of school foolishly makes my stomach flutter.

Before I get too lost within my mind, Zoe exits the building, hurrying down the steps. She looks relieved when she sees me standing next to her car, and she pulls her keys out, unlocking it.

"Thanks for waiting," she breathes. "Chemistry lasted for an eternity. Mr. Bromwell can never seem to shut up."

After sliding into the passenger's side, I remove my hood and pat down my hair. "It's okay."

Zoe turns the key in the ignition, taking the time to make sure she's in reverse before pulling out of her spot. It's silent as she directs us away from the school, and I look out at the streets that are becoming steadily familiar. Pender Falls isn't that big. When you look at it on a map, it appears as though it wouldn't take that long to see all of it. It's odd how a place so small can contain so much mystery. When the wind blows through the trees, it's almost like the sound of secrets being whispered among the leaves.

Zoe peeks at me out of the corner of her eye. "You were with Mason again this morning." I don't respond, squirming in my seat. "You were with him at your party too."

"I'm surprised you noticed."

She crinkles her nose as we round the corner. "Still sore about that, huh?"

"Possibly."

"Is something going on between you? You had that dream about him too."

"No!" I protest, cheeks burning. "Why would you think that? I barely know him."

Zoe shrugs innocently, pulling up to the coffee shop that Audrey and I walked past yesterday. I find myself looking over my shoulder, hoping that Officer Edwards won't make a reappearance. We exit the vehicle, ducking under the overhang of the shop roofs to escape the rain. She pulls open the door to the coffee shop, gesturing for me to go first, and I step inside.

The air inside is significantly warmer, and the smell of espresso and coffee beans reaches my nose, making me feel a little less on edge. For the past week, my body has been a tightly wound coil of tension, and I can't get it to unravel.

"The two of you have a weird vibe," Zoe remarks, and I take a break from perusing the menu to give her a look. "I'm not blind, Allie. I remember you saying you were friends in elementary school, but that was ages ago. What's up with you guys now?"

"I don't really know," I admit.

An unreadable expression crosses over her features. "Kind of odd, isn't it?"

"What is?"

She gestures as if it should be obvious. "You weren't friends for years, and now that you suddenly lost your memory, he wants to reconnect? It just seems kind of suspicious to me."

I frown, pondering the accusation, and she steps up to the counter to order two Americano mistos. As we wait for our drinks at the side, I listen to the gentle music floating down from the speakers and the coffee grinder.

"I don't think that's what he's after," I say. "It doesn't seem like he wants to be my friend."

"All the more reason not to trust him. Who knows what he might have to gain by getting close to you."

She grabs both of our coffees then leads the way to a table near the window, and I feel a surge of annoyance. She doesn't even know Mason—granted, I don't exactly know him either—but the feelings I get from him are genuine. Kind of like Parker, yet different altogether. I've never felt like he's had any ill will toward me.

But maybe I'm being naive. I have no idea what his true intentions are.

I settle into the seat across from her, my mind once again going to the day I was reintroduced to Amber and Whitney. Bringing my mug up to my lips, I let the drink warm my fingers.

"Did anything happen between us?" I ask.

Zoe frowns. "Who?"

"You and me. I just remembered what Whitney said about us making up."

She looks confused for another beat, before laughing and shaking her head. "Whitney doesn't know what she's talking about," she says, waving a hand dismissively. "Allie, we used to get into arguments all the time. They never really meant anything."

As she takes a sip of her drink, I watch her carefully, noting how she keeps her gaze riveted to the table. "Are you sure? Because if I did something to offend you . . ."

"Trust me," she remarks. "I'm not easily offended."

She fixes me with a knowing smile, and I do my best to return it, trying not to let my hesitation show on my face. Audrey hadn't seemed all that surprised about how Zoe treated me at my birthday party, and she essentially implied I used to do similar things to her. *Best friends one moment, at each other's throats the next.* It wouldn't be a stretch to conclude that things might not have been peachy between us before my accident. Maybe it's something Zoe doesn't want me to know, or maybe she's trying to be courteous of my condition by hiding the truth.

"Anyway." She sets her mug on the table, looking at me sympathetically. "I thought you might want to talk about what happened with Damien."

I hold back a groan at the sound of his name, placing a hand to my forehead. My coffee curdles in my stomach as the image of his dejected face pops into my brain. "How is he?"

"He's . . ." she begins, her voice light, before deflating. "Not that great."

"Judging by the way he was looking at me today, I figured as much."

Zoe winces. "You kind of destroyed his heart."

"Wow, thanks."

"It's not your fault," she says quickly. "He feels everything very strongly. And he's used to getting what he wants. Life has been easy for him. His future was looking bright, he got a soccer scholarship to UBC, he was seen as a promising athlete who was going to make it big one day, he had you . . . I think he feels like part of his perfect future is slipping away."

Tension builds in my shoulders. "He wanted too much from me," I say, shaking my head. "I didn't feel like I had any other choice. I understand that you're his friend, so I don't want to make things weird by—"

"Allie." She reaches out, placing her hand over mine. "You're my best friend. You made the right decision. I'm not choosing sides, I'm here for both of you."

"Really?"

"Of course," she emphasizes. "He'll get over it eventually. James and I are your friends. I wanted to tell you that on Friday, but you ran off before I had the chance."

I sag in relief. It'll be hard to figure out how to navigate my relationship with Damien, but school is suddenly sounding a lot less lonely than it felt today. Despite the times when we're at odds with each other, Zoe is essentially my only friend. "Thank you. I was worried you guys might hate me now."

A flash of my nightmare comes back to me, the three of them descending in my direction with soulless eyes, and I clear my throat, suddenly tense.

"Please, we'll never hate you." Zoe swirls her coffee in her mug. "Do you think there's any chance of you guys getting back together?"

"God, no," I choke out, nearly spitting out my drink. Zoe sits up straighter, lips twitching. "If I'm being honest, I don't even understand how we were together in the first place. We just seem so different."

"Good to know," she says lightly.

"I've been meaning to ask you," I start, leaning back in my seat. "People keep telling me I used to get into all kinds of trouble, and I'm assuming you must have been there for at least some of that. Is that true?"

"Oh, absolutely," she remarks, looking amused. "We were real-life partners in crime."

"Tell me more."

"Last summer we spent a week in Vancouver pretending to be other people, sneaking into clubs, and other places we *definitely* shouldn't have been," she says. "Don't even get me started on that guy we met who claimed to be a prince . . ."

As she tells me stories of our scandalous adventures, I realize there are times when I feel at ease being with Zoe. It makes it seem as though all the bad stuff never happened, like I really *can* trust her, almost to the point where I wonder if I've created all the drama in my head. She's self-assured and sturdy, and there's a safety that comes with being in her presence sometimes, like no matter what happens, we'll be able to handle it together.

I wish we had more days like this.

The rain is aggressive by the time Zoe drops me off at home, angry dark clouds hanging low, pummeling the pavement with water, and I make a mad dash for the front door. It's quiet in the house when I enter, and I assume both Audrey and Sofia are at work.

After ditching my coat and shoes by the door, I head up to my bedroom, schoolbooks in tow, hoping to get some work done while I'm alone. It doesn't take long before I'm immersed in my biology textbook, eyebrows creased in concentration.

Out of the blue, my cell phone rings. I dig it out of my backpack, going still when I read the name on the caller ID.

Mason.

My time with Zoe nearly made me forget my conversation with him this morning. A flurry of nerves forms in my belly, and I stare at the phone for another beat before answering it, placing it against my ear.

"Hey," I say timidly.

"There's something I think you should know," he remarks, skipping over the pleasantries. "Meet me outside."

The call disconnects before I can say another word.

13 | REVEAL

Moving to my bedroom window, I peer outside. Beyond the rain-splattered glass, there's a pair of gleaming headlights parked on the street below, a little ways down from the house. I back away, wondering if Mason saw me.

The abrupt nature of his call paired with the urgency of our conversation at school leaves me with a bad feeling, yet I can't tamp down the intrigue I feel at the prospect of having a chance to talk to him alone, uninterrupted.

Taking a deep breath, I look at my reflection in the mirror, suddenly self-conscious. There's no time to do anything about my appearance, so I run my fingers through my hair in an attempt to detangle it.

When I reach the bottom of the stairs, I throw on my raincoat and Blundstones again, preparing to head outside. But the door bursts open before I can, and I move out of the way as Sofia enters, her arms laden with grocery bags, droplets of rainwater resting on the shoulders of her woolen coat.

"Help me with these, would you?" she asks, huffing out a breath.

I quickly relieve her of a couple of bags, follow her into the kitchen, and set them down on the island. Anxiety wriggles into my brain, and I catch a glimpse of the street outside where Mason is waiting in his car. He might leave if I end up taking too long.

Sofia sighs, shrugging out of her coat and draping it over one of the stools. "Can you help me put them away?"

"Actually," I say, fidgeting with my fingers. "I was just on my way out."

She stops moving, looking as though she's properly noticing me for the first time, taking in my jacket and boots. "Where are you going?"

For some reason, I feel compelled to lie, and the words come easily. "I was with Zoe earlier," I say. "I left something in her car and she's dropping it off. We might talk for a while. She's outside already."

Sofia's eyes flicker to the window, noting the pair of headlights. Between the night that's fallen and the rain, it's impossible to tell the make of the car. "Oh," she remarks. "Well, don't stay out too late."

Exhaling subtly, I nod. "I won't."

I hurry to the front door before she can change her mind. When I step outside into the rain, the world feels muted. My boots splash in the steadily forming puddles as I toss my hood over my head and stick my hands into my pockets, trying not to squint at the bright lights.

Reaching the car, I brace myself before grabbing the handle of the passenger door, pulling it open, and sliding inside. I instantly feel the rush of heat blasting from the air vents in the car, and I shiver involuntarily as I push back my hood.

"Hey." The low voice comes from beside me, and I turn to look in Mason's direction for the first time.

His blue-green gaze is riveted to my face, some of his dark hair falling over his forehead, and I can see that the ends are damp, as though he rushed over here and it wasn't all that long ago that he was out in the rain too. I'm suddenly very aware that we're in a small, enclosed space.

"Hey," I return, the word coming out breathier than I intend. "What's going on?"

"I'm sorry for acting so strange."

"You're kind of freaking me out," I admit.

"For weeks, I've wondered if I'm reading too far into things," he remarks. "But I can't shake the feeling that something isn't right."

"What are you talking about?"

"I lied to you." When he sees my look of confusion, he continues. "On your birthday. I didn't actually leave when I said I did."

"Okay," I say slowly. "Why?"

"I had a hunch." He drums his fingers on the steering wheel, agitation emanating from his posture. "Something is off about your friends. Have you noticed?"

"What do you mean?" I press, shifting in my seat to angle myself toward him, listening to the downpour hammer on the hood of his car.

"They're hiding something," Mason says, before looking at me squarely. "I overheard them talking about you."

My fingers tangle themselves together anxiously. "I got into a fight with Damien that night," I confess. "He was really upset. I have no doubt in my mind he was telling them about it."

"It wasn't that."

"You're scaring me," I say again.

"That might be a good thing."

"Mason, just tell me."

He hesitates, an uneasy expression on his face. "They said they were worried about you remembering the truth." A chill runs down my spine. "And that they're going to make sure you don't."

"The truth about what?"

"I don't know," he says, searching my face. "That's all I heard."

Letting out a breathy laugh, I turn away from him and look out at the poorly lit street. It suddenly seems a lot more threatening than it did only moments ago, despite the fact that my house is only a few steps away. "Well, that could be anything," I reason. "Right?"

"It could be," he offers. "But it doesn't sound good."

"Anything can sound bad out of context."

"Alina," he says. "Do you really believe that?"

I don't say anything, and he seems to accept that as an answer.

"There's something in my gut telling me there's more to your accident than what everyone has been told," he finishes. "Have you felt it too?"

In my periphery, it feels like branches are creeping steadily closer to the car, but when I blink, they disappear.

Yes.

I begin to feel lightheaded. "This cop keeps questioning me. I thought it was weird, but . . ."

"Something isn't right," he reiterates.

"Hold on," I say, lifting a hand, feeling my eyebrows pull together tightly. "Are you seriously trying to say that my friends had something to do with it? What reason do they have to do something like this?"

When he doesn't immediately deny my claim, it deepens my feeling of dread. Distantly, I hear a peal of thunder, and it sets my teeth on edge.

The lights from the houses on the opposite side of the street illuminate Mason's face, and he swallows visibly, taking the time to consider his words before answering. I feel a flicker of doubt.

Mason suddenly dropped back into my life after years of being absent from it, and though some of that was my own doing, could that mean he has ulterior motives?

All the more reason not to trust him.

A motion light snaps to life outside my window as a cat saunters by, and it causes me to startle, heart pounding.

"The night of your accident," Mason says, not seeming to notice my uneasiness. "I—I was at the party."

I frown, my fingers inching closer to my door handle. "I thought you didn't like parties."

"I don't." He shakes his head. "I don't know why I went. But I saw you and Zoe get into a fight."

"Apparently, we fight all the time," I counter.

He glances at me warily, not seeming to appreciate my defensive attitude. I can't help it; I'm starting to learn that trusting people blindly isn't a wise thing to do. "It looked serious. Lots of people saw. And when you left that night, you weren't alone."

Panic creeps into my chest again. "How do you know?"

"I saw you leave, Alina," he tells me. "Your friends followed you out. But you were found alone."

The second the words leave his mouth, I'm plunged back to being in Dr. Meyer's office, deep in the throes of complicated visions. *Leave me alone*, I'd heard myself say, my voice clogged with anger, straining to be heard over a pounding bassline as I stalked to the front door. And then I see the scene from my nightmare again, Damien holding on to me with a viselike grip as Zoe and James block the door.

My hands begin to shake, and I look away from Mason's prying stare. "Why are you even telling me this? What's in it for you?"

The atmosphere in the car changes, and out of the corner of my eye, I see him flinch, clearly put off by my accusation.

"You think I'm doing this for me?" His voice is louder now, incredulous.

"I don't know," I mumble.

He scoffs. "Seriously?"

"I don't know you, Mason," I blurt, turning to face him again, and a flicker of hurt dashes across his features. "What am I supposed to think? Who am I supposed to trust?"

Mason's mouth opens and closes before he presses his lips together firmly.

Feeling agitated, I drag my fingers through my hair. "You tell me we used to be friends, but you won't tell me what happened." He looks away. "Maybe you did something to me. Maybe I shouldn't be friends with you. I mean, I don't even know what you think of me. Zoe has supposedly been my best friend for years."

"I didn't . . ." He trails off then shakes his head, his jaw ticking. "I have nothing to gain by telling you this. What reason would I have to lie?"

I shrug stubbornly, turning to look out the window. The conversation has become tense, and I feel the urge to get out of the car and leave him in the rain, but for some reason I can't make myself move. This wasn't what I was expecting when he asked me to meet him.

And despite the accusatory nature of my words, I don't know that it's how I really feel. There's been something drawing me to Mason ever since I saw him on my first day back at school, and it hasn't gone away. Maybe it's my childhood memories coming to the surface. Dr. Meyer told me I needed to learn how to access the information that's stored in my brain and that memories can manifest in different ways.

It could just be that my mind is grasping for anything it can get a proper hold on, and that resulted in latching onto something from years ago, leaving me with positive feelings. But that doesn't mean something terrible couldn't have happened between us and been the reason our relationship crumbled.

"I don't know anything about you," I conclude, looking at him squarely.

"Know that I would never do anything to—" He exhales, frustrated. The intensity of his eyes on mine makes something burn in my chest, sets my pulse racing. "You don't have to trust me. But I think believing me would be in your best interest."

I search for any hints of insincerity on his face, but I'm unable to find them. The silence in the car feels charged, and in spite of my bold words, I begin to give in. "Okay, say I do believe you. What did they do and why did they do it?"

He pauses. "Maybe the fight between you guys went south. Who would want to be implicated in something like that? Your reputation would never recover, and they care a *lot* about reputation. Either way, they clearly know a lot more than they're letting on."

My mind plays through a slideshow of all the times Zoe has told me about the social hierarchy at school as though it were written law and how she explained that the reason Damien is so upset about our breakup is because now his life isn't quite as perfect as it appears. I can feel myself starting to trust Mason, and the thought is frightening. Am I really ready to admit my only friends might be irreversibly tangled up in what happened to me?

"I spoke to you that night," he says, pulling me out of my thoughts. "It was brief, but it was the first time we'd really spoken in years."

"What did you say?"

"You were on your way out," he explains. "You looked really upset, so I felt like I should ask if you were okay. You didn't reveal much, but you said you never wanted to see Zoe again."

I bite my tongue, waiting to hear more before attempting to justify the words, but bold statements like that are sometimes just said for dramatic effect. In my head, I can picture the scene, but it's more imagination, less memory.

"You told me you were going to ruin her."

Ruin.

It's such a loaded word. Unease creeps into the car.

"Alina, I didn't tell you this to try to mess with your head," he says, peering at my face. My throat becomes tight. "I wouldn't be talking to you right now if I thought it was just some wild conspiracy theory. I may not have the facts to prove it yet, but I'm confident what happened that night is more sinister than you think."

The way he says the words sends another torrent of shivers down my spine, and nothing in me wants to believe them.

But I do.

It's already been a while since I left the house, and Sofia told me not to stay out too long, but getting out of the car now and ending the conversation would leave me with too many questions.

"Where was the party?"

Mason frowns. "Iris's house?"

"Can we go there?"

"You want to go there right now?"

I nod.

If anything, it'll help to compare it to the party I keep seeing in my memories and decide whether what I've seen is fact or fiction. To my surprise, Mason doesn't ask any more questions. Instead, he sighs, turns the key in the ignition, and shifts the car into Drive, pulling away from the curb.

The lights of my house disappear in the side mirror, and the windshield wipers are on a continuous loop, doing their best to keep the glass visible. A shudder racks my body again, and Mason peers at me out of the corner of his eye. Reaching forward, he turns up the heat, and I stretch my cold fingers out toward the air vents.

"Thanks," I murmur, feeling my cheeks warm. Even after our argument, he's showing me kindness. I can't figure out how to read him.

We leave my neighborhood, and it's odd to be sitting in a car with someone I don't know anything about. He's focused on the road, and I wonder if he feels as awkward as I do.

"Why are you being nice to me?" I ask.

He laughs shortly, turning a corner, and I watch the streetlights pass over his features. "What kind of question is that? Am I supposed to be mean to you?"

"We're not friends anymore."

"That doesn't mean I'm suddenly a horrible human being."

"So it's just sympathy."

Mason turns to me, studying my expression and looking irritated. "What answer are you looking for, Alina?" Even though the words are spoken with an undertone of frustration, I feel a jolt run down my spine at the sound of my name.

"One that actually explains something," I push. "Like why we drifted apart. I'm trying to understand you."

"You're not going to give that up, are you?"

I give him a flat look.

He drags a hand through his hair as we enter an unfamiliar neighborhood. "You grew up and found other friends. End of story."

But the lack of conviction in his voice doesn't convince me. There's more he's not willing to share. "I don't think that's true."

"Why not?" he asks. "Look at where we both ended up. As soon as we moved to middle school, you and Zoe found each other. The rest is history."

"I'm sure I would've preferred to stay friends with you instead," I say.

He grunts in amusement. "Maybe now, but not back then. I wasn't all that great."

The houses here are definitely not as large and extravagant as the ones in my neighborhood. It feels homier, more lived in, like the people here are down to earth, even in the dark. We drive around for a while until we slow to a stop in front of one house in particular.

"Here we are," Mason announces unceremoniously.

I stiffen, sitting up straight again and peering out of the window. The siding looks yellow, though it's hard to tell in this lighting, and the motion lights are flickering, lending to the unsettling feeling building in my belly. I press my fingers to the glass, focusing all of my attention on the house, trying to see if it will trigger anything or bring something new to the surface.

The front door opens as a man steps out, bringing out the trash, and the action makes my blood run cold. I remember seeing that door.

A foggy image of my hands pushing it open flashes through my brain, and suddenly I feel as though I'm crying, but when I touch my fingers to my cheek to check, they come back dry.

This is definitely the house I've been seeing in my visions. I'm certain I'd remember more if I went inside.

My knee begins to bounce anxiously as I picture myself being followed out by my friends. That doesn't necessarily mean they did something to me. They haven't always been the best people to be around, but they're the only ones who choose to be around me at all. I don't want them to be a part of this.

"Did we just come to stare at the house?" Mason asks, reminding me that I'm still in his car.

"No," I say, staring at the lake that's forming in the driveway. "I just thought seeing it might help."

"And did it?"

I shake my head. "I don't know."

He gives me more time to take in the building before slowly pulling away. I already knew something bad happened to me after I left that house. But what started as a story of my own reckless behavior may be turning into one of deceit and betrayal.

14 | DENY

The skies are dark and angry on Tuesday morning. From my seat next to Audrey in her car in the parking lot, I watch the students file into the school.

"Everything okay?" she asks, leaning forward to catch a glimpse of my expression.

"Yeah," I say, forcing a smile.

In truth, Mason's suspicions have wormed their way deep into my brain, and now they're all I can think about. The idea of having to face my friends makes me feel restless. I should've told Sofia I didn't feel well enough to come today.

Audrey tucks some of her hair behind her ear, not seeming to believe me. "You know you can tell me if something is wrong, right?"

"Of course," I lie. She has no idea what kind of secrets I'm keeping from her. "But seriously, Audrey, I'm fine."

"If you insist," she says. "Maybe I'm just projecting."

She told me that her plan is to give her two weeks' notice at Antonio's today. The thought of having to work with her ex-boyfriend any longer than that was more than she could handle.

"It's going to be okay," I say gently, guilt twisting my insides.

"Eventually," she agrees, before gesturing to the brick building with her chin. "Have a good day."

"You too."

Bracing myself, I step into the rain, squinting as I jog to the front entrance. Pulling the heavy door open, I cross the threshold of Pender Falls High. My legs are shaky as I embark on the journey to my locker.

I see a familiar figure in my periphery, and I turn, locking gazes with Mason. He stands at the other end of the hallway, and students mill about in front of him, unaware of our unspoken conversation. He tips his head in the direction of the infamous threesome standing by Zoe's locker, before sliding his eyes back to me. It's as if he's asking, *Who do you trust?*

Running my suddenly sweaty palms down my jean-clad thighs, I look away, heading in the direction of Zoe and the others. Talking to them is the last thing I want to do, but it might help me figure out what to think.

James is in the middle of saying something that has Damien nearly doubled over his crutches in laughter. They notice me approaching before I reach them, their good humor dying out. Damien's face becomes troubled as I walk over to him, and I try not to think of the last time we spoke. They've gone silent by the time I stand before them, waiting expectantly.

I open my mouth, but all knowledge of speech seems to have vacated my brain, my face growing increasingly hot under their scrutiny.

Damien takes a slow step toward me, limping slightly. "Allie."

They're worried about you remembering the truth. And they're going to make sure you don't.

"I . . ." My sentence dies out as I look between all three of them. Zoe frowns.

James raises an eyebrow. "You good?"

I find Damien's eyes again, remembering the broken look they wore as he apologized for something unknown and the disturbing image of him in my dream. Taking a subconscious step back, I shake my head.

"Sorry," I mumble.

The first bell rings, and I push through the crowd, my hands quickly finding the door to the girls' room and flinging it open. My chest rises and falls rapidly, and I head straight for a stall, locking myself inside.

Closing the lid of the toilet, I sit on top of it, sliding my fingers into my hair. I'm overreacting. Mason is following a hunch. Despite how much I'm inclined to believe him, hunches can be wrong.

I hear the door to the bathroom swing open again, causing me to freeze, and I tuck my legs up on the toilet seat, not wanting anyone to know I'm in here. Looking to the floor, I see a pair of oxfords making their way across the tile.

"Allie?" Zoe calls, and I hold my breath. "You in here?"

Swallowing, I brace my hands against the cool sides of the stall, trying to remain upright.

She walks slowly, stopping in front of my closed door, and my heart constricts, sending a prayer up to the heavens that she'll just go away and leave me alone.

"I don't know what's going on, but you don't have to hide from me," she says, her voice gentle.

It occurs to me then how strange I'm acting. Just yesterday, we were talking together at the coffee shop, and everything was fine. Now, even the thought of looking at her makes me apprehensive. I purse my lips, not daring to breathe.

She leans against the door. "I know it's probably awkward to see Damien. But he's not mad at you. None of us are."

I don't say anything, and she taps on the stall.

"Come on, you can't hide in there all day," she coaxes, and I stifle a groan.

Putting aside my pride, I step down from the seat and unlock the door. Zoe nearly falls backward as it opens. She assesses my appearance, reaching out to push some of my hair behind my shoulder.

"That's better."

I force my lips into a tiny smile, limbs wooden.

"Shall we go to class?"

The idea of seeing Mason right now knowing he witnessed what just happened doesn't appeal to me. I need some time to recover from my embarrassment. "I don't think I'm going to go."

"Is something going on? You can talk to me about it."

The second bell is about to ring, and I eye the door, not knowing what to say.

"It doesn't have to be here," she says quickly, placing a hand on my arm. "Come over after school. Or we don't have to talk about it if you don't want to. I can make you forget what happened."

The bell chimes overhead, and I go still. "Make me forget?"

"Yeah, we can watch movies or something."

"Okay."

I'm unsure of what I believe, but one thing is certain: I'm not setting foot in the Harris house again without talking to Mason first.

At lunch, I wait in the parking lot, arms crossed over my chest, bouncing on the balls of my feet impatiently. The rain has stopped now, but the threat of another downpour remains—like if you took a stick and poked the clouds, it would all come rushing out.

There's a restlessness in my bones that's matched by the wind as I stand next to the car. My conversation with Zoe sparked something within me—an anger. I don't understand why it's there, but I can't spend another second at this school without doing something about it.

I stand up straight as the person I've been waiting for exits the building. Mason steps outside, letting the door fall closed behind him, doing a sweep of the parking lot before spotting me.

He doesn't say anything as he reaches around me to unlock the door, putting us in incredibly close proximity. I stare at the side of his face before his eyes flicker to mine, catching me off guard. Even though we're outside, it feels like we're in an enclosed space with little room to move, and it makes my heart race.

"Get in," he tells me in a low voice, and I obey, moving past him and heading to the passenger's side.

Once we're both inside, he pulls out of the parking lot, and I question why I feel more relaxed in his presence than I have all morning. The tension begins to vacate my body the farther we drive from Pender Falls High. I wonder what he's thinking. I've made it clear I want to talk to him, but now that we're here, I'm not sure what I intended to say.

"Are you hungry?" he asks.

"What?"

"It's lunch."

"Oh," I say, blinking. "I guess."

Mason brings us to the Wendy's drive-thru, and when we get to the pay window, I reach for my backpack, unzipping it to search for my wallet, until I feel his fingers touch my arm.

"I've got it," he tells me smoothly, and I cease my movements, closing my backpack and nodding meekly.

"Thanks."

After we've received our food, he drives to a nearby park, and we sit in the car as the rain begins to fall. I hadn't realized I was hungry until I had the food in front of me, but now the anxiety has worn off and my mouth waters in anticipation. We eat in silence for a while, splitting fries between us and watching the grass become saturated with water, until I finally speak.

"Zoe invited me to come over after school."

"Are you going?"

"I feel like I have to," I say. "I don't want her to know I'm suspicious."

Mason hums thoughtfully. "That's probably smart."

"It could be a chance to have a look around and see if I can find anything," I suggest, balling up the sandwich wrapper in my hands. "But if she found out I was snooping . . ."

"Don't let her."

"I don't even know what I'm expecting to find," I say, doubt creeping into my words. "It's not like there's going to be a note saying *I did it.*"

He gives me an unimpressed look. "Obviously not. But you never know. Text messages, a diary, web search history, things like that."

I suppress a shudder at the thought of trying to do any of that without getting caught. "This is a bad idea."

"You could also try for a conversation. Ask if she can tell you anything more about the night of your accident," he says. "She can't fault you for that. You're just trying to understand what happened to you."

"Maybe."

"Whether it's today or tomorrow or some other day in the future, we're going to find out the truth about what happened," he reassures me, his voice soft.

"We?"

One half of his mouth hitches upward. "I'm far too involved to back out now."

The thought of having someone else on my side—someone to confide in, to theorize with—provides a tantalizing amount of comfort. It may be too early to be making snap decisions, but I desperately want to trust Mason.

I struggle to think of what his ulterior motive for telling me all of this could be, unless he's trying to throw suspicion off himself. But that's not an explanation that makes sense.

"Why are you helping me?"

"The story that was released to the public about your accident has never sat right with me," he says, serious once more. "And I'm not the kind of person who can just ignore the things I overheard."

"The police said the same thing . . ." I trail off, remembering my conversation with Officer Edwards at the bookstore. "They said my accident seemed calculated. They think I'm hiding something."

"What, they think you staged it?"

"Apparently. Or that I'm faking the amnesia to cover something up."

"That's absurd." He shakes his head. "This is what I mean, though. The cops know what really happened, and it's not the bullshit they fed to the media. So why haven't they come out with the truth?"

"It's like they're trying to apply pressure," I muse. "But why threaten me? I'm the victim here. They seem to believe I'm trying to cover for someone. If I knew that someone did this to me, I sure as hell wouldn't be trying to protect them."

Mason considers my words before shaking his head again, looking upset. "It's sick. All of it."

"But maybe I had it coming," I murmur.

He lets out a short laugh of disbelief. "What are you talking about?"

I tear off a tiny piece of the wrapper. "You heard about Jacob Griffin."

Mason makes a low noise of sympathy, sitting back in his seat. "What happened to him was fucked up, but I don't see what that has to do with you."

"People think I did it."

"You didn't."

"How do you know?"

He looks irritated. "Because that doesn't make any sense."

"Zoe told me he was this great actor and I might've felt threatened by him, so I tried to get rid of the competition." Saying the words aloud makes my stomach turn, bile rising in my throat.

Mason is looking at me as though another head has sprouted on my shoulders. "Alina," he remarks. "Jacob wasn't in theater."

I freeze. "What?"

"He was well known for being very academic and playing sports, but he never tried out acting."

"Zoe said—" I stop, mind racing. "She made me believe it was my fault."

Mason is speechless, shaking his head as he watches the torrent of emotions play out on my face. "I'm sorry."

Everything feels as though it's unraveling. That day outside of the school she fed me lies with such conviction that it makes me question whether anything she's told me is true.

A complicated mixture of emotions fights for my attention. I don't know whether to feel relieved or even more confused. Ever since I heard about my possible involvement in what happened to Jacob, I've obsessed over everything, unable to get it out of my head.

But maybe what ties me to Jacob is our shared connection to one person in particular.

The Harris house has a distinct chill to it.

Even in Zoe's bedroom, with the fireplace going, it feels as though there's a breeze moving through the room, causing goose bumps to rise on my skin. I'm lying on her bed, stretched out over my schoolbooks, and she sits at her desk, her posture perfect as always, as music floats from her Bluetooth speaker.

I didn't want to come over, especially after my conversation with Mason, but watching her up close, observing her with this new perspective, could help me reconcile my feelings with reality.

Zoe looks over her shoulder, amused. "Why are you staring at me?"

I shake my head to clear it. "Sorry, spacing out."

She nods her chin in the direction of my history textbook. "How's it going?"

With a sigh, I sit up, flipping the cover closed and crossing my legs. "This is exceptionally boring," I say. It doesn't help that being in the same room with her makes it impossible to think about anything other than our supposed fight that she refuses to tell me about.

And Jacob.

"I'm nearly done, anyway," she remarks, closing her own books and tucking them into her backpack neatly. When she sweeps her long hair behind her shoulders, I notice the locket that rests against her white sweater, catching light from the flickering fire.

"That's pretty," I say, and she looks confused before her fingers encircle the necklace. "Where did you get it?"

"It was a gift."

I tilt my head curiously. "From who?"

Hesitation darts across her delicate features, her cheeks turning pink in an uncharacteristic blush. "Well," she pauses. "From Damien."

Not the answer I was expecting. "Oh."

"It's nothing like that," she explains quickly. "I tutored him in math last year. It was just a way to say thank you."

"That was nice of him."

"Yeah." Reaching into her bag, she grabs a bottle of hand sanitizer, squeezing some onto her palms and rubbing them together. "Do you want to watch a movie?"

"Sure."

Zoe stands from her chair, nodding. "I'll just go ask my mom if it's okay."

"We need your mom's permission to watch a movie?"

Her cheeks flush again. "I—I meant I'll go see if the living room is free," she stammers.

She exits the room in a rush, and a wave of her perfume washes over me. The door clicks shut behind her, and the floorboards creak as her footsteps retreat down the hall.

It doesn't take long before the sound of raised voices drifts upstairs. They obviously belong to Zoe and her mother. I didn't know watching a movie would cause so much controversy, but from what I've seen of Mrs. Harris so far, I'm not a huge fan of the woman. If this is what Zoe's home life is like on the daily, I feel grateful I woke up to Sofia as my mother instead.

Regardless of my tumultuous relationship with the girl, it feels wrong to intrude on her argument with her mother. I stand and reach for her phone, turning up the volume just enough to drown out the voices. When I go to set it down again, I hear a buzzing noise, causing me to freeze.

The cell phone in my hand is dark and unmoving, but the vibrating continues, coming from somewhere within the room.

I peer at the door hesitantly.

Zoe would kill me—maybe literally—if she caught me snooping, but I can't help my burning curiosity. Biting my lip, I gently pull on the handle of the top drawer of her nightstand, sliding it open.

At first, I don't see anything besides a meticulously organized collection of notebooks, but after digging through it a bit, I find what I'm looking for, a phone lying face down at the bottom of the drawer. The buzzing stops.

Slowly, as if it might burn me once it connects with my skin, I flip it over.

Beneath the shattered screen, a photo of Scout stares back at me.

I exhale sharply, fingers trembling, before picking up the device. When I slide my thumb over the home button, it unlocks.

My head spins. I have the desperate urge to get out of the house as soon as possible. Why the fuck does Zoe have my phone? Sofia said nobody could find it, and here it is, lying in Zoe's drawer.

I navigate through the messages but everything has been wiped. It seems she only forgot to change the wallpaper.

Abruptly, the doorknob to the bedroom twists, and I snap into action, tucking the phone into my bag and shoving the drawer shut. By the time the door opens, I'm back in my previous position on the bed.

Zoe steps inside, looking agitated. She glances at me before looking around the room, as though she can tell something is amiss.

"How'd it go?" I say, hoping my breathy tone makes my voice sound light, rather than nauseated.

"Great." Zoe pauses, tension hanging in the air for a moment. "Are you ready?"

"Actually, I think I'll head home now," I say. "My head is pounding. I spent way too long trying to make sense of that textbook."

"Oh," she says. "Okay. I can drive you."

"That's all right," I blurt, then force myself to calm down. I can't let her know anything is wrong. "I feel like walking."

She gestures to the window. "It's raining."

"I don't mind."

Before she can protest, I sling my backpack over my shoulder, call out a good-bye, and brush past her on legs that feel like they'll give out at any moment.

15 | WRECK

I'm standing in the living room of Iris Wen's house.

For once, I notice that no one is looking at me. The music is too loud, and the bass reverberates in my skull as I push my way through sweaty bodies, disoriented. I don't want to be here. I try to make my way to the front door and escape into the wintry night air, but every time I get close, the room seems to shift, and I'm farther away than I was before.

Distress rises and settles in my throat, and it becomes hard to breathe. Breaking free from the crowd, I grab the railing of the stairs. It's not the exit, but at least there's more room here. My limbs are sluggish as I drag myself to the second floor, stepping over a girl sprawled on the carpeted staircase.

I stagger to the bathroom, drawn by the light peeking out from the crack beneath the door. Before I know what I'm doing, I'm pushing it open all the way, and there's a girl inside, washing her hands.

Zoe.

She turns at the sound of me entering, lips curving into a wolfish grin. When she shakes her hands out, blood drips from her fingertips, staining her skin red.

Horrified, I take a step backward, exhaling sharply.

"Alina."

The voice comes from right behind me, causing me to flinch. I turn around to find Mason, a pensive expression on his face as he grabs my arm. The familiar dissonance between his eyes brings me a sense of comfort, but the fear within them sets me on edge.

"We need to get out of here."

I let him guide me back down the stairs, stumbling along behind him and trying not to trip over my own feet. Zoe's presence looms over my shoulder, and when I look back, the red is creeping steadily up her arms, darkening the sleeves of her white blouse.

We reach the living room again, and it's as though the number of bodies in the house has multiplied. Mason's grip on me is broken, and I lose him in the throngs of people.

"Allie," Zoe calls out in a singsong voice. She reaches up to flip her hair, leaving a streak of crimson on her shoulder.

"Leave me alone!" I choke out, elbowing my way to the door.

The living room is lit up in a bright flash of white, and the air fills with screams as everyone dives out of the way. My feet are rooted to the floor, and I can only look on in terror as a car bursts through the outer wall of the house, coming straight for me. I hold my arms up to shield my head, bracing for impact, but it never comes.

Instead, I wake up in my bedroom. I bolt upright, skull pounding, and squint in the early morning sunlight. I glance at the clock; it's a little after six. Too early to be awake, but there's no chance in hell I'm falling back asleep now.

The mattress beneath me is grounding, and my fingers curl around my comforter tightly. I've seen similar scenes in my brain before, but this one felt like it lasted forever.

And in the past, I didn't recognize the faces.

I stayed up late, trying to think of a million logical reasons as to why Zoe might have my cell phone locked away in her bedroom and came up empty. It's one of the missing puzzle pieces I thought

I wanted, but now that I have it, I would rather go back to my igno-rance. At least then I felt relatively safe.

Sliding out of bed, I make my way to the shower downstairs, hoping a good dose of hot water will give me some clarity. As it courses through my hair, I try to will the images of the nightmare away. Maybe if I wish hard enough, all of this will disappear, and I'll wake up in the hospital all over again and start fresh.

But it's foolish to think that way. I've known ever since the moment I first opened my eyes that I was cursed, destined to find darkness around every corner.

Stepping out of the shower, I hurry back to my bedroom to get dressed before grabbing both of the cell phones and my laptop and sliding on my coat and boots. I leave the house quietly, making sure I don't wake anyone. Scout watches me, and when she begins to whine, I bring a finger to my lips, as if she'll understand the gesture. It seems to work, and I'm able to slip away otherwise undetected.

The morning air is brisk, though with each day that passes, the temperature grows warmer as spring settles in. Everyone else at school is starting to worry about prom and graduation, but all of it feels so hollow.

Restless, I stride down the sidewalk, vaguely paying attention to the names of the streets as I make my way through the neighbor-hood. Eventually, the fancier houses become more sparse, and the longer I walk, the more depressing the area around me becomes.

When I get close to my destination, the disparity between the nic-est parts of Pender Falls and the not-so-nice parts makes me feel disheartened.

I stop in the middle of the sidewalk, staring at the tiny house across the street. The siding is white and chipping, and some of the shingles on the roof are beginning to lift. I slide my phone out of my coat pocket, shooting off a hurried text message.

Come outside, it reads, humming as it delivers.

I jump slightly as the front door of the house clicks open, revealing a very perplexed-looking Mason Byrne.

His eyebrows are drawn together as usual, his hair is mussed with sleep, and I would find all of it endearing if I wasn't so uneasy. I walk up the creaky wooden steps of the porch until I'm a couple of feet away, and the shock gracing his features doesn't budge, as if the sight of me standing on his front porch is too strange to comprehend.

"Good morning," I say, stupidly self-conscious all of a sudden.

"Alina." Mason shakes his head, voice husky. "What are you doing here?"

"I needed to talk to you. I couldn't wait until school."

I slide past him, eager to escape the chill, my shoulder brushing against his chest. Once I'm safely inside, he shuts the door behind me. The entryway of the Byrne house is cramped. I find myself trapped between Mason and the front door, though he makes no move to let me inside, and I try to ignore what the close proximity does to my heart.

His mouth flounders, and it seems as though he's not fully awake yet. "How did you even find my house?"

I stave off a wave of embarrassment. "Sofia."

He simply stares at me, bewildered.

"So, can I come inside?" I push.

Mason takes a step back, gesturing for me to follow him. "We can talk in the backyard."

I nod wordlessly, trailing behind him as we creep through the silent corridor, tiptoeing across the creaky kitchen floor until we reach the door to the patio. He slides it open slowly, allowing me to exit, and I do so, greeted by the crisp morning air once more. After he points to the deck stretching out in front of us, I take a seat on a step, set down my backpack, and tuck my hands between my knees to keep them warm. He sits beside me a second later, running a hand through his bedhead.

"Well, Castillo, you certainly have my attention," he says. "What was so important that you needed to ambush me so early in the morning?"

There are traces of amusement in his voice now, but I'm unsettled. I let out a shaky breath. When he sees the look on my face, the mirth disappears from his expression.

"She had my phone," I say, voice unsteady.

"What?"

"I found it at her house yesterday." My pulse is increasingly obnoxious in my throat, getting faster the more I think about what happened last night.

Mason ducks his head toward me, looking concerned. "Alina, what are you talking about?"

"Zoe," I remark, rising in volume before I rein it back in. "She had my cell phone. Sofia told me nobody could find it after the accident, but she had it in her fucking drawer."

I pull out the most incriminating piece of evidence we've stumbled across so far, presenting it to him with trembling fingers.

He leans back, face paling. "Shit."

"I didn't know what to do," I continue. "I freaked and left as soon as I could. I took it with me, but I'm scared she's going to notice it's gone."

"It's good that you grabbed it," he says absently. "Maybe we can put it back before she realizes."

The image of Zoe's bloodstained hands pops into my brain, a cold sweat forming on my forehead. "What am I supposed to do?"

"Hey," he says, voice gentle. "We can find a way to figure this out. Did you take a look at what's on the phone?"

"She wiped it."

His mouth presses into a firm line, and he takes it from my hands after gesturing for me to unlock it with my fingerprint. "That means there was stuff on here she didn't want anyone to find. There has to be a way we can recover what she deleted."

"I have no idea how to do that," I say, reaching over to unzip my backpack, pulling out my laptop. "But I brought this. I haven't actually used it yet, because I didn't know the password. Looking at the phone gives me an idea."

Mason watches as I open the computer and stare at the keyboard. There's a tiny, subtle, black square I hadn't really noticed until now, and I place my forefinger on it lightly.

The screen immediately changes as a new bubble of text pops up. *Welcome back!* I let out a breath of relief. It's amazing how these devices are capable of remembering my fingerprint when I have no recollection of even using them.

"I can't believe I didn't think of that before," I muse.

"We might be able to restore a backup that has the old messages," Mason says eagerly.

After fishing out a cord from the bottom of my backpack, I pass everything off to him, peering over his shoulder as he navigates through my programs, locating iTunes.

"There's only one," he says after a pause. "There's no way to tell what's actually on it, but it's worth a try. It's going to take at least thirty minutes to restore."

My shoulders slump. Thirty minutes feels too long. "Is there anything else you can find on here while we wait?"

He glances at me, and it's only then that I realize how close we're sitting. Mason clears his throat, and I scoot away slightly, embarrassed. "Are you sure you're okay with me looking through your stuff?"

"I don't care anymore. It feels like someone else's life, anyway."

His gaze lingers on me for a moment longer before he turns back to the computer, beginning to look through my documents and photos now that he has my permission. We don't really find anything of significance. The laptop is mostly loaded with school assignments and photos from other parties, like the ones in my room.

After scouring through rows upon rows of folders, Mason sighs in defeat, dragging a hand through his hair. He's about to exit when I stop him, spotting something that causes me to stiffen.

"Wait, what's that?" I point to a folder we didn't notice before, several layers deep within my files, difficult to find.

It's titled "J."

He clicks on it, waiting for the thumbnails of all the photos to load. One is a picture of Jacob Griffin, others appear to be screenshots of articles. I share a worried look with Mason, my pulse kicking into gear. A flicker of doubt nudges my mind, and for a fleeting second, I wonder if I really did have something to do with what happened to him. Having a folder dedicated to the incident certainly doesn't look good.

But then Mason enlarges one of the screenshots, and the main image is a picture of Jacob standing next to Zoe. He's grinning proudly, holding a large trophy, while Zoe looks robotic, clasping a smaller, silver trophy. *Close race between Pender Falls High juniors to be top of the class*, the headline reads.

Wordlessly, we scroll through the rest of the photos, which all detail similar situations, with Jacob and Zoe duking it out to claim the title of the brightest in the class. If nothing else, this proves she could've had a motive if she was the one who intentionally harmed Jacob. I remember the way she framed it when she rationalized why it could've been me, trying to make it out like I wanted to get rid of the competition when I wasn't even competing with him in the first place.

"This looks like it's a conversation between you and Zoe," Mason says, voice low.

I lean closer, squinting at the screenshot. The grey bubbles of text appear to be Zoe, and the first message is either a plea or a demand, sent at midnight.

Delete the video

Allie

I'm serious

You know what I have on you

My reply came a couple of hours later.

This is worse, Zoe

But she was undeterred.

You were there, too, Allie

And I can make them think it was all you

That's all the screenshot shows of the conversation, and I sit back, exhaling, unsure if I want to see any more. Mason hesitates before moving to the next photo, seemingly trying to gauge my reaction. I run my clammy palms down the length of my jeans, my knee bouncing nervously.

"It's like I was trying to build up a defense against her."

"Or a prosecution."

"But why? Who was I going to give this to?"

He shrugs. "Maybe it was just blackmail to have on hand. Look, this must be the video she was talking about."

The thumbnail is a blurry image of what looks like the floor of the cafeteria. After Mason hits Play, I catch sight of my Blundstones before the camera pans up to Zoe. Judging by the angle of the video, she doesn't know she's being filmed.

"What are you doing?" I hear a furious whisper that sounds like mine, but it's hard to make out over the buzz of the crowd in the room.

"Relax, Allie," Zoe returns. "He's always been a drama queen. This will probably help build up his immunity anyway."

"It could kill him! Zoe—Zoe, wait!"

She strides away, ignoring my protests, and then she's lost in the flow of people. But the video keeps rolling until she can be spotted all the way across the room, standing next to a table and smiling down at the boy sitting there. I try to zoom in, but the view is obscured by people walking in front of the camera.

Zoe places a hand on Jacob's shoulder before walking away, the smile slipping effortlessly from her features as soon as he can't see her anymore.

She spots the camera, expression contorting in a mixture of rage and betrayal, and then the video cuts off abruptly.

I continue staring at the screen, though I'm unfocused, mind spinning. "It was her all along," I murmur, voice teetering on the edge of breaking. "Everything was her."

I've made it to the top of every class I'm in by any means necessary.

Mason exhales slowly, speechless.

"She wanted to kill him," I say, as my brain flips through all of the memories I have with Zoe. All the little digs, backhanded remarks, and hints that I didn't pick up on. "She wanted to kill me too."

"We still don't know exactly what happened," he points out. "Or why." He pauses, and when he speaks again, he sounds a lot more hesitant. "Until we have more that we can bring to the police, you should probably stick close to her. Just to keep up appearances. I'm sorry."

"You can't be serious. I don't want her anywhere near me!"

"I know," he says. "That's why you need to be extremely careful. Believe me, I'd feel much better if you never had to cross paths with her again. But if she senses that something is off or that you don't trust her anymore, things could go south very quickly."

"Fuck," I whisper. "I don't know if I can do this."

"You can."

When I meet his eyes, they're full of resolve and belief in me. I wish I felt the same. My reaction last night proves that I'm not as good an actress as everyone says I am. Zoe could definitely tell something was wrong. But finding the phone caught me completely off guard. Maybe if I have more time to prepare, I can do a better job.

Besides, I have anger on my side now.

Mason stands from the deck. "Wait here."

"But—"

He disappears into the house before I can tell him that I really don't want to be left alone. I tuck my knees to my chest, looking at the droplets of dew resting in the grass. A few minutes later, Mason reappears, wearing a deep-green army jacket over his hoodie, his hair styled into its usual messy quiff. I rise to my feet expectantly.

"I have an idea," he remarks. "The restoration says it's going to take an hour now, so we have some time to kill. Come with me."

Those last three words are all it takes for me to follow him back through the house. At this point, I'd probably go anywhere with him if it meant getting a temporary escape.

Raleigh's Junkyard is a wasteland of old, forgotten cars and the smell of oil and gasoline.

I trail behind Mason as he walks through an opening in the chain-link fence, taking in the mountains of car parts and feeling confused. He hadn't told me where we were going, and I trusted him enough not to ask. I'm not sure what good being here will do, but he walks with purpose.

He looks at me as I fall into line with him, sticking his hands into his pockets. "Your car would've been taken here after it was totaled," he explains, keeping his voice low. "I want to see if we can find it."

"I don't even know what kind of car it is."

"It's a 2009 Ford Focus," he says automatically, and I tilt my head, squinting. His lips part, a hint of embarrassment creeping onto his features. "I know cars."

"Okay," I say, drawing out the word, secretly feeling flattered that he paid enough attention to me to have the make and model of my car memorized, despite the fact that we aren't truly friends. "Lucky I have you here, then."

The junkyard is eerily empty, the heavy machinery frozen in time, waiting to be used again. It's closed today, and the fact that Mason was able to find a way in so easily leads me to believe he's done this more than once.

He seems bound and determined to locate the vehicle, dutifully scanning every inch of the yard. All I can see is space junk and hunks of metal, and I feel disgruntled as I step over a loose tire.

After what feels like an eternity of searching, Mason stiffens, pointing straight ahead. "There!"

Sections of black poke out from beneath a large mound of scraps, and I have no clue how he was even able to notice it under all that garbage. He hurries forward, gesturing for me to follow him.

"Help me uncover it," he says.

I obey, doing my best to lift off the debris to get to what's lying beneath. Together, we're able to dig out the hood and passenger side of the car. There's an air freshener hanging on the rearview mirror, and the sight of it makes me feel strange knowing that I was the one to hang it there.

The front of the car is smashed in, one of the headlights missing, and the passenger side is severely dented to the point that it comes dangerously close to the driver's side.

I turn to Mason, taking in the pensive look on his face as he assesses the vehicle. "Well?"

"They said you hit a tree," he says thoughtfully, gesturing to the front, before pointing to the side door. "So why is this damaged too?"

It looks like the car was struck by something else, but that doesn't align with what I've been told.

"Do you really think Zoe is this calculated?" I ask, turning to him again. "Stealing an EpiPen is one thing but staging an entire car accident?"

He contemplates the question for several beats. "She's clearly very clever," he admits. "But Zoe has always struck me as the type of person who would eventually snap."

My phone buzzes in my pocket. Flashing Mason an embarrassed look, I dig it out, shoulders slumping when I see the name on the caller ID.

"Shit," I mumble. "It's my mom."

He grimaces slightly.

"We missed first period. Someone must have called her."

"Are you going to answer?"

"No," I say firmly, dropping the phone back into my pocket. It continues to buzz persistently. Cringing, I dig it out again, grumbling, "Goddamn it."

Mason chuckles softly as I pick up the phone, holding it to my ear.

"Allie?" Sofia's voice is abrupt, bursting in before I can speak. "Where are you? Why aren't you at school?"

"I'm . . ." I hesitate, making eye contact with Mason, "at home."

"*I'm* at home."

Oops.

"Oh."

She sighs in frustration. "I told you to call me when you felt like this. You can't keep skipping school and doing whatever you want."

Feeling embarrassed, I take a step away from Mason, turning my back to him. If I'm about to get chewed out by Sofia, I don't want him to hear.

"I know," I say honestly. "I'm sorry."

Sofia sighs again, sounding tired this time. "Where are you? I'll come get you."

"That's okay. I'll walk home."

"If you're not home in half an hour, I'm forming a search party."

She ends the call abruptly, and I wince, lowering the phone. Slowly, I turn around to face Mason, instantly catching sight of his look of amusement. I open my mouth to speak, but he beats me to the punch.

"Time to head back?" he teases.

"Please," I breathe. "Before I have another death threat to worry about."

I follow him out of the junkyard and back to his car, suddenly getting the feeling that we're not alone.

16 | DECEIVE

Despite the revelation that Zoe has been an evil mastermind this whole time, nothing happens until the middle of the following week.

After combing through it for hours, Mason is unable to find anything of consequence on the backup of my old phone, and it seems that she was several steps ahead of us. We may not have enough to link her directly to my accident just yet, but we certainly have enough to heavily implicate her in what happened to Jacob Griffin.

I feel a tap on my shoulder as I'm depositing my books in my locker on Thursday, causing me to flinch.

Zoe.

Ever since I discovered the cell phone, looking at her makes me apprehensive, whereas I used to feel comforted at best and irritated at worst.

She sidles up next to me as we move through the hallway, her arm jostling against mine, and I work to keep my expression light and neutral. Though try as I might, I can't completely rid my body of the tension that floods into my bones just from being around her.

"Principal Clayborn called this weird assembly," she says, sounding annoyed. "I imagine it's going to be a waste of time."

"Maybe it'll be interesting," I offer, following the flow of people in the direction of the gymnasium.

Zoe scoffs. "Doubtful."

A short distance ahead, I spot Damien and James. Damien is without his crutches, though he moves a little slower than normal. I haven't spoken to him since I embarrassed myself the other day, nor do I want to. Knowing he could've been involved in what happened that night is enough reason for me to want to stay far away. James too. Mason told me my friends had followed me out. Friends, plural. I can't trust any of them.

"You're being really quiet," Zoe says, her tone changing, and the hair rises on the back of my neck.

"I am?"

She shrugs, expression guarded. "Are you mad at me again or something? You've been weird ever since you came over."

"No," I emphasize, heart rate picking up as I try to think of an explanation. "I just have a lot on my mind." She tilts her head. "Stuff at home. With Audrey."

Something flickers across her face. "Ah. I see." She pauses. "Does it have to do with Parker?"

My footsteps falter. Her tone is sympathetic rather than accusatory, but the words feel harsh, like a punch to my gut.

"What makes you say that?"

She gives me a look that toes the line between condescending and understanding. "Allie, I'm your best friend," she remarks. "I know stuff."

Heat floods to my cheeks. I didn't think anyone else knew, and I wanted to keep it that way. I do a quick scan of the hallway, trying to see if anyone is paying attention to us. "No," I protest, my voice hushed. "It has nothing to do with him. That's . . . that's long over."

"Is it?"

"Yes," I say firmly. "I haven't even seen him since he moved out."

"Okay."

The subject is dropped, though I still feel frazzled. We get closer to the gym, where the hallway traffic is more congested, and our pace slows significantly. I begin to feel claustrophobic, trapped with Zoe as people crowd around us, trying to get inside.

She doesn't say anything for a while, but then she bumps my elbow with hers, looking at me conspiratorially.

"Seems like you've got your eye on someone else anyway."

In a way that's both subtle and quite the opposite, she gestures with her chin, tilting her head, and I follow what she's pointing to, landing on Mason a short distance away. He doesn't notice, wearing his trademark brooding expression, and something twists in my chest. She's teased me about him in the past, but I didn't think she was actually being serious.

"Not really," I mumble.

"Don't get me wrong, I totally support moving on from Damien," she says, working to keep her voice down. "But does it have to be with Mason Byrne of all people? I don't trust him."

Pursing my lips, I think back to when she approached us in the hallway the other day before we went out for coffee. She was clearly sizing him up and took the time to give me a word of warning after. I feel myself stiffen. It occurs to me that she might realize he overheard us arguing the night of my accident and is doing anything she can to discredit him.

"He doesn't even matter," I tell her. "I'm not thinking about dating right now."

Much to my relief she backs off, and we finally make our way into the gym, trailing toward the bleachers. Despite wanting to sit anywhere else, I take the seat next to Zoe, perching on the edge of the bench and watching the other students filing in. Mason sits down in the section to my left, looking in my direction briefly. The sight of him, knowing he's nearby, is enough to bring me a small shred of comfort.

A large screen has been pulled down above the stage, and Principal Clayborn stands behind the podium. He's an older man, dancing somewhere on the line between his fifties and sixties, and his hair has gone grey and thin on the top of his head.

When he turns to look over his shoulder, speaking with someone behind him, my body immediately becomes rigid.

Officer Edwards is waiting in the wings, smiling at the principal as they exchange inaudible words. What is he doing here? Inconspicuously, I duck my head, letting my hair fall forward in the hopes that it'll conceal my identity a little.

Zoe gives me a strange look, but she doesn't have time to question my behavior because the assembly is called to attention shortly after.

"Welcome, everyone," Clayborn begins. "Thank you for coming. I know we haven't had an assembly for quite some time, but the Pender Falls Police Department has a presentation for you all."

Having to sit next to someone I now believe tried to kill me was already more than enough, but being forced to listen to Officer Edwards brings my level of discomfort up to new heights. Couldn't they have sent anyone else?

"Without further ado, I'll pass it over to Officer Edwards here," he says, gesturing to the other man and stepping away from the microphone.

Hints of chatter float throughout the room as the policeman saunters up to the mic, and two girls in the row behind me whisper obnoxiously. He scans the crowd, and I dip my head in an attempt to blend into the background. But when I look up again, he's somehow managed to spot me easily, fixating on me with a cold stare.

"Good morning," he says pleasantly, shifting his attention to the rest of the audience again. "I wanted to talk to you about something this morning. Something important."

A hush falls over the room. Up until now, I don't think anyone was taking the assembly seriously. A uniformed officer speaking to a bunch of teenagers candidly about a heavier topic has a sobering effect. Even the girls behind me go silent, sitting at attention. Zoe raises an eyebrow dubiously, though underneath it, she appears to be slightly worried too.

"Now, over the years I'm sure you've all heard time and time again how dangerous it is to get behind the wheel after drinking."

Apparently, he didn't think threatening me in the bookstore was enough, he's taken it upon himself to have a whole assembly in order to presumably guilt trip me into confessing to something I don't even remember.

"But when you're young, you think it will never happen to you," he continues. "I'm here to tell you that it can. Anything can happen when you're inebriated. People make all kinds of mistakes. Dangerous accidents don't discriminate, nobody is invincible, though some of us get off lucky."

His beady eyes fall on me again, making my skin crawl.

"There are severe penalties for driving under the influence, ones that will dramatically alter your life." Officer Edwards glances at the screen behind him, and an image fades into view, blown up large, every detail visible.

My heart comes to a shuddering halt.

It's the car.

My car.

The photograph was taken with the front of the vehicle in the foreground, and I'd recognize the smashed-up hood of the black Ford Focus anywhere. Immediately, I look at Mason, only to find that he's looking at me too.

"This is a photo of a car that was involved in a recent accident," Edwards explains. "The victim was taken to—oh."

He stops abruptly, as some sort of commotion happens near the bottom of the bleachers. Frowning, I strain to get a better view, peering over the tops of people's heads. Someone stumbles to the gymnasium floor, and those around him back up to give him space.

James.

With no warning, he doubles over, vomiting on the linoleum.

Gasps move throughout the room like dominoes, echoed by noises of blatant disgust, and Damien hurries over, putting his hand on his friend's back, trying to usher him to the door. My legs feel shaky; it's odd to see any expression on James's face other than playful indifference, but his dark skin looks ashen, a haunted look filling out his features.

As he staggers to the exit, propped up by Damien, the smell of puke reaches my nose. The audience bursts into loud chatter, theorizing about what just happened, and Clayborn and Edwards both appear to be dumbfounded.

Mason's gaze finds me again, and somehow I know exactly what he's thinking. The picture was a trigger for James. He was *there* that night.

Beside me, Zoe is sitting stock-still, expressionless, though she suddenly looks sickly, too, her gaze riveted to the spot where James last stood.

A few more people bolt to the door, eager to escape the gymnasium. Chaos continues to erupt as the emotional distress in the room heightens, and I try to tune it out, feeling restless.

Finally, Clayborn takes over the microphone again. "We're going to end things here," he says, struggling to be heard over the noise. "Please be careful on your way out."

Everyone stands, hurriedly making their way down the bleachers and to the doors, giving a wide berth to the puddle of vomit on the floor. I'm eager to get out before Edwards can talk to me, though that task proves to be difficult with everyone shoving each other to escape. Zoe trails behind me, dazed and zombielike, and it gives me a sick sense of satisfaction.

Her suffering is justified. I hope that the thought of what she did to me is on her mind at every waking moment, because God knows it's all I can think about now.

When we finally make it out of the gym, Zoe heads straight for the doors leading outside. I follow her. The second we step onto the pavement, she inhales deeply.

"That was disgusting," she says, using her hands to push her hair over her shoulders.

"I hope he's okay," I say. "I'm totally spooked."

"Me too." Zoe shakes her head. "What even was that assembly? Officer Edwards is creepy as hell."

I wonder if she's thinking about what would happen if he found out the truth.

Wrapping my arms around my torso, I shiver slightly, watching the rain come down in sheets beyond the overhang of the roof. "I can't stand him."

"He talked to me once before, but I—" She stops, and my heart beats faster. "I think I need to go home," she declares, keeping her voice steady. "I'm so grossed out. I can't handle watching people get sick."

"Do you want me to come with you?" Leaving with her is very low on the list of things I want to do, but how I react right now is important.

"No, I'll see you later."

Without giving me a chance to say anything else, she heads back inside, disappearing down the hallway, unknowingly confirming her guilt.

As soon as she's gone, Mason slips outside, eyes blazing, and the sense of relief I feel at the sight of him is enormous, my shoulders instantly relaxing.

"What the hell was that?" he says. "What kind of games are the police playing?"

"I don't know," I admit, feeling rattled. "The pressure is increasing."

"The thing is, it didn't seem like they were trying to put pressure on you this time."

"Zoe mentioned Officer Edwards tried to talk to her . . ." I trail off, the hope that springs up in my chest too sudden to tamp down. "Maybe they're trying to get her to confess?"

"That could be," he says, though I can tell both of us are trying not to have too much faith. "And the others."

"James is obviously guilty."

"His reaction certainly doesn't make him look good."

I lean against the brick wall of the building, the material feeling rough against my skin, even through my sweater.

"I just want this to be over," I admit, my voice soft.

"It will be," Mason promises, steely determination evident in his words. "Soon."

Sofia is furious about the events of the assembly when I tell her what happened.

She had been spending most of the day preparing for the business trip she's leaving for tomorrow, but the fact that they showed a picture of my car and the fact that it was Edwards in the first place was enough for her to call the school to make a formal complaint.

Up in my bedroom, I'm wired, buzzing with energy. I feel safer in here, away from everyone at school, like I don't have to be constantly looking over my shoulder. My brain doesn't currently have the mental capacity to focus on homework, but I can't just sit here, doing nothing.

Pacing my room anxiously doesn't help, and finally, when I spot my laptop, my movements cease.

There has to be more on here than what Mason and I found.

Taking a seat at the desk, I open the laptop, using my fingerprint to get in again. A notification greets me immediately. It's an email from a clothing brand, inviting me to shop with them again at a discounted price. The message is inconsequential, but I hadn't thought to look at my email until now. Most of the messages in my inbox are similar to the one I just received, and the others are often me emailing myself documents for school.

I look through my sent folder and junk mail before clicking on my drafts. There aren't as many in this folder, and the one at the top catches my attention.

It's addressed to McGill University with the subject line *Zoe Harris*. A hollow feeling settles in my gut as I open it. The text in the email starts with a Dropbox link. Another click shows me that I've uploaded the entirety of Jacob's folder, including the telltale video.

The text in the email is short and to the point: *Is this really the kind of student you want to represent you?*

Nausea burns in my chest. If Zoe knew I had this in my arsenal, it would be enough for her to want to do something about it. You'd think I would send the evidence to the police instead, but this email proves it had less to do with justice and more to do with power. How did things even get to this point? How does a friendship with someone become so toxic and vile? It seems like all we ever wanted to do was destroy each other.

Maybe she knew I was about to ruin her life, so she took it upon herself to ruin mine instead.

I close the laptop abruptly, placing my head in my hands. I'd convinced myself that Zoe was the evil one. But I've been shown time and time again that there's evil in me too.

17 | GRAVITATE

By the time the weekend rolls around, I feel as though I haven't slept.

My mind is constantly buzzing, intoxicated by the hope that I'm getting close to piecing together the entire puzzle of my accident and paralyzed by the fear that I won't have enough time. It won't be long before Zoe is onto me. A wedge has been placed between us, and day by day, her trust slowly slips out of my grasp.

Audrey bursts into my room unceremoniously on Saturday night, flopping onto the empty space next to me on the bed, causing the mattress to bounce. She stretches out her limbs with a disgruntled look, wearing a white blouse and pencil skirt, eerily reminiscent of Sofia.

"Job hunting is going *great*, thanks for asking," she grumbles.

I crinkle my nose. "I'm sorry."

"You're lucky," she corrects me. "You don't have to think about this stuff yet. But then again, you've only got a few months until you're done with high school for good."

"Don't remind me," I sigh. "What am I supposed to do with myself after graduation?"

Audrey uses her elbows to prop herself up on the bed. "You don't have to figure everything out right away. I mean, look at me. I graduated a couple of years ago and I have nothing figured out. Maybe we'll end up being college freshmen together in five years," she teases.

"Sounds good to me," I reply, grinning.

"Anyway, will you go out with me? I need to drown my sorrows."

"Go out where?"

"To dance and have drinks," she explains, before clasping her hands and batting her eyelashes, sticking out her bottom lip. "Pretty please? You deserve to do something fun, you've looked miserable lately."

"I'm underage," I remind her.

She lets out a bark of laughter, waving a hand in dismissal. "As if that's ever stopped you before."

I open my mouth to protest, before realizing the photos in my room prove her point. "*Touché.*"

"Besides," she says. "You already look nineteen. What difference does a year make? Plus, Mom is on her fancy business trip, so you don't have to worry about being interrogated."

Biting my lip, I will myself to turn down her offer, knowing full well it's the smart thing to do. But the idea of putting all of my worries behind me, even temporarily, is a tantalizing offer, something I've been subconsciously desperate for the past few weeks.

A loud, throbbing club is probably the last place I should be as someone with a lingering head injury, but I'd be willing to endure it for a slight reprieve.

"Well . . ." I halfheartedly try to conjure an excuse to say no.

"You're into the idea," she says, nudging my arm. "I can tell."

Standing up from the bed, she pulls me with her, and I stumble to my feet. "Maybe a little," I say sheepishly.

Her face softens. "I know you said you were okay, but you really have seemed down lately. Is it about Damien?"

It takes everything in me to hold back a laugh. She takes my expression as hesitation and holds a hand up.

"Never mind. We don't have to talk about boys. But you *do* have to go out with me."

I make a show of sighing dramatically. "Fine. If you insist."

"Yes!" she cheers, and it's hard not to share her enthusiasm. "Change into something cute!"

Before I have the chance to pretend to object, she skips from the room, presumably heading to her room to change into something appropriate for a night of clubbing. I turn to my own closet, scouring through it for something to wear. I locate a shimmery black number and hold it up to my body, appraising it in the mirror.

In my reflection, I see the slightest trace of real happiness, which I don't recall ever witnessing before now. It softens my features, making me look less harsh and intimidating, and more like a teenage girl with regular teenage girl problems. I throw off my jeans and sweater and slip into the dress, finding a pair of heels to match, and a necklace. Audrey enters my room soon after, and her squeal when she catches sight of my outfit is enough to reassure me.

We head out to Audrey's car, and I find myself thinking about how ironic it is that an amnesiac wants to spend the night forgetting.

Two hours later, Audrey is drunk out of her mind, and while I'm definitely not far behind in terms of sobriety, I've taken on the role of her babysitter.

As it turns out, she becomes prone to trouble while intoxicated, and if I'm not pulling her off a guy who is clearly taking advantage of her current state, I'm swatting a drink out of her hands to prevent her from getting any worse. The idea of going to a nightclub definitely sounded good in theory, but now that I'm here, I just want to crawl home and fall into bed. There are too many bodies crammed into too small of a space, and the music is so loud I can't even hear myself think. When Audrey declares that she needs to use the bathroom, I'm grateful to have a break.

It's calmer in here, though the song outside pulsates through the walls and makes the floor rumble. I lean against the wall, enjoying the cool feeling of the tile on my warm skin. Closing my eyes, I imagine I'm somewhere else; a place where things are simple, easy. A place where I don't even have to think.

But the sound of Audrey stumbling out of her stall ruins the suspension of disbelief, and I push off the wall. She straightens out her dress and sluggishly makes her way to the sink to wash her hands. The curls have fallen out of her hair, and her eye makeup has smudged, both things she seems to take note of as she assesses her appearance in the mirror.

"I'm so ugly," she states, turning her face to examine it from all angles.

"What are you talking about?" I ask incredulously, coming to stand beside her.

"It's no wonder Parker dumped me," she continues, and the name causes a sense of dread to come over me. I have a bad feeling about the direction this conversation is headed. "I mean, just look at you!"

My heart picks up slightly. "Me?"

She turns away from the mirror to face me, leaning against the sink. "You're gorgeous. You've always been the prettier one. Maybe if I looked more like you, I could actually keep a guy around."

I let out a small breath of relief, grateful that she wasn't making the accusation I thought she was. But my heart sinks when I think about her words. "Audrey, don't be silly. You're beautiful."

She simply pushes off the sink, walking to the exit. "I need another drink," she says, slipping through the door clumsily and dodging the throngs of people outside.

"No, you do not," I call, following her, trying not to lose sight of the back of her head as I push through the crowd.

By the time I actually catch up to her, the bartender is already handing her another shot, which she promptly downs, and I groan, sitting down next to her, and leaning my head on the bar. After taking one look in my direction, she orders another one then slides it over to me, and the cool glass grazes my arm. I lift my head, eyeing it skeptically, and she nods in encouragement. With a sigh, I decide to just fuck it and toss it all back in one quick motion.

I wince as the liquid burns down my throat. "All right," I say, turning to face her. "Can we go home now?"

Audrey pouts, sticking out her bottom lip. "Aw, come on. The night is still young!"

"No," I disagree, grabbing her wrist and dragging her in the direction of the exit. "The night is already way too old."

She continues to grumble to herself, but she lets me tug her along, following without putting up much of a struggle. Once outside and in the fresh air, I grab my phone out of my bag, and, without really thinking about it, dial a number that's quickly becoming very familiar. I place the cool device to my ear, trying to keep moving to prevent myself from getting too chilled.

Mason picks up on the third ring.

"Alina," he says, his voice urgent, "Is everything all right?"

"Totally," I reply, feeling warmth rush to my cheeks. Why did I call him? "Um, totally fine. But could you maybe come pick us up?"

"Us?"

"Me and Audrey."

"Where are you right now?"

I take a few steps away from the door, and Audrey gives me a confused look, shuddering from the cold. Craning my neck, I try to read the name of the place, but my vision is blurry and the font makes it hard to make out any letters. "Not sure. Carb . . . Card something."

"Cardino. Alina," he says again. "Why are you at the club?"

I wince, though I anticipated this reaction. "Well, I'm not exactly . . . sober."

He sighs. "I'll be there in ten."

True to his word, Mason arrives in front of the club ten minutes later, his car slowing to a stop a few feet away from the entrance.

Audrey and I are sitting on a bench, her head resting on my shoulder as she struggles to remain awake, and I work on getting us both upright. Mason exits his car, slamming the door shut behind him. We make eye contact as he approaches but he immediately looks away. A feeling of guilt settles in my chest as I stand, keeping a tight hold on Audrey to prevent her from falling to the ground.

"Let's get her in the car," he says, avoiding my gaze as he slings one of her arms over his shoulder.

"Okay," I say, doing the same, and the three of us slowly make our way over to his car, a somber feeling in the atmosphere.

Mason pulls the door to the backseat open, and I let him safely set Audrey inside. After the door clicks back into place, he turns to me, and I don't shy away from his stare. He's unimpressed. For the briefest of moments, he appraises my appearance. His expression softens for a millisecond as he takes me in, before he slides wordlessly into the car.

I blink a few times, trying to process what just happened, then quickly get into the passenger's seat, not wanting to test his patience.

The drive back to Seymour Avenue is awkward as hell. Once we arrive at home, I follow Mason out of the car. Together, we lift Audrey from the vehicle, bracing her on our shoulders again, and I begin to feel restless from the quiet.

After maneuvering through the door, we slowly make our way to Audrey's bedroom, and with a heave, set her down on the bed. Huffing, I blow a strand of hair out of my face, grateful to not be bearing her weight anymore. For a second, we just stand there, watching as she settles into her covers, a mess of incoherent mutters, before I turn to Mason.

"Let me just make sure she's all right," I say, wanting to dispel the tense atmosphere.

"I'll wait out there."

He turns, exiting the room and heading down the hallway. I wait until his footsteps fade away into nothing before taking a seat on the bed next to my sister. Her hair has fallen into her face, and I reach forward, brushing it aside. This causes her to stir awake, and she squints, lifting her head to look around the room, confusion spreading over her features.

"How did we get home?"

"I got a friend to pick us up," I say, wondering if Mason is within earshot.

"Oh." She yawns. "I feel funny."

I give her a small smile, squeezing her shoulder gently before standing up from the bed to help her take her heels off then pull the covers over her body. "Sleep it off."

"You're a good sister, Allie," she says sincerely. "Thanks for coming out with me tonight."

Warmth makes a home in my stomach, though it's accompanied by the ever-familiar feeling of guilt. I'm not a good sister. "Anytime."

I turn the light off, creep out of her bedroom, and shut the door behind me with a gentle click.

I find Mason in the kitchen, sitting on a stool at the island, his fingers drumming on the counter, the low light casting shadows on his face. The movement of his hands stills when he sees me approach, and I hop onto the stool next to him, resting my elbow on the island and my chin in my hand, looking back at him.

"Well," I start. "Let's hear it."

His lips press together in a firm line, and he chews on the inside of his mouth. "I'm really struggling to understand why you thought it was a good idea to go out and get drunk right now," he says bluntly. "It feels reckless, and we need to stay on our guard. Anything could've happened."

A tired laugh bubbles out of me. "You don't understand."

"Explain it to me."

Emotion builds in my chest, settling in my throat and blurring my vision. I stare straight ahead, trying to keep it under control, and Mason waits for me to translate my torrent of thoughts into proper sentences.

"I needed a break from . . . all of this." I gesture in front of me, as though all of my problems are stacked in a neat pile, and I hate how my voice breaks as I say the words. "Ever since I left the hospital, my life has been a fucking mess. I can't remember anything before the middle of January, I can't sleep at night because of nightmares about my supposed best friend trying to kill me, I'm the reason my sister's relationship is ruined, and I constantly have to bottle it all up and pretend like nothing is wrong."

I take a second to collect myself, swallowing down my tears and trying to catch them as they fall, unable to look at him. "I just wanted one night—one *fucking* night—where I could pretend I was a normal human being who didn't have to deal with any of this, so I'd appreciate it if you didn't give me shit for it."

When I finish speaking, my anger and frustration seem to take up all the space in the room. I knew a breakdown was coming soon, but I'd hoped there wouldn't be anyone to witness it.

Wordlessly, Mason gets up from his stool. Part of me expects him to just walk out and leave me to deal with my own problems, but instead, he grabs the box of tissues on the counter, sits back down, and slides it over to me. Feeling mildly embarrassed, I reach for one, nodding my thanks.

"I do understand," he offers, his voice low. "And I'm sorry."

The unexpected apology catches me off guard, and I find myself unable to think of something coherent to say.

"I just—" he starts, then pauses. "I just don't want anything bad to happen to you."

When he looks at me again, I become hyperaware of how close we're sitting, our knees grazing. "Something bad already happened to me," I murmur distantly, not entirely focused on my words.

"Exactly. I'm trying to keep it from happening again."

We're locked in a weighted silence, and I feel my heart beating in my chest, the pace faster than usual. It looks as though he's going to say something more, but then he snaps out of his trance, clearing his throat. I lean back, and some of the tension in the room melts away, allowing me to breathe easier.

Mason watches me with a frown as I stand from the stool. Heading over to the cupboard, I pull open the doors, taking a bottle of red wine from the top shelf and grabbing two glasses. I set one of them down in front of him, and he raises an eyebrow, looking amused now.

"We could both use an escape," I tell him, unscrewing the lid and pouring some into his glass before he can protest.

Sofia most likely won't be happy that I broke into her precious supply, but I can't find it in me to care. I pour a glass for myself before sitting down and holding up my drink for a toast. Mason seems to war with himself for a few moments, until he gives in, fighting a smile as he clinks his glass against mine. We both take generous sips, and I enjoy the taste of the bitter liquid as it courses down my throat.

After a while, Mason seems to be a bit more at ease, his posture relaxing, and when I lean forward, resting my elbows on the counter, he drapes an arm over the back of my chair languidly.

I peek back at him. "Can you tell me the truth about something?"

"Depends on what it is."

"Why did you stop being my friend?"

Mason drags a hand through his dark hair, and I find myself thinking about how it would feel between my fingers. "I wondered when you were going to bring that up again."

"If I did something to you, or hurt you in any way . . ."

"You didn't," he says. "That was all me."

I study his features, waiting for him to continue.

"We used to be together all the time," he confesses. "But things were rough at home. My dad . . . he was a piece of shit. He didn't treat us like he should've. I loved him, though."

"Of course," I say, my heart already sinking.

"Then he left," he says simply. "Moved out one day and never came back. He sends me cards on my birthday, but I haven't seen him in years. I was crushed, you know? I was just a kid. I wanted him to want me."

Mason shifts his position, folding his arms over his chest, and I mirror his pose, another lump forming in my throat.

"I didn't know how to deal with it, so I pushed everyone away," he remarks. "I told you I didn't want to see you anymore. I didn't see the point of letting anyone get close to me if they were just going to leave one day too."

"I get it."

His eyes flicker to mine again, and I can see the remorse swirling within them as they take in the details of my face. No doubt both of us are thinking about how different things could've been if we hadn't drifted apart.

"I'm sorry," he says gently.

"It's okay." I shake my head. "My dad left us too. I think I probably had the same fears you did. It would explain my choice of friends, at least. The way I treated other people. If I didn't let anyone see the real me, maybe I thought it wouldn't hurt when they left."

"It's a lonely way to live."

Hearing Mason's story and the breakdown of our friendship makes me feel as though I truly do understand the old Allie a bit better. Maybe at the end of the day, she was also misunderstood and scared of letting people in.

"What were things like between us before my accident?" I ask.

"You and me?"

K. Monroe

"Yeah." I tuck my legs up onto the stool, wrapping my arms around them. "Did we really not talk at all?"

"We might as well have been strangers," he admits. "It makes sense, though. What I did to you was a low blow. And once you and Zoe found each other in middle school, I didn't think you'd want anything to do with me. I would never fit in with your circle."

"Consider yourself lucky," I remark. "It's not a good circle to be in."

"I don't understand your dynamic," he says, looking bemused. "Damien was such a crybaby in elementary. Zoe and James went to the school across town, but Damien was in our class. I'm not sure how he became so popular in high school."

I grunt in amusement. "He's a crybaby now too."

Mason cracks a grin, watching me intently. "I've always wondered what it would be like to get to know you again."

I realize then that this could be the reason I feel at ease when I'm with him; he's the only person who didn't have preconceived notions of how I'm supposed to act or any expectations of what a relationship with me should be. He knew me as a child, but we're both new people now.

"And? What's it like?"

His mouth twitches. "Still deciding."

"Let me know when you've made up your mind."

Turning to the clock on the wall, he sighs. "Shit, when did it get this late? I should really get home."

"Um, no," I say bluntly, the atmosphere shifting. "You've had way too much wine, you're not driving."

"Alina," he protests, and I give him a serious look.

"Weren't you listening in that awful assembly? You can sleep on the couch," I tell him, standing up from my own chair and heading in the direction of the hallway closet to grab him some bedding. "Sofia is on a business trip, so you don't have to worry."

Mason follows me, our footsteps padding on the laminate floor, and I locate the closet, sliding the doors open and grabbing a handful of blankets. "At least let me help you," he says, reaching out to take them out of my hands, but I jerk out of his grasp stubbornly.

The sudden movement causes my head to spin and my knees to buckle. He reaches out, his hands flying to my waist to steady me as my breath catches. Startled by the sudden contact, I meet the eyes that always seem to draw me in with a gravitational pull, and he looks equally shocked by our accidental closeness, mere inches apart. Clearing my throat, I take a step back, and his fingers slip from my hips.

"Sorry," I mumble, and he nods before I turn away, heading to the living room and feeling a burn in my cheeks.

We enter the room, and it feels too dark, so I reach over to flick on the lamp above the couch. Unfortunately, the light only serves to bask Mason in a soft glow that does things to my heart, and I quickly look away, setting the blankets down.

"Will you be okay out here?"

"I'll be fine, Alina," he says. "Thank you."

"Good night, Mason."

"Good night."

Leaving him to get settled, I turn away, making for my bedroom. My heart beats a little faster with the knowledge that Mason is just downstairs, and it's both a comforting and terrifying thought. Taking a deep breath, I settle under the covers, willing my heartbeat to slow down, and my blinks become increasingly slower until my eyelids finally fall closed.

And for the first time in a long time, I sleep peacefully.

18 | IMPLODE

When I wake up on Sunday morning, Mason is gone. There's a note lying in the spot he previously occupied on the couch, scrawled in his bold handwriting, as if he knew the first thing I would do in the morning is look for him.

Thank you.

Those two simple words cause something to stir in my chest, and the events of last night come flooding back. For weeks, Mason has felt like this illusive, unreachable part of my past, haunting my dreams and many of my waking thoughts, but all of a sudden, he's real and tangible.

I had been under the impression that we were two vastly different people, but now it seems as though we might've been cut from the same cloth. I wonder how different our lives would've been if we were able to connect through our trauma rather than be driven apart by it.

The majority of the day is slow, the minutes dripping like honey from a jar, and I slum around the house, too lazy to do anything beyond that. I check on Audrey, confirming by her pulse that she's just extremely hungover and not dead. Eventually, I force myself to do some schoolwork, and it isn't until the evening that I finally have the motivation to do something about my hygiene.

Under the piping hot water of the shower, I wash away the less than stellar remnants of the night before. My skull pounds persistently and my limbs move with a zombielike stiffness, proving my body wasn't truly ready for a night of clubbing and drinking.

After stepping out of the shower, I towel off and throw on a sweatshirt and a pair of leggings before heading upstairs, the ends of my hair dampening my shoulders.

The door to my room is open, and to my surprise, Audrey is sitting on my bed, next to a basket of laundry. She looks up as I enter.

"Hey." I greet her, my voice doing little to mask my surprise. "Nice to see you awake and doing things. I didn't think you'd join the land of the living at all today."

She doesn't answer, and I grab a brush from my dresser. Standing in front of the mirror, I run it through my hair, brushing out the tangles, but the sight of Audrey in my periphery stops me in my tracks. Her shoulders are hunched, and she still hasn't said anything.

Finally, she speaks, her voice thick.

"How could you?"

Frowning, I slowly turn around, catching sight of the look on her face. Her expression is crestfallen, tears glittering in her eyes, and a bad feeling rises in my chest. It's only then that I notice the paper she's holding in her trembling hands.

"What is that?"

"You don't have to play innocent anymore, I know the truth," she says bitterly, crumpling it into a ball and shoving it at my chest. I flinch, failing to catch the paper.

It falls to the floor, but she doesn't seem to care, glaring at me with her arms folded. The malice on her face is chilling. I've never seen her look this angry before, and I've definitely never seen this sort of anger directed at me.

"That was under your bed," she spits. "I wasn't going to read it, but I recognized his handwriting."

Crouching, I open it back up, my fingers feeling cold as I pluck it from the floorboards. It's a letter, addressed to me.

From Parker.

The chill from my hands works its way up until my veins feel like ice, and I can't move.

Allie, the letter begins. *I know you said it's over. But I'm moving out tomorrow, and I want you to know that I'll always love you. Always. Everything is already so complicated, and I don't want to keep making it worse. I want the best for you. I'm here if you need me or if you ever want to talk. Who knows, maybe someday things will be different—*

I stop abruptly, not wanting to read any more, heartbeat thundering in my ears. He must've stuck it in my room somewhere before he left. How did I not notice? Dragging my attention away from the letter, I look at the girl in front of me and shake my head.

"Audrey, please let me explain," I begin.

"How long were you going to keep lying to my face?" she asks bluntly. "How long has this been going on?"

I take in a shuddering breath, my nose stinging with oncoming tears. "I—"

"God, I feel like such an idiot." She cuts me off, throwing her hands up in defeat and laughing without humor. "You've been pretending to be the supportive sister, pretending to care about me, when you were keeping this secret the whole time."

"I wasn't pretending," I interject honestly.

"So, you were just being nice to me to make yourself feel better?" she accuses, angling her body away from me, her posture rigid. "I can't even fucking believe you."

"Audrey," I say, voice low, vision blurry. "I'm so sorry. But you have to understand that I don't remember any of this happening. I'm not the same person I was back then."

She whirls around and the blatant hurt on her face makes me feel ill. "If you were truly a different person, you would've told me about it. I don't know why I thought it would be a good idea to give you a second chance," she grinds out. "You've never been trustworthy.

How foolish of me to think you losing your memory would change that. Is this why you broke up with Damien?"

Recoiling as though I've been slapped, I flounder for words. "What? No, that's not—"

"It all makes fucking sense now."

"The stuff with Parker happened before the accident," I explain hurriedly, taking a step forward. "After I came back home, I shut it down as soon as I realized what was going on. He told me it was never anything more than a kiss. I don't even remember any of it."

She holds up a hand. "Spare me the details. It doesn't matter when it happened. You still did it. It was still you."

Her face threatens to break again, her bottom lip quivering. Tension hangs in the air, and I try to swipe away the tears that have begun to freefall. I knew it would be catastrophic when she found out the truth, but I never imagined this.

"He left me for you," she whispers. "I don't want to see you ever again."

"Audrey, please wait!"

Shaking her head vehemently, she brushes past me, causing me to stumble as she storms into the hallway and down the stairs. I follow her, scrambling to keep up as she bursts into her bedroom, going straight for the closet.

When she turns around, there's a large suitcase in her hand. She sets it on the bed, throwing clothes inside haphazardly.

"What are you doing?"

"Getting the hell out of here," she remarks. "I can't stand being in this house anymore."

Fear creeps into my chest. "Where are you going?"

She doesn't answer, and the fear intensifies, making it hard to breathe. Sofia is away for a couple more days. If Audrey goes, too, I'll be alone.

"Audrey?"

"What's it to you?"

"I care about you."

Audrey laughs again. "That's a joke."

She scoops a handful of things from her dresser, dumping them into the suitcase before heading to the bathroom to grab more. The amount of stuff she's taking is worrying, like she doesn't plan on coming back for a long time.

Maybe ever.

"Don't leave," I plead, but I know I'm fighting a losing battle.

Eyeing me, she heads back to her bedroom with her arms loaded with products. "I'm going to stay with friends in Vancouver," she says. "I'll call Mom when I'm on the road."

"You don't have to go, you can stay here," I say. "You can hate me all you want. I promise I'll stay out of your way. Just please don't go."

She slams the lid of the suitcase, fastening it shut aggressively. Wheeling it behind her, she arrives at the front door and grabs her coat and car keys without looking back. Panic makes my bones shake, and I have no idea how to convince her to stay.

When she reaches for the doorknob, I spring forward, grabbing her wrist gently. "I can't be by myself," I admit, barely above a whisper.

For the briefest of seconds, it looks as though she might cave. But then her lips pull into a sneer.

"Maybe you can ask Parker to stay with you. I'm sure it wouldn't be the first time." Her gaze falls to the crumpled paper in my hand, and she scoffs darkly, shaking her head. "I hope you're happy," she tells me. "You two deserve each other. You're both pieces of shit."

With that, Audrey shakes me off, exiting the house and slamming the door behind her.

I remain in place, shell-shocked and frozen. And then I tear up the letter in my hands, letting the fragments flutter to the ground, breathing hard.

Audrey and I were doomed from the beginning—doomed from the moment I kissed Parker, or maybe from the moment I met him. The three of us are irreversibly interwoven, three dominoes that collapsed onto each other until no one was left standing. I don't think there's a way to ever recover the trust that I've broken, even if I lived a million lifetimes.

There's a disconnect between who I am now and who I was back then. It's as though my life has been ruined by someone I've never even met, and I'll spend the rest of it resenting them for what they've done.

But then Audrey's scathing voice comes back to me.

You still did it. It was still you.

The affair, the email to McGill, it was all me. Nobody else can take the blame.

This whole time, I've been thinking of myself as cursed, someone who was dealt a cruel and unfair hand. But maybe this is karma's way of giving me what I'm owed, and there was no hope of redeeming myself in the first place.

The clock ticks quietly in the kitchen, and all I want is for everything to stop. I find the will to move, leaving the entrance on legs that feel as though they've been carved from wood.

Even though I've been home alone several times before, the lack of Audrey's presence feels loud and all encompassing, thick with the weight of not knowing the next time she'll be back. What am I supposed to do now? The circle of people I trust and feel safe with has shrunk significantly, when it was already small to begin with.

I want to talk to Mason, but at the same time, I don't want him to discover this part of me. The thought of him knowing about what happened with Parker is nauseating. I don't want him to look at me any differently than he does now. After the explosion of my relationship with Audrey, I wouldn't be able to handle it.

I would truly be alone.

Calling Sofia to let her know what happened should probably be my next course of action, but I can't find it in me to do it. Telling her would require giving an explanation as to why everything went down the way it did. Cheating was the thing that drove our family apart years ago, and it's the same thing driving it apart now. Imagine how she'd feel if she knew her daughter had followed in the footsteps of the man who broke her heart.

Instead, I grab my raincoat and head outside. Inhaling deeply, I stick my hands in my pockets as I wander down the sidewalk. I've gotten used to grey, overcast skies. It seems fitting for a town like Pender Falls. Gloomy, foreboding, filled with dark secrets. Maybe this place is actually the undiscovered tenth circle of hell. It's as though an evil stems from the roots of the trees and creeps into houses through the floorboards. It certainly wrapped its tendrils around me and Zoe. James and Damien too.

I recall James's disturbing behavior at the assembly. It's clear he was there that night, which means that Damien was likely also an accomplice. Bad things come in threes, and my friends are always together.

When I broke up with Damien, he anguished over wanting to take something back. I imagine nearly killing your girlfriend and lying about it would be pretty high on the list.

As the sun begins to make its descent, the sky becomes increasingly charcoal and the temperature plummets. I keep walking, feeling like if I stop moving, my thoughts will completely spin out and go haywire. And the idea of going back to an empty house is far from appealing. I don't even know how long it's been since I left; it feels like forever and a split second at the same time.

Turning on my heel, I prepare to go back the way I came, though I've walked far, and this part of the neighborhood is unfamiliar. I do my best to retrace my steps in the waning light, starting to regret that I didn't turn back sooner. Staying out after nightfall doesn't feel wise.

I can't tell if it's just the paranoia I've drummed up in my head or something more concrete, but I suddenly have the prickly sensation of being watched.

Casting my eyes around surreptitiously, I peer at the silent streets. Despite not being able to hear much beyond my footsteps on the pavement, I have the feeling that I'm not alone. Curling my fingers into fists, I quicken my pace, eager to get home. At least houses have locks to keep people out.

I glance over my shoulder but the road behind me is empty. There's a rustle in the bushes, and I try to convince myself that it's not real.

A twig snaps, the sound closer this time, and I move even faster. Daylight is running out, and I have to strain to see clearly in the dim light. There are a few street lamps ahead, and I gravitate toward them. It's easy for something to sneak up on you in the dark.

But as I grow closer, one of the lights burns out.

When I think I hear the sound of quick and heavy footsteps, I freeze, whirling around.

The night is static, and I swallow, looking around, my heart beating rapidly in my chest. Without waiting to hear anything else, I take a slow step backward, turning on my heel. It takes everything in me not to sprint, somehow feeling like a strong reaction will only give them more incentive to pursue me.

I might get accused of all of this being a product of an overactive imagination, but I have no doubt that I'm being followed. The image from my dream of Zoe smiling at me with blood staining her hands flashes through my mind.

My shoulders nearly melt in relief when the familiar sight of the house comes into view. The motion light flickers on when I reach the driveway, and I hurry to the front door, shutting it tightly behind me.

With shaking fingers, I twist the lock on the door, then exhale, leaning against it. The peace I feel is fleeting, as I remember there are other points of entry. After going around to lock every door and window and letting Scout inside, I feel only slightly better.

I sit with Scout on the living-room floor, keeping a watchful eye on my surroundings. The silence of the house is stifling, and I'm hyperaware of every tiny noise as it settles, Scout whining softly beside me.

As I stare into the backyard, it looks as though the shadows move. They creep closer to the house, tree branches snaking toward me, sliding under the door. I blink a few times, aware that I'm having another episode, trying to steady my breathing.

But when I think I see a pair of eyes on the other side of the window, I can't take it anymore and reach for my cell phone, calling the one person who makes me feel safe.

19 | PLUNGE

Darkness has completely fallen by the time a car pulls up outside of the house.

I stick close to the wall, peering through the sheer curtain into the outside world and squinting at the brightness of the headlights. The car door clicks open before slamming shut again, and Scout trots over to the window, placing her paws on the sill and standing at attention. There's a knock on the door, and my heart kicks into gear.

I scramble to unlock it, clumsily twisting the doorknob and pulling it open.

Mason stands in the entryway, his hair tousled, cheeks slightly flushed. Scout simply watches him, proving to be useless as a guard dog. I allow him into the house, catching a hint of cologne as he moves past me.

"Thanks for coming," I say, feeling entirely embarrassed.

He steps inside, scanning the room and peering into the kitchen. I close the front door, making sure to lock it once more before trailing after him.

"Where did you say you saw something?"

I look at the French doors leading to the backyard. "There," I say, gesturing to them with my chin, cheeks warming as I fidget. "It was probably nothing, though."

Mason takes my words seriously, glancing over his shoulder. "Wait here. I'll check it out."

He pulls the door open and disappears into the backyard. My pulse races the whole time he's away, and I have to resist the temptation to go outside with him. Even if it means stepping into the potential line of fire, I'd rather not be alone.

When he returns, I let out a subtle exhale of relief. He shakes his head.

"I didn't see anything," he remarks. "But we should keep the doors locked."

I move past him to lock the French doors, testing them to make sure they're fastened shut, before slowly turning around to face him again with a grimace.

"This is so stupid," I say. "I feel like an idiot for making you come here. It's just that Sofia and Audrey both left—"

"Alina, I don't mind. Seriously. You shouldn't have to be alone."

My heart thrums rapidly in my chest, though I'm starting to feel like it has less to do with whatever might be outside my house and more to do with who's currently inside of it.

"Can I get you anything?" I ask, trying to break through the awkwardness.

"No, I'm all right." He pauses, and I begin to feel hot from his scrutiny. "Are you okay?"

Those three words seem to flip a switch inside of me, and immediately the weight of what happened today presses against my eyelids. I'm not okay. Everything keeps blowing up in my face, and there's nothing I can do to stop it.

"Yeah," I mumble, trying for a fleeting smile. But it wobbles, and I quickly turn around, covering my face with my hands. I don't want him to see me like this.

It's quiet for a couple of beats, and I focus on trying to force the tears back into their ducts, until I feel gentle fingers prying my hands away from my face. My stomach flips at his touch.

"Alina," he coaxes softly. "You don't have to pretend to be okay around me."

"I'm sorry, I just—"

"Talk to me." He reaches forward to push some of my hair behind my ear, fingertips skating across my cheek.

For a moment I'm too distracted to register what he said, but when I do, I force myself to take a step back, breaking the spell. With a sigh, I slink onto a stool, and he takes the one next to me, not unlike the night before. I wish we could go back to that.

"I got into this massive fight with Audrey."

"About what?"

"I—I did something awful to her," I say. "But she didn't know until now. She immediately packed up her things and left when she found out."

I peer at him to see his eyebrows have raised, though his face is free from judgment. "Must've been pretty serious."

"I kissed her boyfriend," I admit before I can stop myself, shame burning on my skin. Even though this is an ugly side of me I'd rather not show, there's something about Mason that feels safe. "Before the accident. He wrote a letter to tell me he was in love with me, then he broke up with her and moved out. She found the letter today. I didn't even know it existed."

Mason processes the words, impassive, and nerves twist my insides. "Were you in love with him?" he asks finally.

"I don't know," I say. "I don't think so. He told me we were best friends before. Maybe I was just confused."

"Sounds complicated," he says, and the words are gentle.

"She probably won't ever talk to me again."

"Give her time. I'm sure she'll come around."

I can't help the scoff that escapes me as I shake my head, thinking of the way her voice dripped with venom. "You didn't see the way she looked at me. I fucked up big time."

"We all fuck up," he offers. "That's what second chances are for."

"My entire life before the accident was one big fuckup, and things aren't going well on the second go either."

"I think you should give yourself more credit," he says. "I'm being serious. The person you are now seems a lot different from the person you used to be."

"You're just saying that."

"I'm not," he remarks. "People can change, and you've certainly proven that."

"I don't know if what happened to me counts as actual change. My memories got erased, that's it," I point out. "Who's to say I wouldn't make all those mistakes again if I went through the same stuff now? Clearly I have it in me."

"I think losing your memory has brought you back to the bones of who you are."

"But maybe it's just about circumstance." I pause, thinking. "It seems like I got swept up in things that weren't actually important. Like all I cared about was the way everyone else saw me."

"Either way, you've been given a second chance," he reminds me. "Most people don't get that."

"I guess so."

Mason glances at me, seeing the trepidation on my face. "You should get some rest," he advises. "You look exhausted."

"I always look exhausted," I tease. "It's part of my charm."

He chuckles fondly. "I can set up camp on the couch again."

Standing up, he begins to walk toward the hallway, but I reach out, clutching his arm and surprising both of us. His eyes, lit up with curiosity, flicker to mine, and I flush, pulling my hand back when I realize what I've done.

"Actually," I start, my heart rate picking up with nervousness. The idea of being by myself right now is harrowing, and the living room feels too far away when there are a number of dark rooms in between. "Maybe you could sleep in my room?" I suggest, trying not to cringe when I see his startled look. "I just—I don't want to be alone right now."

"Of course," he says, and it only serves to kick-start my heart again.

"Just give me a minute to change."

He nods. "I'll meet you upstairs."

I rise from my stool, feeling shaky again as I leave the kitchen. I do a quick sweep of my bedroom when I arrive, trying to see if there's anything embarrassing lying about that needs to be tucked away, but it seems to be pretty clean. My heart continues to thump away in my chest, and I try to calm down, reminding myself that he's just going to keep me company; nothing else is going to happen. After changing into something more comfortable, I leave the door open.

At the sound of the wooden stairs wheezing, I hurriedly take a seat on the edge of the bed. He enters the room seconds later, and I watch as he closes the door, listening as it shuts with a muted click, sealing us inside.

"Should I grab some blankets for the floor?" he asks, voice rougher than usual. I can tell by the way he asks that he knows the answer to his question.

"You don't have to sleep on the floor," I tell him, forcing the warmth to leave my face as I say the words. "I don't want you to be uncomfortable."

"Thanks."

He comes around to the other side of the bed, gently peels the covers back, and takes a seat on the mattress. Summoning any amount of courage and peace of mind I can muster, I do the same, sliding beneath the comforter and making an effort to keep my breathing steady. The tension in the air is palpable, and I rest my head on the pillow at a snail's pace.

I can see him in my periphery, though I'm too scared to turn to look at him fully, afraid of what I might do. Instead, I roll over onto my side, facing away. I feel him shuffle and adjust his position on the other side of the bed, and all I can hear is my heart beating, the sound so loud and intrusive he must be able to hear it too. I want to say something, to break the thick atmosphere, but I don't know what.

"Good night," I decide on needlessly, trying to gauge how he's feeling.

"Good night," he returns, giving nothing away.

I stare at the large shadows sprawling across my bedroom wall. All I can think about is him lying next to me, the best kind of distraction and the most dangerous. Gathering up a handful of courage, I roll over to face him slowly. His blue-green eyes are wide open, gazing up at the ceiling, but they flit in my direction after I've completely angled myself toward him. I watch the way they study me, taking in my every detail, and I admire the glow of the lights leaving intricate patterns on his mouth, cheekbones, and jawline.

And then before I know what I'm doing, I'm raising my head from my pillow, lifting a finger to trace that jawline and pressing my lips against that mouth.

His response is instantaneous.

Fingers slide into my hair, his lips eager as they meld against mine, and my heart goes into overdrive as he shifts our position, pushing himself up as he kisses me back desperately, sending tremors of shock down my spine. Following his lead, I roll onto my back and he hovers over top of me, my hands finding their home as I pull his face impossibly closer, wanting there to be no space left between us.

I feel his hand on my waist, causing me to shiver, and it rests on the bare skin where my T-shirt has ridden up. I don't want it to stop; I want to stay on this plane of existence that's become ours, surrounded by an overwhelming sense of euphoria that has my chest feeling both heavy and light at the same time.

But then he pulls away abruptly, and it ends.

"What's the matter?" I ask, breathless and bewildered.

"This is wrong, Alina," he finally tells me, his voice hoarse with emotion, and my frown deepens.

"What?" I blink, unable to keep myself from feeling a sting of hurt. "Why is it wrong?"

He changes his position, releasing me from the cage of his arms and sitting upright instead. I follow suit, pushing myself up until I'm sitting, too, looking at him in confusion. He sighs, resting his head in his hands.

"We shouldn't get distracted," he says. "There's too much going on right now."

I don't believe he intends the words to be hurtful, but the sting multiplies tenfold. "Is that all you think this is for me?"

"That's not what I meant," he tells me, shaking his head, dragging a hand over his face wearily.

"Look, Mason," I say, trying to keep up the courage to wear my heart on my sleeve. "I have feelings for you." The statement hangs in the air, and his expression goes slack. "I'd appreciate it if you were honest with me. Don't give me any excuses, just tell me straight up that you don't feel the same, and then we can move on."

He looks away, taking great interest in the comforter spread out over the bed, running a hand over it. "I can't do that," he says finally.

"Why not?"

"Because I'd be lying."

My breath catches, my heart coming to an abrupt halt once more. Given the way he just ended things, I wasn't anticipating that answer, and it only serves to make me more confused. "Then, why . . . ?"

"It's not the right time," he reiterates, longing evident in his expression. "So much is happening—so much has *already* happened—and you're emotionally vulnerable right now. I'm not going to take advantage of that."

While I understand his reasoning, it doesn't stop the crushing weight of disappointment from crashing down on my chest. Against my will, my bottom lip trembles, and he curses under his breath when he senses the impending breakdown, reaching out to cup my face with his hand, worry etched into his features.

"Hey," he says, thumb grazing my cheek, "it's all right."

I sniffle, reaching up to swipe away the first tear that escapes, trying to think of a way to properly voice my thoughts. "I just wanted one thing," I confess, my voice barely above a broken whisper. "One good thing. I wanted *you*."

Mason gives me a rueful smile, wiping away another tear with the pad of his thumb. "You still have me," he assures me softly, removing his hand from my face to tuck a section of my hair behind my ear. "I think you've had me ever since we were kids, but I didn't realize it until now. I'm very much yours."

His admission causes my lips to curve upward gently, a fluttering sensation growing in my belly. After a little while, we settle back under the covers, and despite our conversation, I curl up next to him, my head on his chest, and he doesn't protest, wrapping his arms around me in a protective embrace.

"You know," I muse. "You're the only one who always calls me Alina. Why is that?"

"Hm." He runs his fingers down the length of my arm, before murmuring, "I suppose I wanted something that was mine."

Warmth blooms in my chest as he presses a kiss to my hair, and for a moment, after I close my eyes, I pretend I'm an ordinary person who stumbled into some semblance of love, instead of someone too frightened to be alone, with the threat of death looming over them like a creeping shadow, and the delusion stays with me until I drift into another sleep free of nightmares.

20 | PRELUDE

The following Friday, one week after the assembly, I find Iris Wen sitting on the front steps of the school at lunch, hunched over a sketchbook.

Her short black hair is pulled into a tiny ponytail at the back of her head, and circular gold frames perch on her nose as she scrawls on the page. She doesn't notice me approaching until I casually take a seat next to her.

I don't know much about Iris; besides the information I gathered just by looking at her Instagram feed, I've learned that her parents are frequently away, making her empty house the de facto venue for weekend parties. For the most part, she blends into the flow of the other students and surprisingly spends most of her lunches outside on the steps by herself, drawing.

Until now, I hadn't really thought to seek her out—from my understanding, the party she hosted on the night of my accident was large, and I don't expect her to know anything more than the average partygoer. But I'm so close to finding the bitter truth about what happened that night; even the tiniest bit of information could help.

"Allie, hey," she says, surprise evident in her voice.

"You're Iris, right?"

"Yeah." She pauses, visibly troubled, before blurting, "I'm sorry."

"What are you sorry for?"

"I wanted to talk to you sooner, to tell you how awful I feel about what happened to you, but I didn't know how," Iris says. "The fact that it happened when you were going home after my party . . . I think about it all the time."

A tug of sympathy pulls at my chest. "It's not your fault," I say sincerely. She doesn't seem sure of whether or not she should accept my words. I jerk my chin in the direction of her sketchbook. "What are you drawing?"

The page is filled with a collection of different pairs of eyes, but they don't seem like random, disconnected doodles. All of them are trained straight forward, intense.

"Oh." Pink floods her cheeks. "It's kind of dark."

"Now I'm even more interested," I say.

"Sometimes I draw things based on emotions. This one is based on guilt." Iris brushes away some stray eraser shavings with her fingers. "I guess it's more about what you might see when you're guilty. Or what you think you see."

I stare at the drawing for a few beats longer, until it really does begin to feel like judgmental eyes are watching my every move. "Damn. You're very talented."

"Thanks."

"There was another drawing of yours I saw on Instagram," I say. "It had these two girls, their eyes looked a bit like this."

An unreadable emotion darts across her features. "Allie, that was a picture of you."

My limbs go still. "What?"

Iris turns the pen around in her hands, looking nervous. "Well, it was you and Zoe. I drew it after the party."

"Why?"

She opens her mouth to say something then closes it quickly as someone passes by us, heading into the school. I recall the caption of the picture: *The End of an Era*. The breeze flutters the pages of her sketchbook and raises the hairs on the back of my neck.

When we're alone again, she ducks her head, leaning closer. "Because your friendship definitely ended that night. You spent most of the party screaming at each other."

"Was I drunk?" I ask.

"No," she says immediately. "Zoe was the drunk one. I don't know what you were fighting about, but it seemed pretty serious. That's why I drew the picture. Both of your emotions were so heightened, I couldn't get it out of my head."

It's similar to what Mason already told me, but it isn't the whole story. The incident with Jacob happened many months prior to all of this, yet the email draft was recent, shortly before the party. What was the tipping point that finally pushed us over the edge?

"Were we always like that before?"

She shakes her head solemnly. "I'd never seen anything that bad. It was on another level."

"Interesting," I say, watching leaves skitter across the pavement. "How do you feel about Zoe? I know most of the people at school aren't my biggest fan, and I've been wondering if it's the same for her."

"To be honest," Iris says, glancing around the front lawn to make sure nobody is within earshot, "Zoe has always creeped me out. She's deluded herself into thinking she's the top tier of the social hierarchy, but it's all just a fantasy. She doesn't realize that nobody really cares about social standing, we're all just trying to get through high school."

I let out a scoff of amusement, thinking back to all the times Zoe explained the school system as if it was fact, making it clear that people like Mason weren't supposed to associate with people like us. But it never occurred to me that she was the only one playing her convoluted games. Or maybe it was the two of us playing together, locked in a perpetual battle of trying to one-up the other.

"She does take her reputation pretty seriously," I admit, trying to remain diplomatic.

"A little too much, if you ask me." Iris leans forward, obscuring the view of the eyes on the page. "She's been acting so weird ever since my party. When I saw you guys fighting, it was pretty obvious you'd never speak to each other again. And then suddenly she started acting like nothing even happened. She got a fancy new car and pretended she didn't know what people were talking about whenever they brought up the fight."

"That's definitely strange." The words "fancy new car" strike me. I vaguely remember Zoe making a comment about that when she nearly hit the fence. Seems like an odd time to buy a new vehicle out of the blue.

Iris blushes again and shakes her head. "She's your best friend, I don't know why I'm saying this to you. I'm sorry."

"Don't apologize," I say quickly. She's turned out to be a bigger fountain of information than I thought, and it would be a shame for her to stop now. "I appreciate the honesty."

Her shoulders sink slightly in relief. Overhead, the lunch bell rings, startling both of us. Iris stands, closing her book and brushing off the front cover, and I do the same, stifling a sigh.

She's about to head into the school when she hesitates. "A bunch of us are going to Boulder Trail tonight," she announces. "I don't know if you heard about it already. It's just for the seniors, and it's the first party we've had since everything happened. It might be weird for you, but you're welcome to come if you feel up for it."

"Thanks, Iris."

With a timid wave, she makes her way inside, and I step into the building shortly after, an idea brewing in the back of my mind. I move through the hallways, searching the crowd for a familiar face in the brief few minutes before my next class begins.

I find Mason exchanging his books at his locker.

"There's a party at Boulder Trail tonight," I say, by way of greeting. "Did you know about it?"

"Alina," he replies. "Hello to you too."

After collecting his books, he sidles up next to me as I head toward study hall, his arm brushing mine. I'm still not sure how to act around him. Things undoubtedly shifted between us when we kissed, but we essentially decided to shelve those feelings for now. Easier said than done.

"I think we should go."

"I thought we'd decided that neither of us like parties," he remarks, skeptical.

"We don't," I agree. "But shit always goes down at parties, right? It could be a chance for secrets to come out."

His face lights up in interest, though he works to control his tone, voice low and smooth. "Good point. You should try to get something out of Damien. He'll be the easiest to crack."

"I don't know," I say, grimacing. "I haven't spoken to him since the breakup. He's definitely not over it."

"Even better. He's probably desperate to talk to you."

Mason takes in the fleeting hesitation that passes across my face and ducks his head toward me, furrowing his eyebrows. We come to a stop outside of study hall, stepping out of the flow of traffic.

"You don't have to worry," he says. "I'll be there too."

"I know," I return gratefully. "But what if it doesn't work?"

"Then we try something else."

The conviction in his voice is hard to ignore. When he speaks the words so confidently, it's easy to believe them.

"We're so close," he presses. "Hang on a little bit longer."

After touching his fingertips to my shoulder gently, he ducks his head, disappearing in the opposite direction.

The sight of him walking away has a foreboding sense of finality to it, like something has been set in motion, and by the next time

I see him, things will have changed. I try not to think about it, going through the rest of my classes with a lack of focus and nagging feelings of anxiety.

When the final bell rings at the end of the day, I grab my backpack, slinging it over my shoulders and hurrying through the school, wanting to catch Zoe before she leaves. Her demeanor has been different ever since the assembly, though I can tell she's trying her best to appear as though nothing is wrong.

I find her nearing the exit, wearing an expensive black raincoat with a hood. There's a pensive expression on her face as she nears the door. We didn't speak much today; I haven't eaten lunch with them in the cafeteria since breaking up with Damien, and I think the photograph of my car traumatized her enough to make her forget about pretending to be my best friend.

"Zoe," I call just as she begins to push the door open.

She stops at the sound of my voice, looking over her shoulder. For a moment, she looks troubled, until she recovers, smiling woodenly. It reminds me of the dream I had. Letting go of the door, she steps back inside, moving out of the way of people exiting the building and waiting for me to reach her.

"What's up?"

"Did you hear about the senior party tonight?" I ask, making an effort to sound casual.

"Yeah," she says slowly. "What about it?"

Shrugging, I give her a strange look, as if it should be obvious. "You're going, right? We could go together."

To my dismay, she crinkles her nose, shaking her head. "I'm not really in the mood."

A gust of wind outside causes a spatter of rain to smack against the window, and my shoulders deflate. "Oh, come on. I thought you loved parties. Why not?"

"The weather is terrible. What makes you think I want to traipse around in the woods?"

It's a weak excuse, and I get the feeling it's more that she doesn't want to spend more time with me. "It's supposed to clear up later," I continue. "Please? I really want to go."

Her expression remains stubborn and steadfast, though she tilts her head, assessing me. "Why do you want to go so bad?"

My pulse picks up, and I try not to let it show on my face as I conjure an excuse out of thin air. "Everything has felt so complicated and confusing lately. I just want a night to let go and have some fun."

It's the same thing I told Mason after going to the club with Audrey, but this time it's a lot less genuine. The look on her face changes, softens, but it's hard to read. A touch more prodding and I'll be able to push her over the edge.

"Remember my birthday?" I say, raising an eyebrow. "Remember when you said you would do *anything* to make it up to me?"

Sighing, she flips her hair over her shoulder. "I was hoping you'd want something that could be paid for with money, not something that requires time and energy."

Clasping my hands, I bat my eyelashes, like she's done several times to me, and she finally caves, her pink lips hitching into a smirk.

"All right, fine." She pulls the hood over her blond tresses. "Be at my house at seven thirty sharp. We can get ready together again."

I step forward as she pushes the door open. "Wait!"

Zoe stops.

Forcing a contrite look on my face, I fidget with my fingers. "Could you convince Damien to come too?"

A flicker of irritation darts across her pretty features, so quick that I'm not sure if I misinterpreted it.

"I'd really like to talk to him," I continue. "I don't want things to be weird anymore."

Zoe watches me, letting the rain splash onto her oxfords. "I'll see what I can do."

With that, she leaves, and satisfaction courses down my spine.

For weeks she's lied straight to my face, parading around as a friend when she was truly my enemy; it feels good to lie to her in return, to lure her into a false sense of security. The thrill I get from pulling off that small performance makes me feel for the first time like I truly was an actress in my past life.

But this was just the rehearsal.

The way I act tonight has the power to either make everything fall into place or destroy everything we've been working toward.

21 | DETONATE

By the time Sofia drives me up the Harrises' sprawling driveway, the rain has stopped and the sun is poking through the clouds, steadily descending toward the horizon, casting the world in warm, golden hues.

There's a sense of foreboding in the air as the house comes into view. Sofia surveys the ornate building, and I'm not sure whether it's out of admiration or envy.

"Well," she says, after she's put the car into Park, staring at the perfectly maintained garden. "I hope you girls get a lot of studying done."

I may have twisted the truth a little bit. I doubt she would have driven me here if I hadn't.

"Me too," I agree.

I reach for the door handle, preparing to get out of the car, but Sofia's voice stops me, gentler this time.

"You haven't heard from Audrey yet?"

The words make my heart sink. It's creeping up on a week since she packed her things and hightailed it out of the house. She called Sofia from the road but hasn't spoken to her since then. I understand it's likely going to take a long time for me to get anywhere close to forgiveness—that doesn't make it sting any less.

"No," I say. "I don't think I'm going to."

"Neither of you will tell me what happened."

Nausea threatens to seep into my chest at the idea of her knowing the truth. I'm sure she'll find out some day, but I hope that day is far off in the future.

"I think it's better if you don't know."

She exhales in frustration. "How am I supposed to help if I don't even know what's going on?"

"This is something we need to figure out on our own," I explain. "You can't fix everything."

Though she seems dissatisfied with that answer, she lets me go, bidding me good-bye, and I step out of the car. I wave as I make my way up the front steps, watching her retreat down the driveway, wanting her to leave before I head inside, in case she somehow picks up on the fact that what we'll be doing tonight is a far cry from studying.

When I can't hear the sound of the car anymore, I turn around, inhaling deeply before knocking on the door. I wait in silence, and nothing happens. Feeling uncomfortable, I knock again.

Still nothing.

My phone shows that it's exactly seven thirty. Zoe told me not to be late, so where is she? Lifting my hand, I prepare to try one more time before the sudden sound of raised voices startles me.

The door swings open abruptly, and Zoe bursts onto the porch, a stormy expression on her face as she brushes past me, making a beeline for her car. A man in a business suit emerges shortly after. His posture radiates pure fury, and all of it is directed at his daughter.

"We're not done here!" he shouts, pointing at her and stalking down the steps.

"I've had enough," Zoe spits out, looking at me over her shoulder. "Come on, Allie."

The familiar melodic chime fills the air as she unlocks the vehicle, and I'm shell-shocked, too stunned to move. But then she pulls her door open, slipping inside, and I snap out of my trance, rushing to follow her. I certainly don't want to be left alone with her father.

I scramble to get into the passenger's side, and Zoe's fingers shake as she struggles to get the key into the ignition.

"Fuck," she whispers, her voice breaking.

"Zoe Elizabeth Harris!" the man roars. "If you drive away right now, I will make damn sure you regret it."

For a moment, it looks as though Zoe hesitates. She ignores her father standing right outside her window, smoke practically coming out of his ears, and she shifts into to Drive.

The car lurches forward, and I rush to fasten my seat belt as we tear down the driveway. Her father manages to slam his fist against the trunk of the car before we're out of his reach, causing both of us to flinch.

After we've made it a distance from the yard, I glance at Zoe timidly, my heart racing. Her jaw is set, and she grips the steering wheel with white knuckles, blazing a path to Boulder Trail.

"Are you okay?"

"Fine, why?"

I swallow. "Do you want to—"

"I hate him," she cuts me off, before shaking her head, getting some of her hair out of her face. Even in the midst of her turmoil, she's stunning. "I fucking hate both of them."

Compassion threatens to wash over me, and it feels horribly misplaced. This is the same person who made an attempt on my life, lied about it, and led me to believe I could trust her. I shouldn't be feeling sorry for her. She doesn't deserve it. But to be treated the way she is by her parents . . . I don't know that I'm cruel enough to say she deserves that.

"Why was he so angry?"

She lets out a ragged breath, face threatening to crumple, revealing the cracks in her nearly perfect facade. "The cops keep showing up at our house," she confesses. "They think I'm involved in your accident somehow. It's ridiculous. I had nothing to do with it!"

The desperation in her eyes makes me feel cold. If I didn't know any better, I'd find her performance convincing. With great difficulty, I work to keep my expression concerned instead of distrusting.

"What the hell?" I shake my head. "Why do you think they're coming after you?"

"I don't know!" she exclaims, looking panicked. The car swerves slightly, and I feel my pulse in my throat. "You're my best friend, Allie. Why would I want to hurt you?"

"You wouldn't."

Zoe thinks for a few beats, not seeming to pay much attention to the road, yet subconsciously managing to take us in the direction of the trail. "They're wasting their time. I'm not the one they should be looking at."

I freeze. "You think someone else is actually involved?"

There's a flicker of fear on her face as she looks between me and the street in quick succession. "If the cops are investigating, obviously something about it is suspicious. And I have a strong feeling I know *exactly* who it was."

This is unexpected. I thought Zoe would just maintain that I simply crashed my car into a tree, that the accident was entirely my own doing. But I suppose after revealing the police are interested in her, throwing the blame on someone else makes sense from a guilty standpoint.

"Who?"

"Mason."

To her credit, she has the gall to look me dead in the eyes, gauging my reaction.

"*Mason?*" I repeat, incredulous. "What makes you think it was him?"

"He was totally obsessed with you," she remarks emphatically.

"I used to always catch him staring. And I never told you this, but you guys talked at the party. You turned him down. He probably never got over you dumping him as a kid and hated seeing you with Damien all the time. Maybe he snapped."

"Really?"

"Think about it," she persists, grip tightening on the wheel. "He immediately slithered back into your life after you lost your memory. Killing you didn't work, so now he's using your amnesia to his advantage. It's disgusting."

I stew in my seat, fidgeting with my fingers. I don't know what to say. The picture she painted of Mason isn't what I see when I look at him. There's no universe where I can imagine him doing any of that. But I don't know if I should pretend to buy into her version of events or the version everyone else believes.

Zoe sniffles, swiping at a tear before it can fall. "Anyway, it's just speculation. You don't have to believe me," she finishes. "Just be careful."

The rest of the drive is stifling. Whatever happened at home seems to have completely distracted her from keeping a close eye on my behavior—she's too rattled to pay attention to how quickly my knee is bouncing.

She pulls into the parking lot of the trail haphazardly. We step outside, and the air is cool as the day creeps closer to nightfall. Zoe trudges onto the path without a word, and I follow, trying not to lose my footing. The deeper we go into the woods, the louder the disembodied shouts and laughter floating toward us become. Sticking my hands into my pockets, I feel a chill rack my body. This place is a lot more welcoming in the daylight.

I hasten to fall in line with Zoe. "Do you know if Damien is coming?"

She refuses to look at me, veering in a different direction than the waterfall. "Who knows?"

We reach a clearing, where flames flicker in a large fire pit. People sit on logs surrounding the fire and dance next to the makeshift sound system, moving in time to the throbbing bassline. The party is in the beginning stages but there are already loads of people here.

A boy I vaguely recognize from my history class is standing next to a folding table, filling up a line of plastic shot glasses. Zoe grabs one without waiting for permission, tossing it back with ease.

The boy watches her, impressed. "Damn, okay."

Wincing slightly, she sets the empty shot glass on the table before reaching for the next one. To my surprise, she passes it to me, letting me know she actually is aware of my presence.

"Oh thanks," I mumble. I don't want to drink a lot tonight. I need to stay focused, but I also need to keep up appearances.

Zoe picks up another glass, tapping it against mine, and together, we throw them back. I can't hold back my grimace as the alcohol burns my throat, and I make a face, sticking my tongue out.

She laughs shortly. "Don't tell me the amnesia made you a light-weight too."

"I'm going to pace myself tonight."

"Suit yourself."

Zoe wanders away, most likely in search of something else to drink, and I take a seat on a tree stump, watching as more people trail into the clearing.

A tap on my shoulder causes me to jump and whirl around, my heart in my throat. Mason holds his hands up in surrender at my overreaction, and I take a deep breath, immediately relaxing.

"Don't do that." I scold him, my cheeks warming.

"My bad. How's it going?"

"Zoe is freaked. She got into a really intense fight with her dad about the cops questioning her before she came here. She spent most of the ride convincing me she's innocent."

I refrain from telling him the part where she tried to pin everything on him.

"Shit," he says, voice low. "We should give her some space then. Any sign of Damien?"

"Not yet."

Mason turns back to look at me, studying my features as a gentle breeze toys with his hair. "You good?"

"Am I ever?"

"Sometimes." He gives me a knowing half smile. The moment hangs in the air, and I let myself imagine what it would be like to be able to step forward and kiss him again.

Mason clears his throat, reaching up to scratch the back of his neck, and I refocus on the task at hand. The music reverberates inside of my skull, making a headache form at my temple. I look to my left in time to see Zoe shotgun a beer while the people around her egg her on.

She finishes, letting the can fall to the ground and lifting her hands up in victory. I've never seen her like this. She's always been poised and put together, unwilling to let anyone see the chips in the marble, but tonight she doesn't appear to care.

"I didn't know you had it in you, Harris," the same boy from before shouts, offering her a high five, and she beams, cheeks rosy as she slaps her hand against his.

A cool breeze hits the exposed skin on my neck, and I shiver, turning in the direction of the mouth of the trail as two more people step into the clearing. Damien and James. They're welcomed by raucous shouts of the other members of the soccer team, and Damien grins, basking in all of the attention.

"The man of the hour has arrived," Mason says sardonically, watching with an unimpressed look on his face.

I grimace, then walk over to the table and return with another shot. Mason watches me, arms folded in amusement as I swallow it, working to keep the disgust off of my face. After taking care of the empty glass, I shake my hands out and bounce on the balls of my feet, feeling queasy.

"All right." I breathe, steeling myself. "Let's do this."

Taking a step in Damien's direction, I don't make it very far before Mason's voice stops me.

"Alina."

I turn back to him expectantly, and he takes a step toward me, causing the space between us to shrink. I wait for him to say something more, but he doesn't. Instead, he lifts a hand, cupping my face and leaving my skin with a tingling sensation.

He taps my bottom lip with his thumb gently before lowering his hand and stepping back again. "Be careful."

"I will."

Feeling a little more reassured now, I turn around to face the party. Damien hasn't noticed me yet, and I'm grateful for that simple fact; I'm sure if he witnessed what just happened, it would ruin our whole plan. He needs to think I'm attainable.

I approach my two former friends where they chat near the fire, lifting a hand to get their attention.

"Hey," I say meekly.

Damien instantly turns at the sound of my voice. I nod at James, and he nods in return, looking curious.

"Allie," Damien breathes, my name sounding reverent coming from his lips.

"I'm glad you guys are here."

"You know I won't miss a party. Especially if *you're* in attendance," James says, apparently over the awkwardness already.

I'd nearly forgotten about his tendency to flirt at every possible opportunity.

"Zoe said you wanted to talk to me." Damien's eyes already look a bit hazy, and when I pay closer attention, James is the same way. Seems like they got the party started before they arrived.

"I do," I say, hoping my expression comes across as sincere. "Can we grab a drink?"

He nods eagerly. "Of course."

Damien fetches us a couple of beers from the cooler, and after bidding good-bye to James, we set off on a different path. Just as we leave the party, I spot Mason in the crowd, and the sight lends me one last surge of courage before he's out of sight completely.

It's significantly quieter here. I can feel my heartbeat in my throat as we traipse down the trail, the noises of the party fading into nothing. I gesture for Damien to take a seat on a nearby log and, while he's not looking, slide my phone out of my pocket, preparing to set up a voice recording.

After tapping the red button, I pocket it again, turning around and taking a seat next to him.

"What'd you want to talk to me about?" he asks, passing me a beer. His voice makes it painfully obvious that he's trying to sound casual and keep his expectations low, but I'm certain he thinks I'm about to ask him to get back together.

He's not entirely wrong.

"I wanted to tell you I was sorry."

His thick eyebrows shoot up in surprise, rising to his curly hairline. "Really?"

"I regret what happened between us," I say, my fingers cooled by the can tucked in my hands. "I just . . . I got so overwhelmed with everything that was going on, I needed to press pause."

There's a childlike sympathy on his face. "I understand why you did it."

"You do?"

"It totally makes sense. And I figured if I gave you space . . ." He trails off, and I feel my eye twitch. "You might come back."

My grip tightens on the beer. "Well, you were right. I miss you, Damien."

Hope sparkles on his features, and he reaches out, taking one of my hands between his. This recording is going to be brutal to listen to later. "I miss you too. So much. I don't want us to be apart anymore."

"Me neither." I squeeze his hand, resisting the urge to drop it like it's on fire. "But I need you to tell me something first."

Damien tilts his head, confused.

I concentrate on keeping my face a combination of soft and stern. I can't sound angry or accusatory because it could scare him away.

"Damien," I say, and his eyebrows pull together. "I need to know what you did."

"What do you mean?"

"When we broke up, you said you wanted to take something back. I need to know what it was."

Slowly, the meaning of my words dawns on him, and his frown clears. He slides his hand out of mine, and I feel my heart clench, worried I've screwed everything up. But then he leans forward, burying his face in his hands.

"Shit," he mutters.

The woods are eerily hushed as I wait for him to continue. He takes in a ragged breath, and I run my clammy palms over my jeans as my legs begin to shake.

"I didn't mean for it to happen," he finally says, voice hollow and muffled.

I lean closer, wanting the audio on the recording to be clear, and place a comforting hand on his back. "For what to happen? You can tell me."

After a lengthy pause, he sits up, on the verge of tears. "I shouldn't have kissed Zoe."

It takes me a second to realize what he said. I blink, giving my head a shake, certain I must have heard wrong. "Huh?"

"It happened on the night of your accident," he continues, sniffling. "You guys were fighting. Zoe got me alone. She was really drunk and she told me everything. About you and Parker."

My stomach flips. "What are you—"

"And then she came onto me," he blurts. "I kissed her back because I was really upset. I felt like I took advantage of her." He sighs, dragging a hand through his hair, looking guilty. "I guess I always kind of knew she had a crush on me. I didn't think it was that serious, though."

I exhale sharply, realization dawning on me like a bucket of cold water. It all makes sense. Zoe is in love with Damien.

When you have something other people want, they hate you for it. But this can't have all been over a *boy*.

"What happened after that?" I ask, trying to keep my breathing steady.

He clamps his mouth shut, and I feel a surge of panic. There's no way I'm letting him stop now.

"Damien," I urge, voice cracking.

He holds my gaze for another beat before continuing, sounding sorrowful. "You caught us. She threatened to tell your sister about the Parker thing. I'd never seen you so angry. You said you never wanted to see either of us again, and then you started going off about sending some email. I had no idea what you were talking about, but it seemed to really spook Zoe. It was weird."

The letter to McGill.

He scoots closer to me, reaching for my hands again. "Allie, I don't care about any of the bad stuff that happened in the past," he remarks. "I don't care that you cheated. None of it matters. All that matters is right now. I just want to be with you."

My head is spinning, and I shake it vehemently. "Damien, tell me what else happened that night."

"I—I can't," he whispers. "It's too awful. And Zoe would get mad."

"Why would she get mad?"

"Just forget about it. That's what I did."

Bile rises up in my throat. I can't play pretend anymore.

Pushing his hands away, I stand up, and he looks at me with a floored expression. "Don't touch me."

"Allie?"

I know I should try to coax more information out of him, but I think it would require giving him more of myself than I would like. Besides, I'm too wired to control my reactions. Hauling in a shaky breath, I turn around to head back to the party, ignoring Damien's calls for me to stay.

Squeezing my eyes shut, I place my hand on a tree trunk, taking a second to calm down. I need to find Mason.

"You know."

The sudden voice from behind me causes the hair on my neck to rise, and I whirl around.

Zoe is standing a short distance away, looking haunted, so still it's like she's made of porcelain. The rest of the trail is empty, and I immediately regret my decision to come out here. The party feels miles away. Panic seizes my bones as I take a trembling step backward.

"Oh hey." I breathe deeply. "You scared me."

Her lips curve into a slow, small smile, and it's as though her soul has been sucked out. "You know what happened."

"What are you talking about?" I feign ignorance. "Are you feeling okay?"

She tilts her head to the side. "You don't have to pretend anymore."

I continue to inch away. "I don't know what you're saying."

Zoe takes a step toward me, a flurry of emotions flying across her delicate features: regret, guilt, sadness, and rage. When she speaks again, her voice is soft.

"I can't let you leave."

The words strike a chord of fear in my chest. She takes another step closer, reaching out a hand. Before I can think about what I'm doing, I shove her off the path and into a tree trunk, and she stumbles against it.

I'm halfway down the trail before she hits the ground.

22 | RECKONING

Adrenaline has my heart in my throat as I move through the trees.

My vision is swaying, fear making it hard to see straight as I make it back to the party, searching for a head of dark hair in the crowd. Mason stands on the outskirts, a red Solo cup in his hand as he surveys the scene. When he sees me and the horrified look on my face, he surges forward, and we meet in the middle.

"Alina—"

"We have to leave!"

Without giving him more of an explanation or a chance to respond, I grab his wrist, dragging him to the trail that leads back to the parking lot, and he stumbles along behind me. The forest feels thick, impenetrable, and never ending.

Mason waits until we're far out of earshot of the party to speak. "What happened?"

"Damien," I say between breaths. "He told me too much. Zoe overheard."

Remembering my phone, I reach into my pocket, stopping the recording. With trembling fingers, I crank up the volume and hold the phone between us. Mason inclines his head toward me as I play it back. A lot of it is hard to hear over our footsteps, the device being in my pocket at the time of recording, and the sorrowful, reserved nature of Damien's confession.

And then it gets close to the end, when Zoe found me. This time it sounds like she says "I can't let you *live*."

I have to suppress the urge to vomit.

Mason is at a loss for words, mouth floundering. "Where are we supposed to go?"

"I don't know," I say, shaking my head. "But we had to get out of there."

My mind is reeling. For nearly two months I've questioned what happened to me, why it happened, and who made it happen at all. To suddenly have the motive and the culprit and an almost confession after all this time is surreal. I never thought she would admit it. I thought it would be vehement denial until there was irrefutable proof.

The truth is in my hands, but I still don't know how we can bring it to light. We have evidence of what she did to Jacob Griffin, though we can't prove she was involved in my accident.

"Shit," Mason says abruptly, making me snap to attention.

He's staring at the woods a short distance away, watching the shadows move. If he sees them, too, that means they're real. My body goes numb as he grabs my hand, tugging me until we're pressed against the other side of a large tree, hidden from view.

"What do we do?" I whisper as he peers around it, jaw set.

"Call the police."

The idea of cops doesn't reassure me. "But Officer Edwards—"

"They're already suspicious of her," he interjects. "We have no other choice."

I swallow, scanning the forest. It's easy to hide in here. In the blue light, my vision plays tricks on me, and I listen to the chirping of the crickets, the rustle of the leaves. It feels like one of my nightmares, one that I can't wake up from. Gripping my phone tightly, I make the call, my pulse loud in my ears.

"Nine-one-one, what's your emergency?"

"I'm being followed," I say hastily, working to keep my voice down.

"My name is Alina Castillo. Two months ago, someone tried to kill me, and now they're following me. I'm at Boulder Trail—"

A sudden flash of blond hair, silver in the moonlight, paralyzes me, and the phone falls to the ground.

Distantly, I can hear the operator's voice, but Mason has clapped his hand over my mouth and pulled my back against his chest. She hasn't spotted us yet. Pine needles and branches crunch beneath her feet as she stalks past our hiding spot, a blade glinting in her hand, and I hold my breath, my thoughts going into a tailspin.

Immediately, an image resurfaces.

I'm in a car that's just been struck by something, spiraling dangerously before lurching to a halt. It takes a few seconds for me to gather my bearings, brain foggy with confusion, though when I register what just happened, I painstakingly shove my door open, stumbling to the ground.

"Allie!" I hear a panicked voice.

Rage settles in my bones as I storm toward it. "What did you do to me?"

"It was an accident, I swear—"

"Like hell it was! You're crazy!"

I turn to make for the forest, wiping blood from my forehead. Three figures follow me into the dark.

"Alina!"

Gasping, I come back to the present, latching onto Mason's voice.

My gaze is blurry and unfocused, and I have to blink rapidly to clear it. His face has paled, hands gripping my arms.

"Are you all right? What the hell is going on?"

I shake my head to get rid of the ghostly sound of tires squealing. "Nothing. I'm fine."

"That wasn't nothing. It looked like you were losing consciousness—"

"Is she gone?"

Mason's jaw ticks. "I think so."

"Then let's keep moving."

With bated breath, we move through the trees as carefully as possible. I concentrate on keeping my footsteps light, avoiding the branches beneath my feet. Far off in the distance, Zoe's singsong voice calls out for me, and it's impossible to discern which direction it's coming from. I don't trust my brain; it's still having difficulty staying in the present.

Out of nowhere, a figure streaks across our path, and I come to a shuddering halt.

James tackles Mason, sending the two of them tumbling to the ground, rolling down the steep incline. I follow them, my hands scraping against bark as I grab branches to keep myself upright, feet sliding in the dirt. Grabbing a fistful of Mason's shirt, James clocks him in the jaw, and my stomach bottoms out.

"Stop!"

"Hey, doll." He grins, eyes bloodshot.

"Let him go, James."

"Wish I could, sweetheart. You know I'd do anything for you. But we're in too deep. It's out of my hands." Pausing, he glances down at Mason. "Metaphorically, of course."

When he reaches out to deliver another blow, Mason blocks it, grabbing James's arm with gritted teeth. Using his free hand, he sucker punches James, winding him, and takes the opportunity to flip over, sitting upright. There's a mess of limbs and elbows, but Mason manages to maintain his advantage.

He turns to me, blood trailing from his nose. "Run," he tells me, voice low. "I can handle him."

Panic makes my throat seize up. "I'm not leaving you—"

"*Run.*"

Acting on a whim, I bolt in the direction of the mouth of the trail. I dart through the trees, veering off the path and jumping over tree trunks and fallen logs, letting out a string of breathy expletives.

"See you later, doll!" James's voice is distant and haunting, echoing through the forest.

One of my boots catches on a root, sending me tumbling down a small overhang of earth, and a strangled yelp leaves my mouth. I land on a large stone, inhaling sharply, and forcing down another scream of pain.

Gritting my teeth, I clench my fists, looking up to the top of the hill I just fell from. The good part about my descent is that I'm shielded from view now. The bad part is everything else.

I try to ignore the searing pain flaring up on every inch of my skin and drag myself along the ground closer to the edge of the hill, blowing away a strand of hair that falls into my face.

My name bounces throughout the woods, like a twisted game of hide and seek, as I reach the wall of earth, sitting up and leaning my back against it. I tuck my knees to my chest, hoping I've concealed myself enough, straining to listen for any sounds of nearby life. My fall was loud, but I don't know where anyone is. Noise is distorted here, coming from all directions, and my muddled brain can't make sense of it.

A loud thud causes me to flinch, and Zoe appears in front of me.

She straightens up, her hair mussed, a couple of leaves tangled among the blond. "There you are."

I struggle to take in a breath, inching away. The blade in her hand catches the light, and she walks leisurely, as if she's in no rush to finish.

"Why are you doing this?" I ask, pleading. If I keep her distracted, it could give me time to think of a plan.

"Because you left me no choice!" she reiterates, the words teetering into hysteria. "You were going to destroy my life. My family. My reputation."

I continue to back up inconspicuously, and she takes a slow step closer. I've never seen someone look so undone.

"Ever since we met, you've been evil." Her expression becomes stormy, eyebrows drawing together. "I told you I loved him, and you slept with him! And then proceeded to flaunt your relationship in front of my face for two years."

Damien.

"Zoe, I'm sorry—"

"Shut up!" she shouts, tension visible in her shoulders. "For once, just listen to me. You didn't even really care about him. You cheated on him with your own sister's boyfriend. What a vile, pathetic excuse for a human being."

"What you did to Jacob is worse," I counter, anger making my body rigid.

"It was necessary," she bites back. "People like him just take up space."

"How can you say that?"

"I don't think you understand what would happen to me if I wasn't the best at every single aspect of my life. I would be nothing. Jacob needed to stop taking what was mine."

A chill courses down my spine at the callous way she talks about the boy she nearly killed. Images similar to the flashback I had before begin to resurface, and I work to ward them off. I need to concentrate.

"Anyway, I found out about your little affair," she sneers, crossing her arms, gripping the knife tightly. "You didn't do a very good job of hiding it. I wanted you to come clean and tell Damien, but you refused. I told you if you wouldn't do it, I'd do it for you, and I'd tell Audrey too.

"You didn't like that. Then you drafted up that god-awful email to McGill to try to get them to revoke my acceptance. You knew it would ruin my life. Everyone would've known what I did to Jacob. My parents, they would've—"

Her face threatens to break at that, and I remember her father pounding on the hood of her car as we sped away. Something akin to sympathy twists in my conscience, and once more I work to tamp it down. This girl is currently monologuing about her failed homicide attempts while brandishing a knife.

"I got drunk at that stupid party. I told Damien everything, and I kissed him," she spits. "When you caught us, you flipped out. You said you were going to send that email. I couldn't let you get away with that."

In the dim light of the moon, I can see her eyes glimmer with held-back tears. It's the most human and vulnerable I've seen her. I hate that I'm feeling any amount of pity. But when I look at her, I see someone who's been treated poorly by nearly everyone around her. That's not to say she didn't deserve some of it.

"I didn't intend for it to happen, but when I saw your car, I couldn't make myself stop. It all happened so fast. I *wanted* to hurt you."

Her voice comes to me again, from that day when we stood outside at the back of the school. *Maybe you got angry and did it before you could really think about it.* She wasn't trying to comfort me, she was trying to comfort herself.

"But then I panicked. You were furious. None of us wanted to get in trouble for what happened. So I took it upon myself to solve the problem and buy us more time." She examines the knife in her hands. "I knocked you out. We smashed your car into a tree, not far from here. I put booze in the trunk so that even if you remembered what happened, nobody would believe you."

It's odd to have the true details of the accident laid out so simply. The flashbacks make sense now: leaving the party upset, getting out of the car, my shouted words of betrayal, the bloodstained hands. She didn't plan for me to survive the crash, so she took matters into her own hands.

"The amnesia was an unexpected bonus," she says, smiling audaciously. "For a while, I felt guilty, so I was nice to you. I thought it would be my penance for what I did. I thought it would throw you off from the truth, even if you did someday get your memory back."

She takes in my feeble position on the ground, sobering up again.

"I realize now that the only way to completely solve the problem is to get rid of you."

When she takes a step toward me, I spring up from the ground and dart into the trees. I hear her growl of frustration as she moves to follow me.

"I thought we established that running was useless," she calls out.

It may be useless, but I have no other choice.

I scramble to get traction on the uneven ground as it inclines upward, clutching roots and trying not to trip over my own feet again. A cacophony of footsteps fills my ears, and though I don't look behind me, I know that Zoe isn't alone anymore. The others must be getting close.

Fingers take hold of my hair and yank me backward, and I scream in pain, trying to stay upright. It doesn't work, and Zoe easily sends me straight back to the ground. My back slams against the dirt, and the movement is a jolt to my rib cage, knocking the wind out of me.

She doesn't give me time to recover, straddling me with her teeth bared, hair falling into her face. I hurriedly lift my arms to protect my chest as she raises the knife, trying to gain clear access to my body. I seize her wrist, feeling the tension in her muscles, squeezing tightly.

"Please don't do this," I beg.

"Stop talking!" Her voice is frantic. Frightened.

The blade scrapes against my arm and red hot pain flares across my skin. I grit my teeth, using all the force I can manage to flip us over, and she grunts as her back hits the ground. Having the upper hand now, I'm able to wrestle the knife away. It slips from her grasp, sliding through the dirt until it comes to a stop somewhere in the underbrush. She rushes to get it, but I pin her arms down, unwilling to let her move.

Her head jerks forward into mine, busting my lip and snapping my head back. While I'm injured, she uses the opportunity to shove me off of her, kicking my stomach and crawling away.

I groan, clutching my torso and tasting blood before using my free hand to push myself up from the ground. Zoe digs through the brush, desperately searching for her weapon. Painstakingly, I force myself to my feet. Locating a large branch, I lunge for it. With Zoe's back facing me, I creep toward her, breathing heavily, and raise the branch above my head.

When she begins to turn around, I bring it down against her skull.

It's not enough to be a fatal blow, but it momentarily incapacitates her, and she collapses to the forest floor with a grunt, landing among the pine needles and leaves.

Leaving her behind, I continue on my journey, racing up the hill, until I have no choice but to stop.

The path no longer stretches on in front of me, and instead I'm standing at the edge of a small cliff, the ground below hard to see through the darkness and distance.

Shit.

"Allie!"

Damien's voice makes me whirl around, and I exhale shakily, watching him race toward me, James in tow. Zoe appears shortly after, looking furious. The one missing face makes my heart clench.

"Stop running," Damien pleads, holding his hands out in surrender, his eyebrows tipping upward. "I never wanted any of this to happen. Please, just stop!"

I want to take a step away, but there's nowhere else to run. Maybe this really is the end.

He motions for the other two to stay behind then continues to walk toward the top of the hill, looking at me imploringly. "Allie, I love you," he says, voice clogged with emotion, looking disheveled. "I told you, I don't care what you did in the past! I've made mistakes too. I'm not proud of what I did. But all I care about is being with you."

Damien extends his arms to me, beckoning me to embrace him. I watch him warily, keeping my guard up.

"If you come with me now, we can put all of this behind us," he says. "I promise I won't let her hurt you anymore."

He gets closer, nearly within reach now. I take the tiniest step back, extremely careful of my footing, knowing full well that one wrong move could send me careening over the edge.

I let him take one of my hands in his. "I just want to have a happy life with you," he declares.

"For Christ's sake." Zoe's irritated voice causes him to flinch. "She doesn't love you, Damien. She never has."

"Yes, she does. Right, Allie?"

I know I should speak, but my heart is pounding too quickly, my head is spinning.

His smile fades, demeanor changing. "Right?" he presses.

"I love you."

The answer makes his eyebrows draw together, though realization takes him a few moments longer. "You're lying," he says, voice breaking. He lets go of my hand. "You've been lying this whole time."

"No, I—"

"How could you?" he shouts, face contorting in rage. "My life *revolves* around you."

Damien grabs my arm roughly. I let out a cry of pain and wriggle to get out of his grasp, dangerously close to the cliff's edge, breathing hard.

"Let go of her!"

The sudden new voice causes all of us to freeze, and my heart leaps. Mason appears, hurrying up the hill, dried blood sticking to his skin and fury visible on his features, even in the low light. The sight of him makes relief swell in my chest.

He's okay.

He storms toward us, never breaking stride for a second. Damien looks between Mason and me, becoming even more outraged.

"This is your fault, isn't it?" he accuses. "You stole her from me! Well, we'll see who gets to have her now."

Damien lunges toward me, a chunk of the dirt beneath my feet falling away as I recoil, and I gasp, seizing a nearby tree trunk to keep myself from tumbling downward. But before Damien can touch me, Mason springs forward, shoving the other boy with great force.

Terror in his eyes, Damien yells, his arms flailing, before he disappears from view, catapulting to the forest floor far below.

23 | FINALE

Everything, all at once.

I black out for what feels like an eternity but must really only be a handful of seconds. For a brief, blinding moment, I'm transported out of the forest and into the deepest of recesses in my brain, revealing my previously unrecoverable memory bank. And, like the persistent rushing of a waterfall, my memories wash over me, hitting me square in the chest and making it hard to breathe. It feels like a remarkable phenomenon, but at the same time, it feels unceremonious.

I remember everything.

Growing up with Audrey, fighting over trivial things like dolls and candy when we were little and then things like boys and clothes when we were older. I remember laughing with her, sharing secrets in the latest hours of the night. I remember drifting apart as we grew older, our conversations quickly dissolving into screaming matches as all of us fumbled through our unresolved problems and abandonment issues.

I remember my dad.

The way he was always the parent I was closest to, how he was my confidant and best friend. Until he betrayed us all in the worst way, choosing a younger woman over the three of us, packing up and disappearing out of our lives without so much as a good-bye. And

I remember how my heart still breaks every year on my birthday when all I receive from him is radio silence.

Images come flooding back, as if I'm recalling them one by one, and I remember bursts of different life stages: My drunken kiss with Parker in the middle of the night, the pounding bassline of a distant party as our soundtrack. The night I ended up falling into bed with Damien and being unable to rid myself of him for the next two years. My camaraderie with James. My curiosity about Mason, the mysterious figure from my childhood who's always had my heart. My ever-growing and dangerous feud with Zoe.

Then there are the more haunting memories. The horrible night of the accident returns to me in flashes I'd rather not dwell on, bearing striking similarities to my current circumstances.

It's as though I'm coming back into my body after a long absence, finally awake and aware of everything. My skin feels like my own again, and it's a relief and a burden at the same time. I'm able to breathe after being starved for air for far too long.

And then I register what's just happened—the reason I blacked out in the first place.

I'm standing at the cliff's edge, hanging on tightly to a tree, the bark rough beneath my skin. I peer over the edge, barely able to make out a disfigured body lying at the bottom. If I squint hard, I can see a gaping mouth and wide eyes that stare at the starless sky, unseeing.

My senses return one by one. Scent follows after touch and eyesight, the smell of pine needles mixing with blood and sweat reaches my nose. Finally, the sound comes back.

Zoe is screaming, crouched on the ground a few feet away, clutching the grass and staring over the edge of the cliff, face caked with dirt and tears. Mason has gone pale, looking haunted, as James vomits into the bushes.

Mason takes a shaky step backward, and I find my gaze drawn to Damien's body again.

"You killed him!" Zoe screams, scrambling to her feet. She fumbles for the knife again, holding it out in front of her, but she's unable to hold it steady.

James quickly approaches her, wiping his mouth with the back of his hand and stepping in front of Mason. "It's over, Zo," he says, voice hollow. "Give it up."

The fight leaves her and she drops the blade, letting it thump to the ground as she collapses against James's chest. In trying to destroy me, the only person she truly cared about wound up getting destroyed instead.

Mason doesn't even seem to notice her, looking in my direction instead, and somehow that's the thing that breaks me. A sob bubbles up from my throat, and I let go of the tree trunk, throwing myself at him. He catches me in his arms, and we stumble backward as he tightens his grip, burying his face in my shoulder.

I can't find it in me to speak, I only continue to wail as I cling to him, my fingers tightening around the material of his sweater. He whispers in my ear, his voice soothing, though it's impossible to hear what he's saying over the sound of my tears.

Both my mind and body are unable to process anything that just happened, and it all feels like a bizarre dream, like something I'd access during a hypnotherapy session with Dr. Meyer: absurd and murky. All I know is that I nearly plummeted to my death, and somebody else took the fall.

I feel Mason stop moving beneath me, pulling away slightly as his body stiffens. I lean back, looking up at him in concern, only to see him looking at something behind me.

I watch as beams of light dart over the trees and the forest floor, followed by the sound of heavy footfalls. A group of officers breaks free from the woods and steps into the clearing, flashlights in hand and guns at the ready.

"Everybody, hands up!" one of them shouts. "Now!"

"Shit," James mumbles.

Mason reluctantly takes a step away from me, lifting his hands and squinting at the bright lights. I follow suit, heart pounding persistently in my chest.

James does the same, but it takes Zoe longer, too caught up in her grief to realize what's happening around her. The cops rush in, wasting no time before wrestling the boys' hands into cuffs. An officer comes up behind me, doing the same, and it's hard to understand them through all the shouting and screaming. My arms ache as they're twisted behind me, the metal cool against my wrists.

Before I'm ushered down the hill, I catch sight of a familiar face.

Officer Edwards watches me, a complicated expression on his harsh features. It's a mixture of guilt and remorse, and it gives me a sick sense of satisfaction as I'm carted away to the back of a police car.

The Pender Falls Police Station is a familiar place.

Months back, I used to spend a lot of time here for various misdemeanors, usually with Zoe in tow. I'd sit next to her, my arms folded, my lips curled in a smug smirk to match hers, knowing that between her father and my mother, they would be able to pull some strings to get us out of facing punishment for whatever we'd just done. It was a strange, addicting kind of power, and back then, I was always searching for power. Even though I despised the girl, at the best of times, we could put it all aside to be partners in crime, the world at our fingertips.

Now Damien is dead, and I'm back in the interrogation room. I sit across from Officer Edwards, burning a hole in his desk with my dismal stare.

I've repeated the events that transpired what must be a million times by now, my voice steady and monotonous, beginning with my arrival and ending with Damien falling to his death. It took even longer to explain all of the context—my tumultuous relationship with Zoe and the truth about what happened to Jacob Griffin. For a lot of it, Edwards appeared to be speechless, sitting back in his chair, shaking his head and running a hand across his face.

Pender Falls is a small town. Nothing like this has ever happened here. Drug busts are usually the most exciting part of a policeman's job. Not three consecutive homicide attempts. This is a high-profile case sure to garner media attention, especially considering the affluence of the Harris family and Zoe herself. Who isn't fascinated by a beautiful teenage girl out for blood?

Different parts of my body ache, and I feel worn out and beaten down. When I catch a glimpse of myself in the bathroom mirror, it is jarring. My pupils are cold and dark, like a frozen lake in the dead of night, splotches of blue and purple have rapidly formed on my jaw, and my bottom lip is red and swollen. I long to crawl into bed and forget any of this ever happened, but I know the images of what happened tonight are forever burned into my brain.

It's ironic—now that my memory has returned, I want nothing more than to forget all over again.

Edwards folds his hands on the table, looking at me squarely. "Allie, I believe an apology is long overdue. I was wrong about you," he says. "About what happened."

He sighs when my expression doesn't change, sitting back again. "I was acting on instinct, and there are some things I did that were out of line. We were getting close to piecing together what really happened, and something told me you played a bigger part in it than you did. But you were the victim, I lost sight of that. I hope you can move past it and won't let my behavior affect your perception of the department."

I nod numbly, and it's all I can offer. Truly accepting his apology feels misguided considering he abused his position of power when he threatened me in the bookstore.

A weighted silence hangs in the room for several beats. "All right," he says firmly, rising to his feet. "I can't allow you to go home just yet, but you can join your family out there."

Relief floods my limbs, and I push up from my chair to follow him out the door. I don't know how long it's been since we left Boulder Trail, but I haven't been in contact with anyone but police and doctors until now. A lump forms in my throat as I step into the main area, tears welling at the idea of this all truly being over and being able to go home and feel safe again. Soon after exiting the interrogation room, I spot a familiar face, and I rush in that direction, enclosing the woman in a tight hug.

"Oh Allie," she says, her voice breaking, and it's my undoing.

"Mom," I choke out, feeling as though I'll fall apart the second she lets go.

She stiffens at my use of the word, and I can feel the shock in her posture. Momentarily, she pulls back to look at me, tendrils of hair slipping from her bun, her cheeks streaked with tears.

The only thing I can manage is a nod, and her face crumples in relief as she clutches me in another embrace that I return.

I've never considered myself as being particularly close to my mom, but I've also never realized how much I crave the comfort of her presence. She's strong and brave, and I truly believe she can fix anything and make bad things go away. Maybe she can make this go away too. I don't want her to let me go.

Eventually, she pulls back, assessing my appearance and pushing some of my hair from my face. "Why didn't you tell me any of this was going on?"

"I didn't know how," I choke out.

"I haven't been around as much as I should've. I've been so busy with work and trying to keep us all afloat that I didn't realize you were suffering. If I'd known, I would've done something—"

"Mom, you can't blame yourself," I tell her tearfully.

"How did this even happen? How did I miss the signs? I let you spend so much time with her—"

"It's not your fault."

She slides her phone out of her pocket, looking at the blank screen with a sigh of frustration. "I haven't heard from Audrey but she's supposed to be on her way here."

Right after she says the words, the girl herself rushes into the room, escorted by another officer who gestures in our direction and lets her go ahead. Audrey's eyes are shiny and red, and she heads straight to us, throwing her arms around me.

"Holy shit," she breathes, voice faltering.

Her presence nearly causes me to break once more. I truly wondered if I would ever see her again, if she would ever look at me with anything other than hatred.

"I'm sorry," I say.

She pulls back, shaking her head eagerly, taking in the various marks on my skin. "I'm so glad you're okay."

"I didn't know if you cared," I admit, my nose beginning to sting.

"Of course I care," she insists, bottom lip trembling. "You're my sister. We can deal with what happened between us later, but right now all that matters is that you're alive."

"Do you know what's going on?" I ask, voice sounding clogged.

"They're still interrogating Zoe and James," Mom says, rubbing my arm soothingly.

It strikes me again that it's over. Damien is dead. Zoe and James are in custody.

My memory is back.

It's not exactly the ending I'd been envisioning, but it's an ending, nonetheless. After far too many weeks of living in the shadows, I'm slowly stepping into the light, and it's blinding. Too blinding, almost.

"What about Mason?"

A flicker of sympathy flashes across her features. "They're questioning him too. Poor boy."

My heart clenches. "Why?"

"Well, he was the one to . . ." She pauses, looking reluctant. "They have to thoroughly investigate."

"But he saved my life," I protest, panic creeping into my chest. "He didn't do anything wrong. Damien would've killed me."

Mom winces at the thought, clearing her throat. "They need to determine whether it was manslaughter, self-defense, or accidental. If it happened the way you told the police it did, he should be fine."

"Can you help him?" Audrey cuts in.

She looks between the two of us, taking in the fear on my face. "If it comes to that, yes."

Her answer eases my anxiety a bit, a numb feeling creeping back into my bones, and I barely register the words as Officer Edwards finally gives us the go-ahead to leave this suffocating building and go home. Mom places her hand on my back, telling Edwards to give her any updates as she ushers me to the exit, Audrey in tow. I come to a halt, causing them to look back at me in concern.

"What's wrong?" Mom asks.

"I don't want to leave without seeing Mason," I say. "We should wait for him."

She opens her mouth to protest, but we're interrupted by a door opening across the room, and Mason exits, looking utterly exhausted, followed by an officer. Releasing myself from my mother's grasp, I head in his direction. He's talking with the officer escorting him, and he doesn't notice me at first. When he does, the hard edge in his heterochromatic eyes softens, a hint of relief evident within them. His face is streaked with blood.

"Hey," I greet softly. "How are you holding up?"

"I don't know yet," he tells me, speaking in a low murmur, and shaking his head. "It's like a never-ending nightmare. It doesn't feel real."

I feel a pressure at the back of my eyelids. "I know what you mean."

"Are you okay?"

"They said I could go home. I was just leaving."

He places a gentle hand on my arm. "You should get out of here before they change their minds."

"I wanted to see you and make sure you were all right," I whisper, vision blurring again, and he swallows visibly. A haunted look passes over his features, and I reach out, taking his hand in mine, intertwining our fingers and bringing them up to my lips.

Mason clears his throat, his lips lifting in a ghost of a smile. "I'll be okay. You can go."

"Okay." I reluctantly let go of his hand. "Call me when you get home."

"I will."

His attention shifts to something behind me, and I turn, seeing a new set of people enter. A worried-looking woman walks in, clutching her purse in front of her, and I recognize her as Mason's mother. But there's another face I vaguely remember, a man in a business suit with the same striking eyes as Mason, though they seem to be laced with something dark. He has a commanding air about him as he strides through the room, and most heads turn in his direction.

His father.

Mason bends forward slightly. "I'll talk to you later," he says through his teeth, nudging my back to push me forward softly, and I take the hint.

I rejoin my family, glancing over my shoulder to see a guarded mask has slipped over Mason's expression as he speaks with his father. He looks at me fleetingly, revealing nothing, before looking away again.

The minute I reach my mother, she guides me out the door. As we walk through the station, I catch a glimpse into one of the interrogation rooms.

Zoe sits alone, her arms resting on the table as she stares despondently at the wall. Her hair is matted, splotches of blood dotting her skin, and her expression looks soulless and vacant. I only see her for a second before I'm ushered outside.

In the parking lot, the night weighs upon me heavily. It feels like a hand is pressed to my chest, making it hard to breathe, a cloud of death and destruction hanging around me. Everything that I thought I knew about myself was ripped away from me and then given back in tattered shreds, and I'm unsure of how to fit it all together again.

But still, it's over.

24 | END / BEGIN

Time passes in a blur, sometimes moving quickly like a violent rush of water and at other times, unbearably slowly. Through all of it, my brain is under a constant cover of fog, and my days are hazy around the edges.

Despite how little I want to go back to school, my mother ensures that I finish out the rest of my senior year. My grades are far from stellar, but nearly dying twice seems to give me a free pass to do as poorly as I please. The hallways of Pender Falls High feel empty even during the busiest times of the day. Without Zoe, Damien, and James roaming them, the school is cavernous and haunting.

It's not the only way Damien haunts me. I often see his decaying face in my dreams.

Every day, I keep my head down, attend all my classes, and go back home to safety. Eventually, Mason comes back, too, and we stick to each other's sides like we're attached at the hip. On prom night we stay in, camping out in my living room and burning through a long list of horror movies. Our relationship has been in a strange form of limbo ever since everything went down—too involved to be just friends, while also having an unspoken agreement that it's not the right time to be anything more than that.

Graduation is a non-event. I walk across the stage, receive my diploma, pose for pictures with my family, and go through all of the motions. As soon as we leave the school, I feel a weight lift from my shoulders knowing that I'll never have to set foot in the building again and constantly be reminded of the worst time in my life.

At first, the case brings in a lot of media attention. All of my trauma is put on display for the world to see and sensationalize. Reporters wait outside our house, chomping at the bit, each of them wanting to be the one who gets the inside story. I don't speak to any of them. Mom tries to hide the newspapers from me, but I see the headlines talking about a deadly love triangle and homicidal teenagers out for revenge. To the general public, it must all seem wildly exciting: a toxic friendship, endless deceit, and a romance gone wrong like a Shakespearean tragedy.

The online theories and speculations about the private details of my life are hard to escape. The scandal is enough to put Pender Falls on the map. People like to refer to me as the girl who escaped death. Twice.

But despite the fact that Zoe has been locked away, far from being able to hurt me or anyone else anymore, I feel a deep sense of unrest in my soul and the unmistakable desire to leave.

The town of Pender Falls is a black hole. The memory of what happened may fade away eventually, but the headlines will always be there and so will the tombstone. Secrets and corruption cling to every corner, hiding in the shadows, and the ghosts of what happened will forever haunt me here.

Getting out is the only thing I can do to save myself.

My relationship with Audrey is far from where I'd like it to be, and there's still a distinct distance between us, but over time, it's slowly healing. Enough so that she's willing to let me crash with her in Vancouver until I find a place of my own. The temptation to start over in a new city where nobody knows anything about me is too tantalizing to resist.

On a warm June morning, I stand on the driveway of our house, gripping the handle of my suitcase and appraising the building, lifting a hand to shield my eyes. Mom watches me, her arms crossed over her chest as she sighs. It took a lot of convincing for her to let me go. Moving with no plans to attend school and no job lined up is less than ideal from her perspective, but she understands my reasoning.

"Just like that, both of my girls will be gone," she says wistfully.

My lips lift in a small smile. "We won't be far."

Scout wags her tail, sniffing at my legs persistently, as though she can sense change in the air. I bend over, sinking my fingers into her fur as a breeze toys with my hair. I'm going to miss having her follow me around.

"And you're absolutely sure about this?"

"Yes, Mom."

Straightening up again, I pull down the hem of my shorts, nerves twisting in my belly. Though this is what I've chosen for myself, I don't know that I'm making the right decision. I don't like that my mother will be alone now, but I'm well aware that she's more than capable of handling herself.

A car pulls into the driveway and I take a deep breath. Bracing myself, I loop my arms around her shoulders, emotion rising to a crest inside of me. We stay that way for a few beats, until the car door slams shut, and I lean back, the end of my nose stinging.

"Take care of yourself," Mom tells me softly.

"I will." I reassure her, though I'm not sure if the words are true.

We step apart, and I look over my shoulder to see Mason waiting next to the vehicle, his hands in his pockets.

"Hello, Mason," Mom says.

He nods his head in greeting. "Hi, Ms. Castillo."

"You've got a long drive ahead of you," she remarks, sniffling. "See if you can convince her to stay."

His eyes meet mine. "I've been trying."

I avert my gaze and give my mother one last squeeze before Mason helps me load my things into his car. Doing my best to hold back the tears, I slide into the passenger seat. Mom and Scout remain in the driveway as we back out, and I wave at them until they're out of sight.

It's quiet as we round the corner. Mason turns on the radio, and I'm grateful for the background noise. Leaning back against the seat, I watch the familiar scenery pass by outside my window. I haven't gotten used to what it's like to have my brain shoved full of memories, both old and new, like I'm remembering the lives of two different people.

I feel as though they've morphed into one now, making me who I am today, but I'm still figuring out who that is.

When we finally make it out of town, I refuse to look in the direction of Boulder Trail. Mason and I have never talked about it. We talked about the stuff that followed, the articles, and the news reporters showing up outside of our houses, but I don't think either of us can bear the conversation. He's been different ever since it happened; we both have. It's impossible to stay the same after going through something so awful.

He rolls down his window a touch, letting the early summer air filter into the car, before glancing between me and the road. "What are you thinking about?"

I turn to him, lifting a shoulder. "Nothing, really."

"Well, I'm thinking that I don't want you to leave."

It's a back and forth we've had for weeks, ever since I decided I was moving. He'd immediately wanted to go with me, but I told him I didn't think it was a good idea.

"Maybe you can come visit me someday."

"Do you want me to?"

"What do you mean?"

He watches the winding road ahead of us. "I just don't know what you actually want."

My heart sinks. "It's complicated."

A tense silence fills the car, backed by the fuzzy rock station cutting in and out as we weave through the mountains.

"You know, you can just tell me the truth," he says, voice low. "That getting your memory back changed the way you feel about me."

"What?"

"You've looked at me differently ever since."

I shake my head resolutely. "That's not true. I care about you, Mason. So much. That's the one thing that hasn't changed."

His expression is clouded over and stormy, as if he's not sure whether to believe me. My heart aches at the thought of hurting him, and I have to turn away, clearing my throat again.

"So, where does that leave us?"

"I think we could both use some space," I murmur honestly. "I just . . . I want to find out who I am outside of all of this. If there was a way for me to do that with you, trust me, I would in a heartbeat. But as of right now, I don't think there is."

He exhales through his nose. "Don't I get a say in this?"

"Mason," I say. "Do you really think we would be happy together?"

"We don't have to *be* together," he argues. "The way things are right now is enough."

"It's not fair to either of us. You told me before that it wasn't the right time, things aren't any different now."

The air in the car has become heavy. Mason laughs shortly without humor, dragging a hand across his face. "Fuck," he remarks. "I guess it's finally my turn to have my heart broken by Alina Castillo."

His final statement is like a slap to the face, and I swallow the lump in my throat.

"I'm sorry," I say, voice breaking. "Please understand."

"If that's what you want."

The rest of the drive is uncomfortable, and I wish it didn't have to end this way. We make our way into the city a couple of hours later, moving slowly through traffic to get to the address Audrey sent me earlier. When we pull up outside of an apartment complex, Mason helps me unload my things onto the sidewalk.

And then all that's left is good-bye.

I stick my hands in my pockets, standing a couple of feet away from him on the pavement, and he looks at me for the first time in what feels like ages. I take in his dark hair and brilliant eyes, committing them to memory, feeling a pang of sadness in my chest.

He studies my face intently, as if he's doing the same, and it causes my vision to blur again. I've never questioned my decision more than I am right now. What am I supposed to do without him?

"I guess that's it," he says, and I'm relieved to hear that the animosity has vanished from his voice.

I bite the inside of my cheek. "I guess so."

"Take care, Alina."

"You too."

He clears his throat, turning to head back to the car, and panic creeps into my throat, spurring me to take a step forward. Before I know what I'm doing, my fingers are curling around his wrist, causing him to freeze. The moment he faces me again, I wrap my arms around his torso, breathing in his familiar scent and basking in the feeling of his arms around me for the last time when he finally returns the embrace.

"Thank you," I whisper. "For everything. I hope when we meet again, it's the right time."

Reluctantly, I let him go, then rise onto my tiptoes to press a lingering kiss to his cheek. His mouth hitches into a half smile, and he runs his thumb along my bottom lip then steps away.

"Me too."

I stay on the sidewalk long after he's gone. There's an inky blackness that's made itself at home inside of me ever since that traumatic night in the woods, and it will take copious amounts of cleaning to get rid of the stain. I've yet to know if I've chosen the right path, and anxiety brews in my stomach at the fear of the unknown.

But for the first time that I can remember, my life feels like it's mine.

ACKNOWLEDGEMENTS

First of all, I want to extend a massive thank-you to my lovely readers. Whether you've been with me for years or just stumbled upon me recently, I appreciate you all the same. Your encouragement, fangirling, constructive criticism, and endless support have gotten me where I am today. This book wouldn't exist without all of you!

I'm eternally grateful to the team at Wattpad for giving me this opportunity and to the platform itself for all that it's brought into my life since I joined in 2012. I've met so many wonderful friends, connected with a slew of amazing writers, and most importantly, I've had a safe space to share my writing and foster my creativity. There's a special kind of magic that comes with telling stories—it's a chance to step into someone else's shoes and live their life for a little while. I consider it a privilege, one that I probably wouldn't have kept up with if it weren't for Wattpad.

Thank you to the friends who helped me do the dang thing: Sarah, for being with the story since day one and supporting it since then without fail, for listening to me read chapters aloud and giving me advice, and for always managing to boost my writing confidence. Taylor, for being someone I greatly admire, for taking the time to look over the book in detail in the midst of your other projects, for answering all of my questions, and for putting up with my stream of shitposts and TikToks. Gabby, for constantly being such a delight even when the FaceTime connection is terrible (sorry), for being the number one *Blackout* hype girl, for listening to me whine about editing, and for being the first to offer to play Alina in the nonexistent movie adaptation (my people will call your people). Simone, for being my soul sister, for believing in this book even when I didn't, for ranting with me whenever the need arises (which is often), and for being someone I will forever want to be more like.

To everyone else who's shaped my writing and online experiences in a positive way: Patty, Shay, and Donovan (the surviving active members of the group chat), Brittany, Ann, Presley, Ivey, and Kate. You've all provided me with friendship, encouragement, and inspiration whether we talk all the time or have only had a handful of conversations.

To my sweet lifelong friends who've been there for me throughout all of this: Anna, Kenzie, and Sharmaine. You guys are the best. Thank you for being excited for me and for cheering me up when I couldn't see the light at the end of the editing tunnel.

To my family, thank you for the unconditional support, even though it took forever and a day to share this part of me with you. You've always given me the freedom to explore my various creative pursuits and have cheered me on from the sidelines, no matter what I'm doing. Thank you for respecting my privacy, even if you didn't understand the need for it, and for allowing me to blaze my own unconventional trail. There are parts of each of you in the foundation of who I am.

To my brilliant editor, Deanna, thank you for helping me whip this book into shape and for giving me the reassurance I needed whenever I was having doubts. Sorry for all of the smiles, glances, eyebrows, grins, waves, pursed lips, and arms wrapped around torsos. To Rebecca, thank you for cleaning up the manuscript and making sure things made sense. To Sergeant Janelle Shoihet, thank you for answering my police questions. To Monica, and Nina, who filled in while Monica was away, to Amanda, and everyone else at HQ I've interacted with in the past, thank you for being lovely points of contact during this process.

And to you, reading this, holding this in your hands—thank you for giving this book a chance.

ABOUT THE AUTHOR

K. Monroe grew up in small-town Saskatchewan and began sharing her work online at the age of fourteen. She attended college in Vancouver, where she earned an associate certificate in graphic design. When she's not writing, you can find her brainstorming ideas, singing along to every song in her music library, and fantasizing about decorating her dream apartment. *Blackout* is her debut novel.

Turn the page to read a preview of

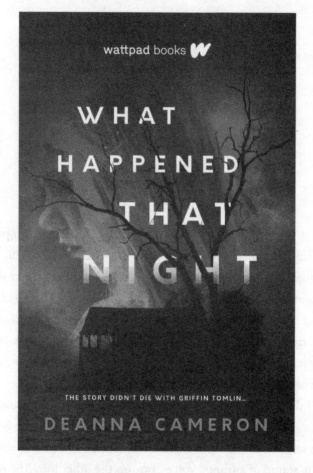

wattpad books

WHAT
HAPPENED
THAT
NIGHT

THE STORY DIDN'T DIE WITH GRIFFIN TOMLIN...

DEANNA CAMERON

chapter one

Bright yellow crime-scene tape blocked the Tomlins' property, looping around the telephone poles and their mailbox, on that Tuesday morning while my family prepared breakfast. Since there were only two police cars parked on the shoulder of the road, my father speculated maybe they were robbed in the middle of night or something. My mother grabbed the phone from the kitchen counter as she cooked, her other hand reaching to turn down the heat on the oven burner as bacon sizzled in a pan.

"I didn't hear their house alarm go off," she was saying to my dad, cradling the phone on her shoulder and flipping the bacon over with a fork. "I'll give them a call. Maybe—" Her face shifted as the sound of a frantic voice came on the other line. The noise (so loud even we could hear it) interrupted my father mid-sip of his coffee. "Hello, Lisa? It's Samantha."

He set down his mug, brow furrowing, as the piercing voice on the other end of the phone continued. "What's going on?"

My mother's hand was still on the burner dial when she let out a breath, a word lost somewhere in the exhale. My father was mouthing something at her. I turned to my sister, Emily, sitting beside me as she stirred her cereal, barely looking up as my mother finally took her hand off the dial to cover her mouth, a gasp issuing through her teeth.

My chest tensed.

My mother was focused on something in front of her, like if she stared at the handle of her frying pan intently enough, she'd be able to understand whatever was being said. The bacon started to burn, so my father turned off the heat and moved the pan, still looking at my mother, raising his eyebrows whenever she met his gaze, her lips still agape.

Finally she tilted the phone away from her mouth as the voice on the other end quietened slightly, and she craned her neck to look at my father. I was annoyed with Emily because she was chewing so loudly on her cereal, I couldn't hear Mrs. Tomlin on the phone.

Mom's eyes were beginning to turn pink and water as she told us, "Griffin died last night."

"*What?*" my dad asked, eyes widening. The pan slid out of his hand and fell into the sink with a deafening crash. "What happened? How did he die?"

I was too shocked to say anything at all. *Griffin died last night.* But he couldn't have. I'd seen him last night, playing Marco Polo, eating hot dogs at our neighborhood's Labor Day party.

Dad leaned closer to Mom, like he thought he'd heard her wrong, he must have heard her wrong, before she started crying silently, her hand over her lips. Then he glanced over at us,

Deanna Cameron

as if just now realizing that we were still sitting there, watching. "Clara, Emily, head up to your rooms, okay?"

"What about school?" Emily asked. "We have to leave in, like, ten minutes."

My father shot her a look as he placed both his hands on Mom's shoulders, squeezing as she cried into the phone receiver.

I looked over my shoulder, through the window to the Tomlins' house across the street, almost expecting there to be visual proof of this impossible event—that Griffin was dead, that he was really gone. But all I saw were the same two police cars still parked alongside the curb, the crime-scene tape fluttering in the breeze.

A hollowness opened in my chest as I heard my mother tearfully ask what had happened to him . . . we'd just seen him the night before, and he'd been fine. Then a numbness settled into my fingers and extended to my arms and my legs and everywhere in between. I slumped against the back of the chair and listened to the faint sound of the hysterical voice through the phone, feeling as if nothing was sinking in. Everything felt blank and unreal.

Griffin Tomlin was dead.

270

chapter *two*

four months later

I heard my mother entering the house through the patio door downstairs from my bedroom, the *shwoop* of the door closing behind her, and the clomping of her boots against the floor as she maneuvered around the table and chairs in the dining room. I imagined her peeling off her dirt-caked gardening gloves as she walked into the kitchen, past a chair no one sat in anymore, and dropping them on the counter.

In the three months since Emily had been arrested, my mother had become more obsessed with gardening than ever before, spending hours outside as she tugged out weeds, planted autumn flowers, and filled her watering can with the hose. The head of her trowel was dented and white at the edges from scratching against pebbles in the dirt, and the elastic of her gardening gloves was worn and stretched. The back of her neck was sunburned from spending so many hours tending to the flower beds. They used to bloom with vibrant petals but now, in January, there was nothing for her to plant. Nothing for her to nurture.

I thought maybe she would've tried to convince my father to buy her a greenhouse so she could continue her intensified obsession with botany and not focus on the fact that her daughter was awaiting trial for the murder of her best friend's son. Instead she would go outside, brush the snow from her garden, and stab her trowel through it to crumble the frozen dirt. The only garden she hadn't touched was my father's vegetable garden. Most of the vegetables had been dug up by an animal last August, but the rest died in October when Emily was arrested and, unlike my mother, my father stopped caring about plant life.

A few of our neighbors—ones who used to be friends—peered out from the safety of their windows and watched her crouch in front of the flower beds, always a glimmer of anxiousness in their eyes. It was the first murder committed here in Shiloh in years, the first in decades committed by an actual resident. Everyone looked at my mother and thought, *This is your fault. You raised her. How could you not know?*

But no one had thought my sister, Emily Porterfield, was messed up. They'd thought she was perfectly normal too, with her cheerleading uniform and her pom-poms waving frantically in the air like fireworks at the games. She'd babysat their children. She'd sold Girl Scout cookies to them in the spring. She'd walked their dogs and even scooped up their poop instead of leaving it there. Emily Porterfield just wasn't messed up.

Downstairs, I heard our answering machine playing a message left half an hour ago, while she was outside and I was in my bedroom. The message was from my father, apologizing for working late again tonight, mumbling we should eat dinner without him, don't wait up. A moment later, my mother pressed the Delete Message button.

Sometimes she asked me if I knew why Emily had killed Griffin Tomlin, if it was just an accident, if I knew why Emily had snuck out of the house and crept across the street into the Tomlins' backyard that night. Every time she asked me a question about her, about him, about them, I would tell her no, even when it wasn't true. No, I didn't know why she'd done it. No, I didn't know why she went there. No, no, no. Sometimes I imagined Emily in a white cinder-block room, dressed in a jailhouse uniform instead of her cheerleader one, and her lips mouthing the word *liar* at me.

Because I knew why she'd done it.

I knew that Emily hated Griffin Tomlin the moment I'd told her something I never should have.

My parents and I haven't talked about it, but every day I've driven Emily's car to school.

Before she was arrested, we drove to school together. We'd stop at the Starbucks across the street and order mocha lattes, listening to Carrie Underwood songs. After she was arrested, my parents seemed to have an unspoken agreement that no one touched her things.

Her bedroom door remained closed at the end of the hall; her granola bars were still in the cupboard, pushed to the back, hidden behind soup cans; one of her socks was still on the floor in front of the washing machine.

But after Emily's defense attorney managed to convince the police to release her car after it had been impounded (on the grounds that no evidence was found related to the case), I started driving it to school every morning. The first morning I did it, a part of me hoped it would still sort of smell like her inside, like if she couldn't be there, then maybe the fruity notes of her perfume would be, clinging to the seats. Instead it smelled like cleaning products, the scent stinging my nose. Everything of hers had been taken out, even the trash in the glove compartment. It was like a totally new car, complete with a pine-scented air freshener, but with old memories lingering in the cracks between the seats, like crumbs.

When I pulled into the school parking lot, there were still a few kids sitting in the comfort of their heated cars. The heater in Emily's car was broken, just like everything else seemed to be. I turned the engine off and sat there drinking my latte, feeling its warmth against my fingertips. Through the windshield, I spotted Kolby Rutledge trudging through the slush.

He was wearing a black puffer vest with a collar and a pair of jeans that were a little worn in the knees. His beanie was pulled over the tops of his ears, his brown hair poking out from underneath, and his Timberlands were damp from walking through slush and snow. His cheeks were rosy from the cold.

I felt a pang of guilt watching him jog up to the school's front doors. Griffin Tomlin used to give him a ride every morning after Kolby had totaled his car last winter skidding on black ice. Kolby's parents couldn't buy him another car, and the insurance didn't amount to much, so Griffin had driven him to school—until last September, anyway.

I reached across the console and grabbed my backpack from the passenger seat. A few of the kids hanging out in their cars looked over when they heard me slam my door, then quickly glanced away. My classmates usually ignored me, just like they had when Emily was in the driver's seat and I was in the passenger's, where we'd both belonged.

I expected everyone to treat me differently after my sister's arrest, to shove me around, sneer, and mutter under their breath as I walked past them in the hallways, torturing me in lieu of my sister, but they didn't. They mostly just stared and whispered to each other whenever they saw me. A few asked if I knew why she'd done it or if she could get the death penalty, oblivious to the fact that New York State abolished it years ago. Somehow this felt worse than if they'd been bullying me for what Emily did, because maybe that would've been something I deserved. I would have been prepared for it. Instead they just stared, their eyes full of pity and morbid curiosity.

But they wouldn't just stare if they knew what I knew.

After I walked inside and started heading down the hall, I noticed a girl standing in front of Emily's old locker, her fingers twisting the dial of a hot-pink lock. Her skin was the color of deepened amber and her hair was ebony in a fishtail braid. She was dressed in a pale pink sweater with a rose-gold choker necklace, and had peach nail polish on her fingers. Her sneakers were pink too.

I stared at her for a moment, feeling thrown by all the pink she wore as she opened the locker, the hinges creaking in such a familiar way I felt an ache in my chest at the sound.

After Emily had been arrested, the police had cleaned out her locker for evidence, as if during Math and Biology classes she had been scribbling her homicidal plans for Griffin Tomlin or something. For a few months, it was left empty and vacant. Someone—I didn't know who—scribbled in black marker *YOU SHOULD BE DEAD* on it a few months ago. It was gone now, scrubbed clean, but it still felt like the words were there, festering unseen.

The girl grabbed a pink notebook from inside her—Emily's— locker and a pen before closing the door, turning to head down the hallway.

At home, Emily was preserved, almost like petals pressed between book pages. Last month, when I'd grabbed the one mug Emily used to use for her tea, my mother's eyes brimmed with tears. She lied in a wobbling voice that it was okay for me to use it, but I put it back anyway.

It felt so surreal that here, out in the world, people were actually beginning to move on from Emily Porterfield.

After last period, as I walked out into the parking lot, I noticed a dark figure lingering around the hood of my sister's Mini Cooper.

He was tall, with broad shoulders, and wearing a familiar black puffer vest.

Kolby Rutledge.

I felt a slight twinge of panic seeing him there. His hands were stuffed into his pockets and his nose was turning pink as he half-heartedly kicked his boot into a pile of slush. I hadn't really spoken to him since Griffin Tomlin's funeral.

He'd come a few minutes into the service and stood in the back of the church, since all the pews were full. He'd been supposed to sit with the Tomlins, because they said Kolby was like a brother to Griffin, but when he hadn't shown up, my mother took his place beside Mrs. Tomlin, squeezing her hand. A part of me wondered if he was late so he wouldn't have to sit with them, so close to the open casket, and listen to the overwhelming sound of Mrs. Tomlin trying to stifle her sobs or Mr. Tomlin constantly clearing his throat.

He'd left soon after the funeral, too, lingering only for a couple of minutes to give Mrs. Tomlin a quick and awkward hug. He nearly bumped into me on his way out, and I mumbled a soft *sorry* I don't think he heard. If I had known then, I would've apologized for more than just getting in his way.

I barely knew Kolby. He was always with Griffin, like they were a package deal or something, and while he wasn't really *shy*, he didn't speak much either. I didn't really know that much about him, except that he and Griffin had become friends on the baseball team in middle school. They were on the high school team, too, but after Griffin died, Kolby quit.

I never really spoke to Kolby unless Griffin was there between us, like some sort of bridge.

Except for the night of the Tomlins' Super Bowl party. And now, apparently.

Kolby had taken off the beanie I'd seen him wearing earlier, and a few snowflakes were caught in his hair. His eyes were a deep shade of brown, the kind that reminded you of coffee with cream and sugar. I had always thought his eyes fit with Griffin's, which were a remarkable ocean blue—and that if irises were elements, then Griffin's were water and Kolby's were earth.

"Hey," he said.

"Hey."

I unlocked the passenger door and tossed my backpack inside, glancing at him over the hood of the car as his eyes focused on the tires, and I felt the urge to say something. Like I should apologize because now he has to walk to school in the middle of January. Or that my sister killed his best friend. But instead I asked, "Admiring Black Beauty?"

"The car's red," he said, his voice flat.

I shrugged uncomfortably, feeling his gaze on me as I started to brush the snow off the windshield with my hand. Kolby paused before taking his hand from his pocket and brushing the snow from the driver's window, his fingers ashen as they glistened with snow. Every few seconds he would stop to shake his hand, as if to warm it up. I wanted to say he didn't have to clean the snow off with me, but whenever I tried, I'd look at him and lose my nerve.

"Emily named it that. Something about a horse—I don't know." I did know, though, but I wasn't sure if this was okay, talking about Emily, especially to him.

He nodded, the muscles in his jaw clenched as he shoved his

pale, wet hand back into his pocket. The prickling feeling of dis-
quiet intensified with every second as he stood only a few feet
away from me.

"Did she . . . has she ever said—?"

"No," I interrupted, shaking my head and looking away,
already knowing what he was about to ask. His eyes held a sense
of vulnerability in them that made my chest ache out of guilt for
lying to him. But if I couldn't even tell my mom, then I definitely
couldn't tell him.

"No," he repeated, the word almost a sigh.

"No," I reaffirmed.

The clouds concealed the blue sky, turning it a shade of white
that made me feel heavy and tired as I pulled into the driveway.
Shouldering my backpack, I caught a glimpse of something in
the rearview mirror. Standing in front of his mailbox, in a pair
of plaid pajama pants and snow boots, was Brandon Tomlin. His
back was turned to me as he grabbed the mail; the same tousled
curly black hair that Griffin had had reached his shoulders now.

Brandon was five years older than me and acted like he thought
he was cooler sometimes, even though he was twenty-two and
still living with his parents, working at the local movie theater. I'd
seen him at the funeral, sitting beside his father, rubbing his eyes
throughout the service. When our family was about to leave and
we'd hugged the Tomlins good-bye, his breath stank of something
sickly sweet as he wrapped his arms around me. He was wobbling,

teetering on his toes, and I held on to him tighter when I caught Mrs. Tomlin looking over at us, not wanting her to know her now-only child was drunk at her youngest son's funeral.

Now, he shoved the mail under his arm and swatted his hand against the mailbox lid to close it before heading back up the driveway.

I almost wanted to tell him why she'd taken Griffin away from him and his parents. But I knew none of them would believe me about what happened between Griffin and me.

I never would've believed it either.

And don't miss Deanna Cameron's
Homewrecker

Available now in print and ebook,
wherever books are sold.